The Green Grass

by

BIBI K

authorHOUSE®

AuthorHouse™
1663 Liberty Drive
Bloomington, IN 47403
www.authorhouse.com
Phone: 1-800-839-8640

Published by AuthorHouse 7/31/2012

ISBN: 978-1-4772-4875-1 (e)
ISBN: 978-1-4772-4877-5 (hc)
ISBN: 978-1-4772-4876-8 (sc)

Library of Congress Control Number: 2012913086

DEDICATED TO:

The loving memory of my parents
AND
To my two darling children, who were the
guiding force that made this all possible!!

Table of Contents

Prologue

Since I have been working for you, I have seen your breathtakingly beautiful house, but have I ever envied you? NO!!

I have seen you driving away in your brand new silver grey convertible, but have I ever envied you being the one driving it? Again, NO!!

I have seen you wearing some huge "rocks" and drop dead gorgeous designer clothes, but have I ever envied you any of these? Again, a resounding, NO.!!

But, I have seen you pass your hand through your child's hair; I have seen you welcome your child home from school sometimes; I have seen you hug your child and I have heard you say "I love you" to each other: Did I envy you these? Absolutely!

These were the moments that have broken my heart into tiny fragments; wishing and yearning for the day when I could have the luxury of doing these things with my children.

Please believe me when I say, that you were not to be blamed for my circumstances. I was not sure, who, if anyone was to blame. Maybe because I was born in a different part of the world or under different economic circumstances I believed that I had no choice but to endure if I wanted to succeed.

Be it as it may, I found myself in my current situation, and as one human being to another, I was not sure if you could blame me for wanting a better life for my children. Come with me on my journey, and you could decide for yourself if you would have made this ultimate sacrifice or if you would have given up from the very first moment of separation!

Chapter One

Leaving, Me?

Even if I live to be a hundred years old, I think this image would be as clear in my mind as it was today. It was a day filled with brilliant sunshine and I was standing in a big open playground, the wooden school building on my left, the sea dam on my right, and the leaves of lush, green trees blowing in the wind to the South. I looked towards the fence and I saw my daughter, three years and 10 months old carefully making her way across an old log so that she could take the short cut to my school. Her brown uniform was smudged and her white shirt was no longer white as she had been cleaning furniture in preparation for Mashramani – Republic Celebrations in Guyana.

Suddenly she recognized me among the students who were playing in the field and she started to run towards me with her arms outstretched, her face beaming! As I bent down to scoop her up in my arms, I looked up to see my friend, Rachel, looking at me. With a tear running down her right cheek, she said,

"I really do not know how you are able to do this", before turning to walk back to the school building.

I picked up my little girl and I held her tight, savoring the moment, burying my head in her neck and fighting all inclinations to break down and weep. As I looked towards the fence again, I saw my son running across the field also. He was 10 years old and he was my little "man".

I bent down to hug him. He was too grown for me to pick him up, which was what I would really have liked to do. He looked at the way I was holding his sister and he said,

"Have you told her yet, Ma?"

I could only answer with a shake of my head, as I was choking up with tears. He then said,

"Do not worry Ma, we will figure something out."

This picture was stamped in my brain and on my mind on Friday, February 19, 1988. It was good that I could not see into the future and realize the numerous heartaches and turmoil that would engulf my family and me.

How do I explain the circumstances that led to this day?

I had a decent life – a husband, two kids and a good job teaching just a stone's throw from where I lived. Being the youngest of eight siblings, with both my parents and five of my brothers living in the same village I was very sheltered. I was surrounded by a great network of family and friends who always looked out for me.

I never had any dreams or wishes of going overseas and if I were to answer a question as to where and when I made this decision, I could not give an honest answer. All I know was that this was a period of political unrest in our country and if you were not part of the ruling PNC party, you were subject to many unpleasant, even somewhat dangerous situations; not only on your job but also in your everyday life.

My husband came home one day and said that one of us should really try to get a Visa to go to America as life was getting harder and harder and that our children would not have a chance in life. Well, that one of us had to be me because he was too weak to take risks in life and I lay no blame anywhere. I was a grown woman with a mind of my own, and I agreed to try.

Obtaining a Visa to visit the USA was a very daunting task. We had no immediate relatives in the USA except for a nephew who had migrated a few years earlier; and a family friend whom I had met only once when she had visited Guyana to attend a wedding.

We had no experience with this process and everyone we spoke with had a different suggestion. They recommended purchasing a car and other items of great value so that the Interviewing Officer at the US Embassy would be satisfied that we had enough assets to bring us back to Guyana. I discussed the issue with my father and he offered to go with me to one of his friends (a high-ranking official) in the city.

This man gave the sanest advice. He told my father not to purchase anything because the folks at the embassy were not stupid. They would see the date of purchase and know that this was just a set up for the Visa application process. He said to go with whatever assets we had, which included our house, a motorcycle and some cash in the bank and I had a job and two young children.

I then went to the bank to get a statement. However, they would not give it to me in my hand. They said that the embassy would only accept a bank statement that was delivered directly from the bank. I even had to speak with the manager because the clerk would not give me a receipt.

My argument was, supposing the embassy did not receive my bank statement,

"What proof would I have that I requested one?"

Eventually the manager saw my point and gave me a receipt for the $15.00 that they charged for a bank statement.

On Monday, January 25, 1988 one day after my 31st birthday, my husband and I left our home in the countryside at 4:00 a.m. in the morning so that we could get to the Embassy and secure a place in the line to apply for a Visa. We left on our motorcycle and after about fifteen minutes, it started to rain. We joked that we were getting blessings from above.

Very soon, the light drizzle became a downpour and we had to scurry under a shop's awning for cover so that we would not be drenched. Eventually we made our way to the US Embassy in Main Street Georgotown. Even though we were so early that the sun had not even risen yet, there were already five people in line ahead of us.

Well, everyone was tense, nervous and anxious but soon conversations started flowing and since I had no one to speak with (my husband had gone across the sidewalk chatting with another guy), I kept listening to everyone around me. I immediately felt like a misfit and wanted to turn around and go back home.

All these people had so many assets and so many relatives in America. They seemed like the perfect candidates to receive a Visa while I only had my limited resources. One woman who had accompanied a relative seemed to know every detail about the application process and as soon as she saw me, she said that there was no way that I would get a Visa. She said that I looked too young and the officers would know that I would not be returning. There went my self-confidence, but I figured since I was already here I might as well go ahead; if only for the experience.

I started praying and tried not to let the conversations unsettle me further. Then the doors opened and we were now all very quiet, waiting for the dreaded moment when our fates would be decided. There were three windows and while standing in line waiting to be called, I could overhear the answers of the person right in front of me.

This elderly woman was saying,

"We have a grocery store and we sell rice, flour, coffee, etc. We also have a fishing boat that brings in income every week."

I was not sure what the officer said to her, but I could hear her raised voice saying,

"How can you say this? I came here before, they told me to get all these things, and now you are still telling me that this is not enough?"

I guess she did not get her Visa and I later found out that I was correct.

I was next in line and I was not sure if it was the way I answered my questions, or if it was the documents I produced or what the criteria was, but the Officer took my passport and said,

"Come back at 3:00 p.m. today."

As I was was walking out of the embassy, the security officer looked at me and asked,

"Did you get through?"

I replied, "I do not know."

He looked at me somewhat funny and said,

"What do you mean, you do not know? What happened?"

I then told him that the officer told me to come back at 3:00 p.m. He started laughing. "You really do not know, do you?"

4

I shook my head. When he realized that I was being honest, he explained,

"Do not worry. That means that you would get a Visa." I was stunned!

As I exited the embassy, my husband was standing there and four of the people who were ahead of me in line were waiting because they wanted to find out how I had fared. Apparently, one of them heard me answering my questions and he came out and told the others that I would get through.

I then relayed the conversation with the security guard and everyone was happy for me except the older woman who started to say she could not understand how I could be so young and still get a Visa. She had been told that you had to be older to get a Visa. I did not let her anger bother me. I was still in shock. I was the first person on that day to get a Visa and as it soon started to sink in, I was not sure what my emotions were. In addition, at this point I was only going on what the security guard had said; I really wanted to wait until I returned at 3:00 p.m.

It was still early in the day; my husband gave me a bunch of errands to run in the city, while he went to work. I finished my errands early so I decided to go to the movies – an Indian movie called "Ek Dujhe Ke Liye" was showing at Empire cinema and it would finish just in time for me to get back to the Embassy at 3:00 p.m.

I cried and cried during the entire movie – the story was about two young lovers who eventually committed suicide because they could not be together in life. I would have cried about the story anyways, (I always cry in movies) but I think this triggered something in me and once I started crying, I could not stop. Anyway, I had the privacy and the cover of darkness in the movie theater and I took full advantage of it. It was very cathartic and soon I made my way back to the Embassy.

When I got to the Embassy, it was closed so I went over to a nearby building where they had some outdoor tables with umbrellas. I sat down for some relief from the sun and a very pretty, older woman soon joined me. She was also waiting to get her passport back from the Embassy.

We talked about lots of things – she had a permanent Visa to Canada and after several attempts, she was now finally getting a Visa to the States. She then told me that I seemed to have a really good soul and that I should not worry, that there would be lots of changes in my life, but that I would come out of it triumphantly. If only she knew.

Soon it was time for us to pick up our passports – mine was stamped with a B12 multiple Visa valid for 1 year. I looked at it and it did not register. The enormity of the changes that were about to take place in my life seemed distant. I think I was unconsciously tyring to minimize this moment. I did not think I was ready to deal with the reality of what I was holding in my hands. Was this really happening to me, or was I having an out of body experience? Was I really going to go away and leave my children, my parents, and my life, as I knew it?

I soon returned home and did not know how to break the news. The only person I told was my babysitter and of course, my husband knew. That night I lay down in my son's bed and I told him that I had a Visa to go to America.

His first words were, "Are you going alone, Ma?"

I explained everything as best as I knew at the time and told him that if I went to America and got a babysitting job I would be able to sponsor him, his sister and his dad, and that we could all be together again in three to three and a half years.

He seemed satisfied with that, but when I said,

"I am not sure about the time. It could even take up to five years."

He replied, "So long Ma?"

As for my baby girl, I had no clue as to how to explain it to her, and so she was oblivious to the fact that I was leaving soon.

I busied myself with work and obtaining Police clearance and all the necessary documents. At the Income Tax Office, I met a relative who was also leaving. It so happened that he was scheduled to leave on the same flight as mine and he told me not to worry, if no one came to the airport to get me in America I could go with him and we would figure something out.

The reason for this offer was because I had written to my nephew with all the details of my travel plans, but I had not yet had any response from him. I did not know if he received my letter and to speak to him via telephone at this time was very difficult. I had also written a letter to the family friend who I had met at a wedding in Guyana the year before. However, no response from her either.

When I got home from the city after my visit to the Income Tax Office, my dad was sitting in the hammock under the awning of my home. I looked at him and my eyes started tearing up. Immediately he knew. I sat on a small bench next to him and I told him everything. He did not immediately answer, but when he did; his first question was

"How are you going to tell your mother?"

I then told him that I would need his help with that. We decided that after his evening prayers, I would meet him at the mosque and we would go home together so I could break the news to my mother.

She was sitting on the veranda and the moon was up. She asked if I would like some dinner and I declined. We started talking about anything and everything except what I came to tell her. My father realized that I did not know where to begin so he said to me,

"Why don't you tell your mother the secret?" She was baffled, what secret she wanted to know.

I then used the relative that I had met at the Income Tax Office and I asked her if she could remember him. Of course, she knew him. So I told her that he had offered to take me to America and that I was planning on going.

"What do you think?" I asked her. Her first thought was about my children.

"How are you going to live without your children, mama (as she used to call me)?"

I responded, "Will you help to take care of them?"

She said, "Of course." I soon realized that she was crying very quietly and I hugged her and said,

"I need your blessings, Ma. Will you give that to me?"

As only a mother could she said,

"You will always have my blessings as long as you live."

Then she begged, "Please do not ever forget me."

As if that was ever possible in this lifetime but I reassured her that I never would. I stayed with her for a little while longer and finally decided to go home. My father followed me and on the way we discussed how we thought she had taken the news really well. Or did she just pretend to be ok to spare my feelings?

I was making all this preparation for my impending departure, but I did not know if I would be admitted to the USA. I was told that I could have a Visa from the American Embassy in Guyana, but that when I had to clear immigration in America, I was not guaranteed entry. It was almost like going through a second interview and then the Immigration Officer would determine if I would be allowed to enter the country and for how long or if I should be put on the next plane back to Guyana.

With this information at the back of my mind, I could not broadcast my impending departure. I did not want to be embarrassed. I did not want to be the laughing stock of my village –

"Oh my God, did you hear, she went to America and she was sent back home?"

So, as much as I wanted to tell my students and friends at work, I could not. The only person I told and swore her to secrecy was my friend Rachel.

Immediate family members were told that I was tyring to go to America and I was not sure of the outcome. My two children and I visited my aunt in the city and told her goodbye, and I visited the family where my brother and I had stayed in the city to go to College.

On our way back home, we went to the most famous restaurant in the city and had a late lunch. My daughter was very chatty with the waiter and she followed him to the kitchen to pay. I was going through all these motions with a smile on my face, but my heart was a solid block of ice. I think if I had let it feel too much at this time, I would not have been able to follow through with leaving.

Sunday, February 21, 1988 I had a religious function at my home with immediate relatives and friends to ask God for his blessings and to get everyone together so that I could say a semi goodbye. There were many hugs and good wishes, but everyone was asked to keep all the details as quiet as possible – as much as such a large group of people could be expected to keep a secret. I was profoundly saddened by the fact that none of us knew whether we would be seeing each other ever again, or what the future held.

Monday, February 22, 1988 I went to my school for the last time. I was there trying to listen to everything that was going on – there was a concert in commemoration of Mashramani, but nothing registered. I was immersed in my thoughts. If I were allowed to enter the USA then today was the last day that I would be among this group of people.

My students whom I shared a wonderful relationship with – would they be mad at me for not saying goodbye, would they ever understand that I could not say goodbye? My fellow teachers among whom I had some long lasting friends, we had shared so many great times together. Would they forgive me for not letting them know? How would I deal with this separation?

I left school for the last time that afternoon with a very heavy heart and the most difficult part was that I could not let anyone see my feelings. I had to pretend that I was leaving just as any other day. I said goodbye to everyone, a little lingeringly, but only I knew this. They had not a clue as to why I kept turning around and saying goodbye once again.

I hurried home to my children who did not go to school that day.

My son had said, "Ma you go I will stay and play with my sister".

As soon as I got home he greeted me with a big smile and said,

"Ma, guess what I did?"

I said "what did you do?"

All excitedly, he said, "I told her! I told her!"

I was all ears now and as he saw the question in my look as to her response, he said,

"Do not worry. I told her Ma would be going to America and that she would send you lots of dolls – big ones, talking ones, and all sorts of toys and candies and fancy clothes and she was really happy and excited Ma."

I hugged them both and thanked my son – I was grateful that he was able to tell her – only from one child to another. How much she understood was yet to be determined.

On Tuesday, February 23, 1988, we were all home. It was a National Holiday – Mashramani – Guyana's Republic anniversary. My sisters-in-law and a few immediate relatives visited for one last goodbye. My sister-in-law who had relatives abroad was more cognizant wtih travel and so on. When she saw the suitcase that I had bought, she said it was too big and that she had the ideal size at home.

She suggested that I should send my babysitter with her to get the smaller one. Her explanation was that if I took too large a suitcase with too much clothes then the Immigration Officer at JFK would assume that I was going to stay forever and could deny me entry into the USA.

I took her advice and Roma prepared to go with her to Parika where she lived. Fiyaz followed them to the main road with his brand new BMX which he was very anxious to ride at any given opportunity. As soon as the adults got into a car and were on their way, Fiyaz was attacked by a young man who slapped him a few times and took away his bicycle.

Fiyaz tried to push the guy off, but his tiny body was no match for an adult male. He did not give up that easily but ran after the thief who rode off on his bicycle. He followed him until he saw him turn into a side street away from the main road.

Unfortunately, Fiyaz ran out of breath and could not keep up. He ran as fast as he could to our home and he came panting into the yard, sweat and tears streaming down his face. He had only been wearing some trunks and his little body was quivering in fear, not only about his ordeal but also about his father's reaction. I was petrified by this sight. I ran and grabbed him, words flailing on top of each other in my anxiety to find out what was going on.

Eventually I was able to get the full story and I tried to reassure him. I hastily made my way towards my brother's house where I knew his father was tyring to gather up some fruits for me to take the next day. I yelled for him to come quickly!

He sensed the urgency in my voice and hearing what was going on, he burst into action. He jumped on his motor cycle; my brother climbing on quickly behind him. Luckily, Fiyaz had followed the robber and he was able to direct his father exactly where the robber had turned into the side street.

By now, a crowd had gathered in front of our house – the usual scenario in the countryside – anything happened everyone was there to find out what was going on and to lend support or get tid bits for gossip later. It was not long before we could hear the motor cycle humming its way around the corner. Next to my husband was my brother with the bicycle and the "criminal". They soon reached us and the first thing that the robber stammered was,

"Oh my God, Miss, I did not know it was your son".

"What difference does that make – you should not be robbing anyone".

As a teacher, everyone called me Miss in our village.

The crowd was getting bigger and they were all offering suggestions as to what to do with him – lock him up and throw away the key, etc. Some of them got in a few good punches here and there. They would have given him a sound trashing, but my husband, who was a Corporal with the Guystac division, stopped them.

My neighbor, a respected elderly woman came up to me and said quietly,

"Do not let your husband get involved with this entire Police red tape right now, just remember that you have to leave early in the morning and you want to leave in as much peace as possible."

I was not sure why, but I listened to her and my husband let the thief go with a very stern warning. Needless to say, I was even more bewildered and anguished about my impending departure now with this additional worry about my children's safety.

I did not sleep much on the evening of Tuesday, February 23, 1988. With everything that happened with my son during the day, I was having nightmares. Along with my heartache at leaving, I now had to worry about how traumatic this experience would be for him and how it would affect him.

Would he get nightmares? How would he deal with this ordeal on top of me leaving? What was this young mother to do? The only thing I always resorted to: I prayed and prayed and asked God for guidance and stamina to withstand all this upheaval in my tranquil world.

All too soon, it was 3:00 a.m. I had to get dressed and we had to leave at 4:00 a.m. to go to the Airport. I was on a standby flight – so it was imperative that I got there early. There were so many uncertainties about my departure that I brought an ordinary dress in my hand luggage so that if I did not get on the plane, I would change and just pretend that I went to the city for some business.

The car arrived and my husband, our two children and I scrambled in as we were running late. We picked up one brother and then went to my parents' home where we would pick up another brother and my mom. My father would not go with me to the airport and he came to meet me under the house.

I hugged him and we said our goodbyes. I did know then if it would be the last time I would see him. I would exchange letters with him, I would speak to him on the phone, but this person whom I had known from birth, would I ever see him again? So many morbid thoughts!

Soon we were on our way to the airport and we were making small talk, but no one discussed the real issue. I was leaving, really leaving. I did not know yet if I would get on the plane, if I would be granted entry into the USA or if my nephew was going to meet me at the airport. These were all things that occupied my mind and in its own way helped to take away the pain of separation.

We got to the airport and as we were sitting waiting, Fiyaz and Zara were playing. Could you imagine my heartache when she said to Fiyaz?

"Come see this plane; this is the plane that Ma and I are going to America with."

We had felt great about how Fiyaz had told her, but her innocent mind had not comprehended the enormity of the situation. She was happy about Ma going to America, but she did not understand that Ma was going ALONE. What could I do or say to make her understand? Could I even try?

By now, the airport was buzzing with activity. We were rushing around with the officials, tyring to determine whether I would get on the plane or not. Finally, I was told that I needed to check my bags and prepare to clear Immigration.

I hugged my brothers – one of them I would see four years later in America as he was sponsored by his son. The other one I would see after twelve years. My mother, I would have to depend on my brothers to read my letter to her and I may get to speak to her on the phone. I hugged her again and again. This was my lifeline – I was attached to her from birth throughout my life. Would this be my final goodbye to her?

I looked at Zara and she smiled hesitatingly. She did not understand why I was crying. I picked her up and she said,

"Ma, why are you crying?"

I was unable to answer. Fiyaz looked at me, tears streaming down his face. I hugged him and said,

"I love you babe – be good to your sister."

I then hugged my husband one last time. Now came the crucial time. Her father had to take Zara from me. She did not want to go; she believed she was coming with me. He pried her away from my arms. She was crying and screaming for me.

"Ma, don't go! Come back, Come back! I want to come with you. Ma, you have to take me with you!"

With her voice ringing in my ears, barely able to see through my tears I made my way to the plane. My handkerchief was soaked; it was unable to absorb any more moisture. I used the back of my hands to wipe away the tears that were blinding me. I got a window seat and when the plane turned around on the runway, I saw a very small image of them on the Pavilion of the airport. I huddled in my corner and tried not to focus on the emotions that were tearing me apart. Was I in my right senses? What was I doing on a plane when my children were on their way home?

My two little angels; I had never been separated from them since their birth, except once. The only time I had ever been away from Fiyaz was when I was in the hospital to give birth to Zara. We had been inseparable. Besides our daily routine, school, work, chores, play, etc. sometimes, in the afternoons when their father went to work, I would go with them to visit my parents.

They had this absurd thing in common. They would be fine away from home during the day. However, come evening, as soon as the lamps were lit, they wanted to go home. No matter how happy or comfortable they were, they wanted to be home. We would then walk home, Fiyaz tyring to help carry Zara but she would not let him.

Her favorite way to be carried home was on my shoulders, looking down at Fiyaz and laughing with him. Sometimes we would sing little songs as we made our way home. That was the way we were. All of that would now change. What agony for a young mother on her way to America!

Feeding into my emotions was too painful and so I tried to focus on mundane things – the airhostess, the passengers getting on board and tyring to fit their carry-on luggage into the overhead bins. I was extremely nervous, as this was my first time on a plane.

I marvelled at the engineering feats of humankind that they were able to make such a huge object fly in the air. Suddenly, we were moving and the plane was gaining speed on the runway. I was ill prepared for the way my stomach would react when we lifted off and as we started to gain altitude, I held on for dear life!

My ears were popping and I was scared, really scared. But, I gritted my teeth and told myself that if all these people could do this, then so could I. This may sound strange with all the pain in my heart that I could still feel a sense of exhilaration … I was flying in a plane for the first time in my life!

I was fascinated by the fact that we were actually flying among the clouds. I kept looking out of the window but soon everything was the same and I dozed off as I was emotionally drained and had little sleep the past couple of nights.

I remembered waking up to the sound of the pilot's voice and he was telling us that we were passing over the Bermuda triangle. I was now all ears because I had read a little about the whole mystery of the Bermuda triangle; how planes would disappear without a trace in this region. Needless to say, I was petrified wondering if our plane would also disappear and that I would never see my family again.

I breathed a sigh of relief as the pilot advised that we had passed through the Bermuda triangle. I could go back to sleep as this helped me to escape my wandering mind and my tumultuous heart, which always reverted to the fact that I was on my way, ALONE, to America. Believe me I knew this was a great opportunity as many relatives and friends had verbalized that they wished they had. It was only the circumstances that were "gut" wrenching. What greater torture could be inflicted on a mother than being separated from her children?

Not only was I being separated from my children, I was also a wife, a sister and above all, a daughter myself. I knew that my parents were feeling as much pain for me as I was for my children. I knew they would worry about me a whole lot more especially since I was going to a strange land where no immediate family member had visited and returned to talk about.

Chapter Two

Culture Shock

I was leaving everything that was familiar and safe; and venturing into a great vastness of uncertainties. I felt like a huge oak that was being uprooted and thrown out into a turbulent sea to go as it would wherever the waters took it. This was my mindset as we touched down at JFK International Airport.

There was no more time for moroseness or self-pity. It was time for action! I had to be alert and ready to answer questions from the Immigration Officer. Was I anxious? You bet. I retrieved my suitcase and stood in line to face the man or woman who would determine my fate.

My officer was a middle aged, short, semi balding guy who seemed kind enough. He was actually smiling as I approached. He asked me some routine questions as to where I was going to stay and so on. Did I have anything in my suitcase that I should not have?

"How long do you plan to stay?" He continued.

"One month," I replied.

"Would you be able to stay away from your family for that long?"

"That I am not sure about, I may want to run back after a few days."

(I think these were the tricky parts in the questioning process and I tried to answer as best as I could.) I really felt like I wanted to turn around right there and run back home. Lo and behold, he stamped my passport – he had given me six months to stay in the USA.

I now had to be checked by the customs officer who opened up my suitcase and took away some of the fruit that I had brought. My brother had gone through a whole lot of trouble to get these special delicacies for his son, unfortunately it was not meant to be.

I was very happy to see my nephew waiting for me beyond the ropes for visitors and as I was walking towards him, I heard someone saying,

"Miss, Miss, wait!"

I looked around and stopped dead in my tracks. The officer who just interviewed me was running after me. Oh my God, what was going to happen now? Was he going to take back the Visa? Was I going to have to go back home and hang my head in shame?

He caught up to me and said,

"Oh Miss, you left your $40.00 on my desk."

(You were allowed to bring $40.00 Guyana dollars with you). Phew!! What a relief! But, what a way to enter America! This was the first of many kindnesses that were bestowed on me in this great land of America. There were so many rumors of people being very unkind and rude; that was dispelled in my first day here. This officer was just coming off duty and he realized that I had left my money there. He did not have to, but he took the time and effort to return it to me.

I thanked him profusely and walked out to my nephew's waiting arms and a thick, warm jacket. Thank God he had the foresight to bring a jacket, because I had started feeling the cold even before the plane landed.

We had a lot of catching up to do. We talked about all the folks back home and reminisced about our encounters with so and so as their names came up. The one topic that we did not dwell on too much was how I was feeling. We were now passing through Queens from JFK to go to New Jersey where my nephew resided.

I was all the while observing the landscape and the scenery around. Nothing to impress me yet – everything was all gray and desolate looking. There were some tall buildings but nothing like I had heard about. It was the heart of winter, February 24, and I saw all these trees, which I thought, were dead because all the leaves had fallen off.

Right away, my mind jumped to my mom.

"Oh my God, Ma, if you could see all the "dry" wood you would go crazy."

I was back in my childhood with her when we used to go to the sea shore and the woody areas surrounding it to cut fire wood for the "fireside" Not the fireplace that gave heat during the winter time, but the fireside that was used to cook all our meals.

This was a special object that was created using bricks and mud that was shaped like a "lop sided L". There would be an opening in the front where the firewood would be placed and then two round openings along the other end of the formation. Pots would be placed in the front opening as well as on the two other holes. The heat from flames of the fire going through these openings would cook all our meals.

There was a special art in building these firesides and when a new one was to be built, we would recruit a special lady in the neighborhood. These services were all done as a favor and it was considered an honor to build or repair a really good fireside for a neighbor or relative.

My bout with nostalgia was short lived as my nephew was saying something to me and I had to ask him to repeat it. We were now approaching the Verrazano Bridge and I was enthralled by the magnificence of this structure. I had never seen anything as intricate and as imposing in all my life.

Guyana had bridges, it even had a floating bridge, but the size, the height and magnitude of this was overwhelming. The vastness of this great land was also overwhelming to me. My idea of America was of "A concrete jungle". I had this vision from my exposure to films like the "Towering Inferno" which was shot in a city location. All these open land spaces were like an enigma to me.

We eventually arrived at my nephew's wife's home. (The reason I say this was because they were having some problems and he was currently living with a group of guys in another part of New Jersey.) I had never met his wife, Roxanne, and I had a little misgiving about the reception.

However, I need not have worried. She was very welcoming and she had prepared a delicious meal for us. Roxanne had a very darling little baby boy who was a little shy with me at first but soon I was able to hold him and play a little bit.

Later that evening her father came down to the basement where she lived to say hello. He was very kind and he gave me $20.00 US dollars. I was embarrassed to take money from him but they assured me that it was OK – it seemed that this was something customary when someone newly arrived in America.

This was confirmed when Roxanne's sister, Monica, came home from work and gave me a beautiful outfit as well as $10.00 US. Anyone who knew me well knew that I was more of a giver and not a taker and I was having a hard time accepting all these gifts and money, but I did not want to appear ungrateful. They were tyring to make me feel welcome and I thanked them sincerely.

On Thursday morning, my nephew took me to his job to meet his boss – he thought with all my qualifications from back home it would be very easy for me to get a decent job in their company. As we were leaving the apartment, which was in a basement, Roxanne told me to make sure I wrapped my scarf properly around my neck. I looked out the window and saw the sun shining, and I was thinking to myself, what was she talking about? The sun was shining, how could it be cold?

Typical mentality of someone just "off the boat". Anyone coming from tropical countries associated bright sunshine with warmth. I guess I was in for a culture shock; or should I say weather shock? As soon as I opened the storm door and came outside the wind whipped my face and I literally took a step back. My God, it was cold! My eyes started watering after the short trip to the corner where my nephew had parked his car.

He offered to buy me coffee as soon as we got to his job as I was shivering by now, but I did not drink coffee and I declined. Soon we met his boss who was quite impressed - I had my teaching degree, shorthand, typing, accounting and English certificates from Pitman and London Chamber of Commerce. His boss offered me a job as the receptionist but I could not start until my nephew could clear some paperwork

Friday I stayed home with Roxanne and her baby and with not much to do I was left to watch TV. What else was on but commercials with little girls running in the sunshine, playing with toys or some outdoor activity to sell some object or the other? You could imagine how this affected me.

I was overcome with grief and did not know how to deal with it. I had always been very low keyed in expressing my emotions. My brother died unexpectedly in 1983 under tragic circumstances and whilst my sister was whaling and following the coffin and so on, I stood there with tears streaming down my face, my heart breaking into a million tiny pieces.

The anguish in my heart that was created by my separation from my children was way above and beyond anything I had experienced before. Gone was the serene person who could be stoic about an extremely sad situation. This grief was bigger than I was. I did not know how to deal with it – I wanted to rant and rave and shout and yell at anything or anyone and yet I was mindful of being private.

And so, the only thing I could think of to assuage my heartache was to go to the bathroom and turn on the shower and then I wailed and banged my head against the wall, until I was spent and drained. I would then wash my face and come back out, only to see another commercial and go through the same ritual all over again. Years later, I found out that Roxanne used to hear me; and not knowing how to help or what to say, she thought it best to leave me alone.

On Friday afternoon when my nephew came home from work, he and Roxanne took me to the mall to buy me some warm clothes. The few dresses that I had brought from Guyana were almost useless because they could only be used here in the summer time.

They bought me a coat and a pair of sneakers along with some socks and sweat pants and shirts. Shopping done, Roxanne insisted that we should get Pizza. She loved it and wanted so badly to introduce me to it. I ate it because she was so enthusiastic, but to this day, it has not become one of my favorite "American" dishes. I would from time to time enjoy a vegetable slice with extra white cheese.

On Saturday, a few of Roxanne's relatives stopped by to say hello and the day went by very fast. Towards early evening, I started to get a slight fever and an earache. By 10:30 p.m. I was in excruciating pain. My head felt ready to burst and my ears were pounding non-stop.

Roxanne gave me some aspirin and I tried to sleep but had a very fitful night. I woke up and my mind was working overtime. I kept thinking,

"Dear God, please do not let me leave my children in Guyana to come here and die." I guess I was being melodramatic, but in my current state of mind, everything seemed larger than life.

Sunday morning I was writhing in pain. I could hardly see straight and Roxanne called my nephew to come over. She thought I needed to go to a doctor. They took me to an old family doctor who said that my ears were literally too "clean" and that the cold air was able to penetrate deep down inside. He gave us a prescription and I was very relieved.

I had really felt that I was going to die and not see my children again. I was now convinced that the greatest punishment that could be meted out to a woman was to separate her from her children.

On Tuesday, I went with my nephew to his job where I was to be the Receptionist. I was slowly getting the hang of the phone system and the language differences. Even though we all spoke "English" there was a vast difference in our accents and needed a period of getting used to. On our way home on Wednesday afternoon my nephew and I started discussing the possibility of bringing my family over.

He looked at me really sadly and said,

"Girl, I have been talking to some people and I think the only way you can be sponsored, would be to work as a housekeeper and/or babysitter."

It was hard for him to think of me having to become someone's babysitter when I had my own babysitter back in Guyana. I looked at him and said that whatever it took, so long as I was making an honest living, I was willing to do it for my children's future.

So on Thursday afternoon I explained to my nephew's boss- that unfortunately, I would not be able to continue with his generous offer of being the receptionist. I explained my situation briefly and he was very sympathetic and wished me all the luck in the world. I said my farewells on Friday after receiving my first paycheck of $200.00 in the USA. I made sure that I gave Roxanne enough money to pay for the phone calls that I had made to my country and then I did something that my mom taught me to do always.

I asked my nephew to pick up some cards for me and I put money in each of them to my husband, my father and my mother. I also gave my nephew $5.00. My mom had always made me do this whenever I had a new job as she felt that I would derive blessings from my loved ones. (I could not afford to send to all my brothers and sister from this paycheck, as I had five brothers and one sister).

In order to send the money in the cards, I had to get some carbon paper and place the money in between, so that no one would pilfer the envelopes. The only person who received the card with her $10.00 in it was my mother. I was disappointed about the others, but overjoyed that my mother had received hers. At least, she would know that I did not forget her teachings and I was assured that she would give me her blessings.

Now I had to look for a babysitting/housekepting job. Roxanne had a relative who knew someone who may know someone who may have some information about babysitting/housekepting jobs. We were given a number to call on Saturday and my nephew and Roxanne went with me to an interview.

I thought we drove all day to get to that place. We did not get there until around 7:30 p.m. that night, having got lost a few times along the way. I met with the family who had two children, a four-year-old son and a baby daughter. The little boy showed me his pet ants and his mother was impressed that he was opening up to me. Nothing came of this interview however, as the lady called to say that she and her husband were going through a divorce and she was not sure about the financial situation at that time.

On Sunday, we got another number and we called to set up an interview. The lady of the house, Mrs. Wilheim, arranged for me to go on Tuesday morning. I did not know that her phone number had been posted at a bus stop. Later I would find out that if they had to resort to posting in bus stopps, it meant that they were the worst employers and that they could not depend on word of mouth recommendations.

Anyway, I was very anxious, and grateful. On Tuesday morning, my nephew came to pick me up and he dropped me off at the bus in Journal Square, a huge bus depot. As I was standing on the steps to board the bus he reached up and touched my shoulder and with a watery glint in his eye, he wished me good luck. I knew this was hard for him because in Guyana, everyone looked up to me as the little scholar and now here I was: having to go look for work as a "servant".

I wrote down my destination on a piece of paper and I showed it to the

Bus driver. He promised to let me know when we got there. I would have many of these encounters with bus drivers, showing them an address and all my experiences with them had been very fulfilling. They had never failed to be kind and to show me which side of the street I needed to be on to get the next bus for where I needed to be.

After what seemed like ages, he soon yelled out Tenafly. Once I got off the bus, I was to go to the phone booth and call Mrs. Wilheim. I felt like I was in the movies now, describing what I was wearing – I had a coat with a yellow scarf and I had a small brown suitcase, etc.

I waited for about fifteen minutes and then she got out of a really luxurious looking silver grey car. She had no trouble recognizing me and on the way to her house, she conducted a mini interview. When she learned that I was a teacher in my country she appeared to be satisfied.

Soon we were going up an incline on a driveway that led to a humongous house. Then she did this thing that seemed like a miracle to me – I had only read about stuff like this in novels. She opened her garage door with a remote control. I was mystified.

Anyway, I did not have much time to muse about remote controls and garage doors as she immediately asked me to pick up the garbage bins that were left by the sidewalk. This was how my life was going to be from now on. No pleasantries; no niceties or courtesies; at least not from her.

We got into the house and it was gorgeous. To this day, after so many years in this country, I still consider this house to be one of the most beautiful I had seen. However, the beauty came at a price. I would soon learn that it took a lot of labor to maintain off-white tiles in the kitchen.

The first floor had a huge living room with tan leather sofas and a built in 52-inch TV screen. In 1988, this was considered a rare privilege of the rich and famous. There was a sitting room with mirrors from floor to ceiling along one wall and then there was a dining room. This room impressed me the most and it was not until a few months later when they had a dinner that I realized how truly exceptional it was.

The table had a glass center with a beautiful cherry wood glassy finish about one foot around the edge. On the wall all around this room this cherry wood finish appeared to be a decorative ledge – however, during the dinner

I realized that this was a lift off covering for a heating panel where the trays of food were placed to be kept warm. I thought this was awesome!

However, for now, I had no time to enjoy the beauty, as Mrs. Wilheim was all business. She did not have a housekepter for almost two weeks and there were loads of laundry to be done. She did not hesitate to take me to the laundry room and at the same time show me where to put my belongings – my room was right across from the laundry room.

She then made me change into a uniform from a stack that was hung in the closet in my room. She said she expected me to wear a uniform everyday. Within minutes, I was literally going upstairs with her to bring down clothes to be laundered. As soon as the washing machine was started, we went to the kitchen and began emptying the dishwasher, thus giving her a chance to show me where everything was kept.

After about an hour and a half, Mrs. Wilheim left me to finish all the chores she had assigned and went out to run errands. I took a moment to get something to drink, as I had not eaten anything all morning, leaving home so early with my nephew to get on the bus. Mrs. W. (my way of addressing her) soon returns in time to receive the girls from school at 3:00 p.m.

The girls, Aleya 16 and Kayla 10 were very polite, saying hello before going up to their room. Around 5:30 p.m. I was still in the laundry room folding clothes when I heard Mrs. W and the girls in the kitchen. She was cooking dinner and I got a little excited about having a decent meal, because I was starving by this time.

I was in for a big disappointment. The girls had finished eating and they went back to their rooms to do their homework and other activities in the den upstairs. Mrs. W. told me that I could clean up the kitchen and that I could have some of the left over. I looked in the pot and all I could see was some boiled spaghetti.

I did not know that you could add spaghetti sauce and cheese, and this would be a meal. I looked around for something else but I did not see anything. The way we would prepare this would be to sauté meat and vegetables with lots of spices and add the spaghetti before eating it as a meal. However, beggars could not be choosers; I was starving and I choked down some of this tasteless food and tried to be content.

Very soon Mrs. W. came back downstairs all dressed up. She told me that she was meeting Mr. W. and they would not be back until late so I would be home with the girls. I finished cleaning up the kitchen and then went to my room. There was a small bed, a dresser with a 13-inch TV on it which was turned on and off by a knob. Then there was closet where the uniforms were kept. I did not unpack my suitcase, as I was extremely tired.

I took a long shower before going upstairs to ask the girls if they needed anything. I tried to make a little conversation with them but they were busy with their schoolwork and, not wanting to be disruptive, I told them if they needed anything to please call me.

I was not sure what my role here was now. Did I stay around the girls and have them think I was interfering or did I go back to my room, or what? I felt responsible and did not want to be too far away and my room was all the way downstairs and to the back of the house. So, I decided to sit in the living room where I could easily run up the stairs if the girls needed me.

The girls were no problem at all. I could hear them moving around and soon they retired to their respective rooms. I went up the stairs quietly and called out to them to see if they needed anything.

Aleya said, "Could you please not be too loud when you wake me in the morning."

I said "Ok, goodnight" and then went to my room.

It was the dead of winter and I lay down in my bed, which was placed against the wall. I was freezing. I huddled into my blanket and could not fall asleep. I was thinking about my children; missing them with an intensity that was too strong for words. I could sleep because it was so cold and I got up and felt against the wall next to my bed.

Lo and behold, I felt the vent that felt a little warm, but not warm enough. I turned on the lights and I saw this round gadget, which I would later find out was a thermostat. Guess what? I turned it all the way to the right and then I went back and lay down. Soon it started to get warm and I was so tired that I fell into a deep sleep.

I jumped up with a start. There was this whirring noise. I was disoriented and I was scared. What could this sound be? After my racing heart quieted down, I heard the door leading from the garage to the house opening. Oh, that was the noise! It was the garage door opening. I felt such a sense of relief. For two reasons: one the noise was nothing threatening and two, Mr. and Mrs. W. were home. I soon drifted back to sleep.

I woke up in a sweat! I was burning up and my back, which was pressed against the wall in my sleep, was hot to the touch. Apparently, in my ignorance, I had turned the heat up way too high and I could have burnt my body if I had not woken up. Thank God, my body was trying to protect itself by waking me up when I did. I fidgeted with the thermostat and I finally got it to a normal temperature. Whatever the ordeal, I survived my first night in a strange home, doing a job that no one in my family would have ever anticipated me doing.

The next morning I was up at 5:30 a.m. I washed up, dressed in my uniform, and made my way to the kitchen. I set up the coffee as Mrs. W. had showed me the day before and I got out the English muffins, which the girls would eat for breakfast. I then treaded lightly upstairs and tried to wake the girls.

Aleya turned over and went right back to sleep; Kayla, rubbing sleep out of her eyes, looked at me and said she would be up. She soon got up and went to the bathroom. I was hovering by Aleya's door – did I wake her up again? She had specifically asked me the night before not to be loud and now she was not waking up.

How did I, a perfect stranger wake up a 16 year old? Would she yell at me? I figured I might as well find out. I tried to wake her up again and by now Mrs. W. was up. She began to fuss that the girls would be late and that I should be up earlier. Aleya went into the bathroom and did not come down when her mother was yelling for her. She could not hear because she was blow-drying her hair. She had a luscious head of blond curly hair about which she would forever be complaining. I thought it was gorgeous; she thought it was too wild.

Anyway, she finally came down and had no time to eat, as it was time for the bus. Kayla was already out the door for her bus. Aleya got into a fight with her mother about running late and she said that no one woke her up. I looked directly at her and she had the decency to look away because she knew that I woke her up earlier.

It was my first morning with them and I did not say anything. Mrs.

W. without saying as much implied that I was the reason for Aleya being late. She then let me know clearly that I had to be up earlier and that I was responsible for the girls being up in time to have breakfast and still make their bus. I thought she was being unfair since I was so new, but I did not say anything.

The girls gone, Mrs. W. sat with me and gave me a list of chores that I had to do on a daily basis. Everyday, I had to do laundry. The linen in the girls rooms were to be washed alternately with the linen in her bedroom. Along with those, towels from both bathrooms and the clothes from the day before were to be washed daily.

The sheets and pillowcases from the girls' beds were simple wash and fold. However, the ones from her bed not only had to be washed but they had to be ironed as well. Then vacuuming of the upstairs and downstairs was to be alternated daily. The kitchen needed to be swept and mopped twice daily – in the morning and at night after doing the dinner dishes.

The beautiful sitting room that I had admired earlier had a wall of mirrors from floor to ceiling. This had to be shined daily. The garbage had to be taken out from the kitchen to the garage every evening. Once I took out the garbage bag from the bin, I had to wipe the bin with a wet rag before spraying it with a disinfectant. Once that was done I had to now rub on another substance on the whole garbage bin before replacing a garbage bag. On Tuesdays and Thursdays, I had to wake up at 5:00 a.m. and run out in the cold to put the garbage out onto the curb.

The bathrooms had to be cleaned daily. This entailed picking up all the towels that they left on the floor and taking all the clothes from the hampers to be washed. Scrubbing the tub and toilet bowl; then mopping the floors. The sinks and the mirrors needed to be polished and shined. Once Mrs. W. had completed this task of assigning my duties, she went upstairs.

Mr. W. who was a very reknowned doctor and had a very prestigious position in a major hospital came down and this was the first time I was meeting him. He greeted me with great kindness in his voice and welcomed me warmly to their home. He drank a cup of coffee and he left for work. Soon after Mrs. W. left to go to her tennis game and then lunch with her friends.

My toils were about to begin. I ran upstairs and made the girls' beds.

Two twin beds were quickly taken care of. I then went to Mrs. W's bedroom. She had a king bed and there was a huge coverlet that came custom made as part of the décor with the drapes. This was on the floor.

I first had to take off the fitted sheet, top sheet and pillowcases. Today I had to wash and iron the linen from her bed. I then had to replace the fitted sheet, top sheet, and pillowcases; then there was an extra blanket that had to be folded and tucked in a special way. Now came the hard part of getting the huge, heavy coverlet onto the bed.

I pulled and tugged at it until I finally got it to fit neatly onto the bed. By the time I was done making this bed, I was panting for breath. I lay down on the floor for about five minutes in order to regroup before I could start again. Those five minutes on the floor would be my morning break from that day onward.

I would then move to the bathrooms and I would run down with a load of towels and started the washing machine with the first load of laundry while I ran back upstairs to clean the tubs, sinks, floor and mirrors in both bathrooms. The bedrooms had to be vacuumed everyday.

The stairs also had to be vacuumed and this required a little technical expertise because I had to attach a special nozzle to the vacuum cleaner to get into the thick interwoven rug. I was not sure if I did not have the proper technique; but this chore was quite troublesome. I would be tyring to balance this heavy vacuum cleaner and operate the extension all at the same time and I never mastered this art for as long as I worked there.

About 12:25 p.m., my nephew called when he was on his lunch break. I soon broke down in tears and told him that I was very hungry.

"What do you mean you are hungry?"

"Exactly what I say", I replied.

He listened to me explaining that I had not had a decent meal. He tried to talk me into finding stuff that I could eat. He had me looking in the fridge.

"Tell me what you see." he said!

"I do not see anything that I can eat."

He made me look in the pantry and there I found cases of soda and in one of the overhead cupboards, I found a packet of cookies.

On top of feeling bad for me about the food situation, my nephew had to give me bad news. In order for me to stay with Roxanne he had to go and get permission from her father who owned the house. Supposedly, he and Roxanne's father were not speaking to each other and he was not willing to swallow his pride and ask for favors.

I could hear his voice cracking up as he told me that he had to go back to work and that he was sorry for everything. I reassured him that it was not his fault and that I would figure something out. Even though I said that to him, this was something else I had to worry about – where was I going to stay if I could not stay with Roxanne? I could not go with him in his Bachelor quarters that he shared with three males.

I labored my way through the week and I acquired a great respect for housework. I never had imagined that regular household chores could make one so tired at the end of the day. I guessed if you did not have to do the same things over and over everyday, it could be less taxing on your body.

On Saturday, I called the friend who I had sent the letter to and had not received a response and she was surprised and excited to hear from me. She was very welcoming and comforting. She said that I was welcome to stay with her and that I should call her on Sunday. This was very reassuring – at least I had somewhere to go for the moment.

Chapter Three

Lost

On Sunday morning, I woke up at five and I had to call a taxicab to take me to the bus stop. Mrs. W. had put my wages on the table – it was $175.00 and I was very grateful. I wrote a little "Thank You" note from one of their notepads and left it on the table. From this, I had to pay $5.00 to the taxi and then the bus fare, which was $1.50. Later, I would find out that most other employers used to give their babysitters/housekepters their passage aside from the regular wages.

I was surprised at the number of women at the bus stop that first Sunday morning. Later, I would name this bus, the "Crying bus" because once we started to know each other; everyone had a different tale of woe. Many of us had come to try to build a better future for our families but most important; all of us were here, ALONE! Some lived with relatives, others shared apartments but none of us had a husband and children to go home to.

Well, this was my first morning in the USA on a bus, 6:00 a.m. the first week in March. I changed from one bus to another and then I had to get off at Linden Avenue. I was doing great. I got off at Linden Avenue. I saw flurries for the first time and I was fascinated. It was as if a bunch of tiny

29

white butterflies were chasing each other. The flurries soon turned into a steady snowfall.

When I got off the bus, I walked in the wrong direction to get to Roxanne's home. Because it was snowing, I put my suitcase on my head to shelter me from the snow and tried to wrap my scarf very tightly around my neck. I did not have gloves and my fingers were getting very cold as I tried to hold my suitcase on top of my head. It seemed as if I had been walking forever yet I could not see the address. I had not been here long enough to understand that I was walking away from the address rather than going toward it.

It was dark and desolate. There was not a living soul in sight. What should I do? This was not yet the age of cell phones and I did not see a pay phone nearby. Thank God for Sunday morning papers and the ability to speak English. An elderly gentleman peeked out his door and reached for his papers and not sure how I acted so quickly with a perfect stranger, I yelled out to him.

"Mister! Mister!" He was quite startled.

He did not know where this voice was coming from and it took him a little while to focus on me. He was in the act of closing his door but he stopped and waited until I reached to his fence.

"Please, Sir, could you tell me where this address is?"

When he heard the address, he looked at me with pity in his eyes and said,

"I am so sorry, but you have walked five avenues away from where you need to be. You have to turn around and go back all the way and then cross over Linden Avenue on the opposite side. From there you should start looking for the number."

I thanked him wholeheartedly and did as he suggested.

Freezing to the bone, I soon rang the doorbell to Roxanne's apartment. Her sister who lived on the first floor opened the door. She looked at me and said,

"You were lost".

They had called the people who had told them about the job and they informed them of the bus schedule. They waited for me and they knew I had to be lost when I did not arrive by a certain time. As I am writing this,

I could almost feel the cold in my fingers from that first morning when I was lost in America.

I soon had some hot chocolate and a home cooked meal warmed up from the evening before. I was so grateful to Roxanne and to this day, I would never forget her kindnesses during my days of despair and suffering. As soon as I was settled, we all went back to bed as it was Sunday morning. I would soon learn to sleep in late on Sundays, like most people did.

Around 1:00 p.m. on Sunday, Leila, my friend who I had spoken with on Saturday called. She wanted to know how I was doing and if I was still interested in staying by her. I told her that I was not sure what to do as I had not seen my nephew since I came home. As soon as Roxanne heard this, she spoke with her sister and her brother-in-law and they were willing to take me to the Bronx where my friend lived. They called back Leila, got directions, and let her know that they would take me to her.

I was in a quandary. I had only met my "friend Leila", once before at this wedding in Guyana. I did not know her husband and their circumstances in the USA. I was not sure how I was going to get to work back and forth from the Bronx to NJ. I was debating whether I should beg Roxanne to let me stay with her, but soon I was caught up in a whirlwind of hustle and bustle. Everyone was getting dressed and it seemed as if the decision had been made for me. I decided to go with the flow and soon we were on our way to the Bronx.

Upon arrival, my friend opened her door, her arms and her heart to me. She lived in a one-bedroom apartment and as she opened the door, there was not enough room for it to be opened fully. She had some friends over and she invited Roxanne and her family to come in. I think they declined because the apartment was so crowded, but they made the excuse that they were not familiar with the Bronx and wanted to head back early. I thanked them repeatedly before they left.

Soon I was being introduced, first to Leila's husband and her son, and then to all the relatives and friends who to this day I could not understand how they all fit into that small space. I was then given one dish after another to eat but I could only eat a small amount, as Roxanne had made sure I had a good meal before I left her home. Once everyone had left, we had our quiet moment to catch up on all the details from back home.

It was now time to go to sleep. Leila gave up her bedroom to me and her son and she and her husband slept on the sofa bed in the living room. You had to understand that once the sofa bed opened up in the living room, it engulfed all the space. The TV and a sewing machine with a chair made it very difficult to move around. I felt guilty for occupying their bedroom while they slept in the living room, but I was not comfortable enough around them to insist and I went along with the arrangement.

On Monday, I did not have to go to work as my workweek was from Tuesday mornings to Sunday mornings, but Leila and her family had work and school. Leila worked only a few blocks away and she promised to call me. I basked in the ability to lie down a little longer without thinking about all the chores I needed to finish. Leila came home for lunch and I offered to help around the house if she would let me know what she would like to get done. She put some clothes in a washing machine, which surprisingly she was able to fit in her tiny kitchen.

I started the dinner and picked up clothes from the line before hanging out the others on a line to dry. She had a clothesline that was connected to a pulley gadget that could be reached from her kitchen window. I folded all the clothes neatly and tidied up her kitchen. She called around 4:00 p.m. and when she realized that I had finished most of her chores she told me to get dressed, we would go for a walk as soon as she got out of work. She took me to the Boulevard where there was a great shopping area and we window shopped for a little before she bought me an outfit; some fruit and my favorite Cadbury chocolate.

We were chatting away excitedly, and we held hands like little girls did as we walked along. Suddenly, she snatched her hand away from mine and looked around nervously. I was startled and looked at her with a frown.

"What was that for?"

I was now going to be exposed to public mentality on "gays".

She said, "Oh, My God, do you want these people to think we are gay?"

I must say that I grew up very much protected and I was extremely naïve in these matters. It took me a little while to register what she as implying but I soon got the gist of what she was tyring to say. However, she had a very bubbly personality and talked a lot with her hands; so very soon we were holding hands again, before she would suddenly become conscious and let go of my hand. I thought this was very funny.

We got home and after dinner that evening she called up information to find out what was the best way for me to get to my job in New Jersey. I had to take a bus from her street to George Washington Bridge and then from there take a bus to Tenafly. Once I got to Tenafly then I would need to either take the taxi service or call Mrs. W. to come and get me. I was relieved that it was not that much of a hassle; in fact, it was a shorter route even though I was in the Bronx now.

Before we went to sleep, I insisted that I sleep on the sofa and that she, her husband, and her son reclaim their bedroom. At first, they were hesitant, but when I explained that I had to leave at 5:30 a.m. in the morning and how would I get through the door with them still sleeping, they acquiesced. I was very relieved. At least I would not feel like such an intruder.

Before they went off to their room, she offered to pull out the sofa bed for me, but I told them that I would. However, I just lay down and slept in the sofa. It was not the most comfortable sofa as it had some old springs that were poking out, but I was extremely grateful for a place to stay that I could have slept on the floor and would not have minded.

On Tuesday morning, I got up early and tried to be as quiet as possible, not wanting to wake up the others. Leila had shown me where everything was in the kitchen and that I should made myself breakfast and take something with me, but it was so early and for fear of making noise in the kitchen which was right off of the bedroom and the bathroom I did not eat anything or bring anything with me.

I dressed quickly and left to get the first bus. It was still dark outside. The directions that Leila gave me were very clear and I had little trouble getting to work. The only problem I had was that even though I had on a jacket, waiting in the cold for the bus was something I was not accustomed to and I soon started to shiver.

At George Washington Bridge, I felt a sense of belonging in a strange sort of way. There were many other women waiting on line for the bus. I was no longer scared. There were some coffee shops downstairs and I ran down and bought a hot chocolate, as I was not a coffee drinker. I also bought a packaged piece of cake. The next bus ride was pretty uneventful with little tidbits of quiet conversation going on. We soon reached Tenafly and since there was a half hour wait for taxicabs, I called Mrs. W. She recommended that I wait, as she was not yet dressed.

I soon arrived to a house that was out of a housekepter for two whole days. I must say that it looked fine to a normal onlooker, but according to Mrs. W. it was filthy and everything had to be cleaned thoroughly. I rushed to my room and dropped my suitcase (yes, I was still carrying it around with me) in a corner before quickly changing into my uniform.

My arduous tasks were about to begin. I almost had no time to think: I started upstairs in the girls' bedrooms as they had already left for school. From Laundry to bathrooms to vacuuming, I was busy all day. When I went downstairs to clean up the sitting room, I had to shine this whole wall of mirrors. I did a balancing act, standing on a step stool with the rag and the Windex in my hands. I rubbed on Windex, then I polished, and then I stepped down.

However, every time I looked at the mirror, there seemed to be another spot that I did not get. From different angles, the mirror looked streaky and I started all over again to get it glistening. It took me a couple of weeks to learn to trick this arduous task. I soon learnt that if I took a feather duster and brushed really hard, then the mirror would get cleaned. Occasionally, I needed to apply Windex and rub it until it literally shone.

I was back and forth doing laundry, cleaning up the kitchen and all the other chores that were on my list of duties. At 3:15 p.m., I was in the laundry room when the doorbell rang and Kayla was the first one home from school. I only had to give her a little snack and she was OK. She sat in the living room and watched TV. I was not far away in the laundry room.

I was doing some ironing and I took extra care to make sure that Aleya's jeans got some well-creased seams in the front. I need not have bothered as she did not like it, but did not want to offend me and asked her mother to make me stop putting seams in her jeans. I was not complaining. It was a little less work for me.

Aleya soon came home and declined any snacks but went straight to her room. I picked up both their bags from near the doorway and put them on the stairs. Mrs. W. soon came home and she made dinner for the girls. Same "old" spaghetti. This time she purees broccoli to go on top. Another night when I had to have dinner from canned foods which I would more often than not, eat right from the can. I was too tired to pour it out and have to do an extra dish.

That night when I went into the kitchen to clean up after dinner, I asked Mrs. W. if I could please use her phone the next day to call home; this would be a long distance call. I told her that I would pay the bill when it came. She wanted to know how would I know how much to pay and I explained, as Roxanne had told me that the long distance bill would come on a separate page.

She said if that was the case, then I could use the phone. I finished cleaning up and soon went to bed, where I fell asleep quickly since I was so tired. I would consider sleep to be my salvation in these times. In the daytime, I was so busy with work but my mind was still occupied by thoughts of my children. At night, I escaped from it all through sleep; relaxing, replenishing, blessed sleep!

I had my daily routine under control. I was up at 5:00 a.m. and I ran around all day juggling chores to make sure that I finished everything to the standard that was expected by Mrs. W. On Friday, at around 2:00 p.m. I tried to call home and I was thrilled that I got through on the first try. My husband picked up the phone and as soon as I heard his voice, I started to cry. I got so emotional; begging him to let me come home. I could not deal with this separation. I crouched on the floor and I was rolling around in tears pleading,

"Please, please, let me come back home!"

I allowed him to convince me to stay for the benefit of the children and for all of us. And so, after about fifteen minutes, I hung up and had a really hard time getting back on track.

I could not stop crying. My eyes were red and swollen. Mrs. W. came, I told her that I did call home and that as soon as the bill came she should let me know, and I would pay her. She looked at me and said OK. That night, even though I was tired as usual, I could not fall asleep. I was tossing and turning and I cried myself to sleep more so than on the other nights. When I woke up on Saturday morning, my eyes were all red and puffy. I started to clean up downstairs, as no one was up early.

Mrs. W. was the first one to come down but she did not notice anything unusual. When Kayla came down, she took one look at me and asked what was wrong with my eyes. I told her that it was nothing. Later in the day, Mrs. W. was on the phone with one of her friends and they told her that their daughter had "Pink eye".

She immediately came downstairs and later I would find out that she just made up an excuse to get me away from the children. She told me that they had a skiing trip the following week and that I should not come to work, as no one would be home.

On Sunday morning, I left as usual and I was very concerned about the fact that I did not have a job for the following week. I was responsible for sending money home to pay off for the plane ticket and to help with the mortgage payments on our home as well as taking care of the children. When I got to the Bronx, it was only 7:30 a.m. and I felt bad about waking my friend up so early on a Sunday morning. So, I went into the corner Deli and tried to wait around a little bit. I bought a few snack items but when the owner started looking at me as if to say,

"Why are you still here?" I decided to leave.

I had no choice but to press the buzzer to Leila's apartment. She soon buzzed me up and opened the door when I reached up. She let me in and realized that all was not well. At first I tried to make light of it and said that nothing was wrong, but she persisted and then I told her about not having a job for the following week. As always, she was very comforting; she said that I should not worry that everything would be OK. She eventually went back to her room and I lay dowb in the sofa and soon fell asleep myself.

As soon as we woke up, she got on the phone to call a woman whom she had met in the supermarket recently. The lady was from our country and she said her daughter needed a babysitter. Leila soon arranged for me to meet her daughter and in the afternoon, they took me to her apartment. She was living on the first floor of the house that was owned by her parents with her husband and two children.

As soon as we were seated, Shaira became very business like and conducted a very thorough interview. She wanted to know my education, what job I did in my country, etc. Leila's husband later joked on the way back that he thought I was being interviewed for a bank job. He did not seem to like her very much but Leila and I both convinced him that I would be among my own kind of people and that I would be in the Bronx, not too far from them.

I was to start on Monday morning and Leila's husband dropped me off at 6:30 a.m. before he went to work. Shaira showed me around the apartment and gave me a list of things she expected me to do during the day. I put my suitcase in the corner of the space that I was to occupy. I did not have a room of my own. Off the passageway from the kitchen to the living room, a plastic screen separated my sleeping quarters. I was thinking that this was a small price to pay for being around people who were from my own background.

I had been in the states for over two weeks now and I had the hang of doing household chores. Cleaning the apartment and taking care of the little three-year-old girl was not that difficult. But, could you imagine the havoc that was being wreaked with my emotions? My own little girl back home was only three years and 10 months and every time I looked at this little girl, I felt like bawling my eyes out. Nevertheless, I prayed and asked God to help me to do my job as best as I could.

On Tuesday, I went on a field trip with the 7-year-old boy. His class was going to an Indian Reservation and Shaira's mother drove us to the school where we would get the bus. I had a very enjoyable day; I felt a sense of belonging being around the teachers and the children and I learnt quite a few interesting facts about the American Indians.

Unfortunately, I could not say the same for the evening. Shaira came home from work and everything seemed to be going well until she said she could not find a check that she just placed on the table. She started to get louder and louder saying that she could not understand how the check could disappear when she just placed it there.

With the noise that she was making, her mother from upstairs ran down to find out what was going on. I did not know what to do – did I help her look and if so, what was I really looking for? I was so scared because everything she was saying seemed to be pointing to me – that I was the only one who could have taken it.

Her mother tried to get her to calm down, and they began to search for the "missing" check. I was tyring to help but honestly, I was not sure how. I was hovering there and I felt as if I was more of a hindrance than a help.

Eventually, her mother found an envelope in a book that was on the table and in the envelope was her precious check. She took it and tried to justify her behavior by saying that she knew she put it on the table. Her mother soon went back upstairs and they retired to their quarters while I lay in my bed tyring to fall asleep.

She woke up the next morning as if nothing had happened the evening before. After she left for work her mother came down to take the boy to school. When she returned, she did not immediately go upstairs but came to me. She told me not to take her daughter seriously, that she had a very quick temper. I told her that I would be OK, but that I felt terrible because Shaira was almost openly accusing me. She said she understood.

On Wednesday evening when Shaira arrived home, she took me to the kitchen and taught me how to make their dinners. She made a big fuss about the rice cooker and the microwave oven and that I had to be so precise in the settings, if not I could damage them. I listened to her and it did not escape me that she was speaking to me as if I were a retard.

But, I was a very patient person in general and in my special circumstances, I realized that I had to be more tolerant and passive. Later that evening I sat in my little corner off the living room writing a letter to my son. Shaira passed by and told me that I should not forget to turn off the light. What did she think; I was a little nitwit? She felt that I was up too late and that I would be running up her electric bill or something.

The week was almost over and I was looking forward to Friday for many reasons, besides going home to Leila. When I had called home on Sunday, I was told that on Friday after Juma (weekly services in the mosque) my father would go to my home and say prayers. This was a special month in our Holy calendar when we said extra prayers and asked for forgiveness for the dead. I could not say any prayers myself during the week, as I was menstruating. However, on Friday, that would all be over. I planned to wake up early and finish my chores so that I could take a shower and when they would be praying back home, I would sit quietly and recite some prayers myself.

Nothing worked out the way that I had envisioned. First of all, Shaira decided not to go to work on Friday. She ordered a large amount of meat and she had me in the kitchen with her making small parcels to store in the freezer. While we were doing this, she kept reminding me that she went to the trouble to order this specially blessed meat because of me. She then had me cleaning the kitchen thoroughly even taking out the lint from the dryer and pulling out the machines so that we could sweep behind.

I was still hoping that we would finish in time so that I could take a shower before saying a few prayers around the same time that my father would be at our home. This was not to be. We went from the kitchen to the bathroom and back to the kitchen with a load of laundry to be done. (The washer and dryer were in the kitchen). As I was looking at the clock in the kitchen and thinking my father would have just finished the special prayers, the doorbell rang and her mother came in.

She had gone to the mosque for Friday prayers and she had brought some sweet meat, called "Halwa" and she offered me some. At this exact moment, they would be serving this same delicacy at my home. The coincidence was too much. It was almost as if I were there with them except that I could not partake in the prayers. I was overwhelmed by the precise timing and my eyes started to water.

Shaira's mom noticed my tears and she asked me what was wrong. I shook my head, nothing, because if I tried to speak, then I would break down and sob. She nodded understandingly and left to go back upstairs.

Unfortunately, that was not the end of the incident. Later that evening, Shaira called me into the living room and asked me why I had been crying. I tried to explain to her that the arrival of her mom with the "Halwa" at the exact time that it would have been served in my home made me sad and I could not help the tears.

Well, let me tell you, I had to sit there and wish for the earth to open up and maybe swallow me to save me from the tirade that followed. Shaira started saying that she knew that she was a hard task master and that the people at her job called her a "bitch" but she believed that people should work for every penny that they earned. She could not have someone who would cry around her children and on and on and that she would have to "try" me out for another week before she would decide whether to keep me or not. She refused to accept my explanation as to why I cried. To her that was no reason to cry.

Around 10:00 a.m. on Saturday morning, Leila and her husband came to pick me up and I took my suitcase with me. I had made up my mind that

I would not come back to her job. She was going to pay me $30.00 less and I had been willing to accept it just because I thought I would be comfortable being around people of my own background. Sometimes, they were the worst ones to be around.

Leila kept asking me if everything was OK and if "that girl" referring to Shaira had been mean to me. I reassured her that everything was great but that I was having a hard time being around the little 3 year old as it reminded me too much of my daughter. She seemed to buy that and I let it be. I did not want to create problems between her and Shaira's mom, who had become a respectable elder in her life.

On Sunday morning, Leila called Shaira and told her that I would not be coming as my nephew had found me a "good job" in New Jersey. A good job would be referring to something in terms of the clerical field. This was not really true, but it was a white lie intended to maintain harmony. Shaira had the nerve to go off again, saying that she could not understand why I would not want to come back and that that was why she did not like to deal with people from my country. Leila, who was usually a feisty one, surprisingly, let her have her say before hanging up.

On Sunday evening, Mrs. W. called Roxanne's home and she then gave her Leila's number to call me. She and the girls were back from "The Trip". She also wanted to find out if I was OK to come to work on Tuesday. I told her yes and she said she would expect me at the usual time. And so, I ended up going back to work for Mrs. W. even though she was a very hard taskmaster. Maybe if I had someone who could provide for me for a little while, I could have taken some time to get a better job. However, my circumstances did not give me much choice and so I got up early on Tuesday morning to start my grueling week once again.

This time though, I was a little more prepared. On Monday evening, Leila packed some leftovers for me to take. She also gave me the curry and other seasonings that were required to make chicken curry. She told me that when Mrs. W. was not home I should made sure I cooked something that I could eat at night in my room. She explained to me that if I turned on the fan over the stove, there would be no lingering smell in the kitchen when Mrs. W. came home. I looked forward to these meals and they helped to sustain my strength for my grueling tasks every day.

As soon as April came around Mrs. W. had me cleaning all the lawn chairs by the pool in the backyard. There was a huge pool and even though they had not taken off the covers, she still instructed me to clean the lawn furniture. This was another backbreaking task.

I had to rub soap on it, hose it down, dry it, and then rub another liquid to make it shiny. Sometimes, when she was not home and I was scheduled to clean around the pool, I would sit down on one of the chairs and if a plane passed by, I would day dream about going home and bringing my children back with me. Futile dreams at that time, and they only made me shed more quiet tears.

I realized that you are probably thinking that I was portraying Mrs. W. as a mean person, but believe me, she was. One Saturday morning, she told me to clean the chairs again, even though I had done them on Thursday because she had friends coming over and they would use the pool. The doctor was home that morning and she realized that since they would all be in the house I would not get to do many of my chores so instead of me enjoying some quiet time with nothing to do, she told me to clean the outdoor furniture.

For some reason, Dr. W. came outside and saw me cleaning the furniture. He asked me why I was cleaning them again. I told him that Mrs. W. said some friends would be coming over to use the pool. He looked at me and by the puzzled look on his face, I knew that there were no friends coming over and that it was just a ruse on her part to keep me occupied and always working.

The weeks and days went. The girls and I got along really well and I spent many evenings sitting with Kayla in the den watching television. Sometimes when we were watching Wheel of Fortune, which I watch to this day, I would answer the puzzle very quickly and she would always be amazed. She would say to me:

"You should be on that show; you are so smart."

She also had a computer, which she allowed me to type on one evening. When she saw how fast I could type, she was speechless. Sometimes I would help her with her Math homework.

In the afternoons when Kayla came home from school, she would sit in the living room watching cartoons. I used to be in the laundry room folding clothes just a few feet away from her. Until one day, I decided to bring my clothes in the basket and sit with her while I folded them. Well, I did not realize that this was a big "No! No!" Mrs. W. soon came home and saw me there folding clothes. She promptly told me never to bring the clothes in the living room again.

From then on, I started taking the clothes into my room to sit on my bed and fold them. When Kayla came home, she missed me sitting in the living room with her and she came into my room asking me if she could come and sit with me. Of course, I did not have a problem with her being next to me. She cuddled up next to me and she soon fell asleep. Oops! Mrs. W. came in from the garage and found Kayla sleeping in my bed with her head in my lap. She did not say anything to me.

However, I would soon find out that she did not like that because the next time Kayla came to my room she said to me,

"If I fall asleep, you have to promise to wake me up and get me to the living room as soon as you hear the garage door opening".

Immediately, I knew why. I was torn. Did I dare incur the anger of my employer or should I offend an innocent child, who only wanted to be around me. I opted for not offending the child and so I let her stay in my room.

Chapter Four

The Guest Bathroom

Little by little, I tried to do different things with Kayla when she got home from school. I realized that her mother did not like her to be in my room and so instead of folding clothes in the afternoon when she got home, I left the clothes and sat with her in the living room and we watched TV together. She was a sweet child and we soon bonded to the extent that when she went to a trade fair she had them carve my name out of wood. I had that gift moving from place to place – I finally lost it to my great sadness during one of my moves.

One Saturday the doctor was home again. He was being honored for outstanding achievement in his field of medicine. I was very proud to be working for someone so distinguished. There was a lot of fanfare in getting dressed up for the big occasion. Hairdressers and make up specialists came to pamper Mrs. W. and the girls and they all looked extremely beautiful. Dr. W. looked very handsome.

It seemed like a fairy tale for me to watch them leaving in the big limousine that had been hired for the occasion. I was like Cinderella looking at everyone dressed up leaving for the ball and I had to clean up after them. Except as in the Cinderella story, I did not have a Prince Charming to take me away from all of this misery.

My weeks were tied up with work and on the weekends, I stayed at Leila who took me with her family wherever they were going. One week she called me at work and told me to ask Mrs. W. if she would let me come home on Friday evening. They were going to PA on Saturday and would not

be returning until Sunday evening. She wanted to take me with them not only for the drive but also, if I did not go with them, how would I get into her apartment on Sunday morning when I came home?

Well, my fears were confirmed as when I asked Mrs. W. she said an emphatic

"No, I need you on Saturday evenings."

When Leila heard this, she was a little annoyed but she said that I should not worry, she would try to get me a key. These were generous, selfless acts that I would always cherish to the end of my days. Leila cut a set of keys for me and gave it to her neighbors in her apartment building - people whom she did not know very well before, except to say hi in the hallways.

She knocked on their door and told them that someone would come early Sunday morning, could they please give her these keys. Who did stuff like that? Just so that I could get into her apartment, she gave her house keys to a complete stranger to deliver to me.

I got in and promptly went to sleep. Waking up around noon, I soon cleaned up her apartment, folded all the clothes, and put them on her bed. Sometimes, if I called her now, she would say that she was just thinking about me, because she had to fold clothes and when I was around, I always folded all her laundry. Anyway, I soon finished and thoughts just engulfed me and, of course, I cried a lot. I took a shower and everything, but I could not disguise the redness or puffiness in my eyes.

Soon Leila called and told me that they were leaving PA to come back to NY and she gave me an estimated time when they should be home. I thought I would surprise them and instead of cooking dinner, I ordered in from a Chinese menu that was on their refrigerator. Luckily, I had only done so about 10 minutes before they arrived home. I did not know what I was ordering and ended up ordering pork. Because of our religion, none of us could eat pork. Leila's husband had a good laugh but still had the presence of mind to call and change the order to something that we could all enjoy.

While we were waiting on the food to be delivered, Leila started chatting about their trip and suddenly she took my face in her hands and tilted my head toward the light. She said,

"You were crying, right?"

I tried to deny it, but my eyes told a different story. Her husband then came and sat next to us and he said to me in a very gentle manner,

"We know how hard this is for you, but please do not cry so much. Please know that we will always be here for you, always."

His words were very kind and sincere and over the years, I have come to admire and respect him as one of the kindest, most genuine human beings one could meet in this world. I was with them once when he went about fifteen minutes out of his way at night just to show a stranger how to get to a highway so that they could find their way home.

He was such a family man, always there for his wife and his children. I had seen him just come in the door from a hard day at work, and if one of his children did not like what was made for dinner, he would go right back out to get them something so that they would not go to bed hungry. He was the one who would remember his children's school PTA metings before his wife did.

My job was still very tiring, but I was getting adjusted to my routine now. I was also learning to cope with being here alone. In one of my cleaning escapades, I had found an old typewriter in the big storage closet. Many days, when I finished some of my chores, I would close the drapes around 11:00 a.m., bring the typewriter to the kitchen table and practice my typing. I would pick up magazines and just try to type a passage in as short a time as possible. This would help me later when I applied for a secretarial job. I would then carefully put away the typewriter, open back the drapes and continue my other chores.

One day, I was so tired from trying to shine the mirrors, (I had not learnt the trick of using the feather duster yet) and doing the laundry and taking them up and down the stairs that I decided not to clean the guest bathroom. I figured no one had used it anyway.

I have to tell you this was a beautiful bathroom. It was black marble and it had ceiling mirrors and mirrors at different angles on the walls. Well, as soon as Mrs. W arrived home she came to the doorway of my room where I was folding the last load of laundry.

She asked me, "Did you clean the guest bathroom?"

I was taken aback. How did she know but I quickly answered, "No, ma'am".

Apparently, when she came home she went all around the house to smell everything to make sure I did it all. That was how she knew the guest bathroom was not cleaned.

She then said, "Make sure you clean the guest bathroom, everyday!"

I immediately got up and went to the closet to get the bucket and the cleaning objects and all the liquids that I had to rub on the toilet bowl, etc. I did not know how to explain what was going through my mind. Here I was cleaning toilets and I used to be a teacher in my country with my own babysitter.

I felt so belittled and degraded that day and I could assure you that I cleaned the toilet with soap and water as well as eye water. My tears just flowed freely and I let them. I did not even try to stop. I huddled in a corner of that bathroom and prayed with every fiber of my being,

"Dear God, help me, please give me the courage to endure this self imposed prison and torture."

For indeed this was emotional torture. Growing up, everyone had said,

"Make sure you take your education and you would not have to labor in the fields and do menial tasks in order to make a living."

Well, I did everything that was expected of me and I had passed every exam that I could possibly have taken at my age. Yet, here I was, being wasted away and not being able to do anything to stop it.

All the same, when I wrote to my father, (my mom could not read or write) I did not let him know any of this. I sugar coated my circumstances and told him that all was great and that I had my own room and my own TV and everything. I did not want them to worry. I preferred to do the worrying. Of course I was tyring to tell my husband, begging him for me to go back home, but he would not listen; he had his own agenda going at this time.

Worry I did, as there was just cause. It was now summer and Mrs. W.

told me that since the girls would be away at camp she would not need me for the full five days, but that she would only need me for three days. What was I supposed to do for work and money for the additonal two days? She had a friend who might take me for the other two days. I was happy to meet her friend, who was an angel.

So on Wednesdays and Fridays, I went to Mrs. Limbeck's house and did the cleaning while I slept at Mrs. W. from Tuesday evening, leaving to go back to the Bronx on Sunday mornings. I loved going to Mrs. Limbeck. I practically looked forward to Wednesday mornings when one of her sons would come to get me. As soon as I arrived, she would always have something for me to snack on and she would have started the laundry.

Mrs. Limbeck was a petite, beautiful woman who had two sons, one was in College and the other was in his senior year at high school. I had to say that her sons thought the world of her and they would pick her up and hug her and were always making her laugh. She was so lucky with them.

However, like most good people, she was unlucky with her husband. I heard Mrs. Limbeck confiding in Mrs. W. that he was having an affair. This was a side of Mrs. W. I learnt to respect. She was always there for her friend.

Despite her troubled marriage, Mrs. Limbeck was a very loving person. Once we started talking and she realized that I had two kids back home, she offered to buy some stuff and mail it to them for me. I was so touched by her offer, but I realized that she was not that rich. She had just started working part time in a boutique and I told her that when I was ready to send stuff home, I would let her know.

Working for her on those two days of the week was a safe haven for me. Her house was dainty, with a beautiful fireplace set in the living room surrounded by some colorful rock formations. This house was so charming that many times when I was eating some lunch, which Mrs. Limbeck would always leave in the fridge for me, I would daydream, about someday having a cute little house like that.

I guess her warmth and affection were also contributing factors to making me feel at peace in her home. I never once felt like a servant, and because of that, I went out of my way to clean her home and made it sparkling for when she returned.

Whilst the girls were away at summer camp, Mr. and Mrs. W. went away for a week. The weekend before they left, I heard about a sponsorship program that was being run by the Board of Education in NY. Supposedly, once you were a qualified foreign teacher, you could be sponsored to work in NY State and your family could join you immediately. I was extremely excited about this news!

On Monday, I called and found out the address and all the details about how to get to the Board of Education in downtown Brooklyn. I was having trouble sleeping; I was so excited that I would be able to get my children. I started calling up the airlines to find out about ticket prices and so on.

Tuesday when I got in to work there was no way I could come back to Brooklyn and on Wednesday, I was committed to work with Mrs. Limbeck. So, on Thursday, I got up at 5:00 a.m. and made my way to the New York City Subway to Brooklyn. I had written down all the information about how to get to the Board of Education and I soon arrived without too much hassle.

When I got to the receptionist, she told me that I could only meet someone by appointment. I begged her to let me see someone as I was coming from NJ and would not get another day off.

I think she recognized the desperation in my pleas and decided to let me see the director of the program. But, all to no avail. He was sorry, but the program had met its quota and they were not sponsoring any one else. I realized the futility of begging and got up to leave. I think he was genuinely sorry that he could not get me the coveted sponsorship that I was desperately seeking.

He offered to help me to get in to Lehman College in the Bronx to obtain a NYS teacher's license and with that, I could get a job as a teacher. This offer was not going to help me. I had no one in the States who could support me while I went to school full time and I did not think about the possibility of going to school part-time in the Bronx while I was working in NJ.

I was crushed. All my fantasies about being reunited with my family within a very short period of time had been dashed to smithereens. I felt very dejected. I had been building castles in the air and now it was all crumbling around me. I finally got to Tenafly and I took the taxi on the final leg of my return trip.

When I got out of the cab, I asked the driver to wait because I was not sure if I could get the keys to open the door. I had never been good with keys. To this day, I am still not good with opening doors. He waited and indeed, he had to help me to open the lock. I rushed into the home and turned off the alarm before it went off. In hindsight, I realized that I had exposed myself to a lot of danger – I should never have let a stranger open the door for me, but that just went to show how trusting I was and how utterly naïve.

As soon as I got into the house, I just sat on the steps, listless. I was emotionally drained. It was as if a truck had just run over me. I could not even cry – I just sat there, staring into space. I finally made my way to my room and as always, I turned to sleep as a means of escape. If only for a couple of hours: I had to get up and start cleaning as Mr. and Mrs. W. would be returning on Saturday evening.

The following week, Mrs. W. told me that she was going to pick up Aleya who would be the first one coming back from camp. I had no problem with that, as the girls were never mean to me; I was a little more concerned about not going back to Ms. Limbeck's. On Saturday, when she was leaving to pick up Dr. W. to go out for the evening, she told me that Aleya had permission to have a few friends over.

Whenever you see teenage movies with kids partying while their parents were away, sometimes you think it was being exaggerated. Believe me it was not. Around 6:00 p.m., a few friends did come over and they ordered pizza. I thought this was it. Aleya was 16 years old and I did not hover around them, I retired to my room, but I was still within reach if they needed me.

There was a big party at the end of the street and very soon, friends of the friends started to come to the backyard. There was no fence around the yard and they had free access to the pool. Later, I would find out that the friends who were coming were bringing six packs of beer. Pretty soon there was a huge crowd outside and Aleya and her friends had joined them. By now Aleya had disarmed the alarm system from one of the exit doors.

The kids were having a great time throwing each other in the pool and horsing around until one of them tried to get into the house by another door, which was not disarmed. The alarm went off and I ran to the kitchen and got there the same time that Aleya did. I called the cops and told them it was a false alarm. The kids went back out and continued having fun. But then another kid was tyring to get through the glass doors leading into the living room. Remember I told you how I used to have to shine glasses and mirrors all the time?

The glass doors were so shiny and he was so wasted that he thought it was an open space and tried to walk through it. What do you know? The alarm went off again and Aleya ran in again. She was scared now, because the cops would definitely come and she would get into trouble with her parents. She freaked out and started to let out some expletives – she quickly realized that she did not know half these people who were now streaming through her kitchen with wet clothes and shoes. She got angry and yelled at everyone to leave with some choice words.

I ran into the kitchen after the second alarm went off and the friends whom she did know were soliciting my help in putting their clothes and their sneakers in the dryer. I found it very funny that sixteen-year-old girls did not know how to operate the dryer. Thankfully, the others who had just stopped by, left just the way they came, without a fuss. They cut back out through the backyard and were gone before the cops came around, even though we had called a second time to say it was a false alarm.

Could you imagine the beige kitchen tiles after a bunch of wet teenagers had romped through it? I felt sorry for Aleya, because I knew, she had not expected this situation to turn out the way it had. Therefore, I cleaned up the kitchen and I swear that in the freezer section of the refrigerator I found broken twigs. I also helped the girls to get their clothes dried and decent for them to wear home. Aleya thanked me and shortly afterward, her parents came home. We thought that was the end of it, because I had no intention of complaining.

Guess not! On Sunday morning, Dr. W. went to the backyard and he soon came into the house and called for me. (I did not leave as usual on Sunday morning because Mrs. W. told me she needed me to stay over as she was having some friends over for dinner.) I was the only one up.

He looked at me and said to me that I should not get scared and that I should tell him what happened last night. I said I did not know, that he should ask Aleya. He then asked me to accompany him upstairs and he told me that whatever I heard him say, I should not be worried. I knew he was getting more and more upset as he continued to speak

.

He woke Aleya up and I was standing in the doorway when he asked her to tell him exactly what happened the night before. She said that nothing happened.

"Dad, I told you nothing happened."

He kept insisting that she should tell him the truth. He was getting a little louder as he spoke and she maintained that nothing happened. When he walked out of her room, she looked at me and mouthed a silent

"Thank you". I knew she was eternally grateful. We later found out that the neighbor had told her dad about the ruckus the night before, and here I thought, only people from my country used to tattle.

Well, everyone was gloomy all day and Mrs. W. was banging pots and pans the whole time. She had started cooking some stuff since Friday and I think she used every pot that she owned to make that one dinner. I was busy all day tyring to clean up after her and by the time the guests arrived the house was spotless. I helped her to bring dishes upon dishes into the dining room. I would soon be left speechless when I saw the true magnificence of this room.

I think I had told you how beautiful this room was. There was a huge table with a glass top. The middle was pure glass and the border of about one foot wide was of a rich cherry colored wood. Around the walls of this room was a one-foot wide ledge with this same beautiful cherry wood. It sparkled when it was cleaned. The reason I was stunned was that this ledge was not an ordinary ledge. It was a cover for a heating panel!

As I was helping Mrs. W. to bring in the dishes, I saw her take off this panel and place them neatly in the corner. Then the dishes that were to be served hot were placed on the heater and once she turned on an electric switch, the food was kept hot. What ingenuity! Wow! I was blown away!!

After dinner that evening which ended around midnight, I was extremely tired and had hoped to go to sleep soon after. Wrong! Mrs. W. insisted that I wash and dry all the dishes – she had taken out her good china and she did not put these in the dishwasher. Mr. W. even suggested that I soak the pots and leave them.

She ordered him out of her kitchen and he left to go upstairs. Once she had given her orders, Mrs. W. then also went upstairs. I finished the pots, pans and the garbage until 2:30 a.m. I felt as if I had barely put my head on my pillow before I had to wake up at 5:00 a.m. to leave for the Bronx. This week I had to come back on Wednesday, instead of Tuesday as she did not want to pay me an extra day for staying over on Sunday.

On the following Tuesday Mrs. W. picked up Kayla and brought home ALL the clothes that she had used during the summer. I did not know at the time, but when the other mothers came home from summer camp with their kids, they would drop off the clothes at the cleaners to be washed and ironed.

Not Mrs. W.! She knew that I would be there on Wednesday, and so for quite a number of days, I was washing and ironing a ton of cotton clothing that was not easy to iron. In addition, the laundry room did not have AC and in the summer time, it was HOT.

This was a different kind of fatigue. I still had to finish all my other chores and since it was still warm outside, I was required to clean the pool furniture. I did not think I had ever worked as hard in my life as I did during that first summer after I came to the USA. I started to develop a severe back pain, which only got worse by me sleeping in the sofa at Leila's house where I was still welcome with open arms on the weekends.

With both girls back and my schedule back to normal with Mrs. W. I could not go to Mrs. Limbeck on Wednesdays and Fridays. She missed me as I did her. She called one day to speak with Mrs. W. and I picked up the phone. We then arranged for me to come back to NJ on Mondays (one of my regular days off) to clean her home. I was happy to do this for her and I would be making an extra $35.00.

It was not easy though, as I had to leave the Bronx at 5:00 a.m. and come back all the way to NJ. Her boys were in school and no one was there to pick me up or drop me off to the bus stop. In the mornings, it was quite easy, as I was going downhill to where she lived. However, in the afternoons, I had to walk about half a mile uphill to get the bus. I would console myself on my way to the bus stop by converting my $35.00 US dollars into my local currency. In my mind, this would make it all worthwhile. I would try to figure out what this money could buy for the kids back home and if I did not do this extra work, where would it come from?

So far, I have not had a chance to go back to visit my nephew in NJ. Roxanne and I spoke often on the phone and one day she invited me to a prayer service to commemorate the one-year anniversary of her mother's death. On that same day, another friend whom I had known since I was a child in my country had a prayer service to commemorate her father's death anniversary as well.

I felt obligated to attend both. One was in the morning at 9:00 a.m., the other one was in the afternoon, and it was at 3:00 p.m. I brought "good" clothes with me when I came to work and on Sunday morning, I left Mrs. W. as usual. I took the buses that would bring me to Jersey City instead of to the Bronx.

When I got off at the bus stop to go to Roxanne's home, I was careful not to make the same mistake that I did when I had walked in the opposite direction in the cold. It was so different getting off the bus in the summer time and I had no problem getting to her home.

After this ceremony, I was to go to the Bronx where my friend's husband would pick me up from Leila's home to go to their service. It was not an imposition because he had to come to the Bronx to pick up the officiating priest. Everyone at Roxanne's home was busy so no one could give me a ride to the bus stop. One of her brothers told me to take the bus to Journal Square and then take the train to Hoboken. When I got out at Hoboken, I would get a bus to the Bronx. He told me the number of the bus and I wrote it all down.

I made it quite well to Hoboken, but when I got up on the street to get the bus, the trouble began. I was standing on a corner of a gas station that separated a four-lane highway. Traffic was hectic. I waited; and I waited; and I waited; for this particular bus to arrive.

Buses came; buses went; and then one driver stopped and called me to his bus. He said to me,

"This is the third time I am passing and you are still standing here, where do you need to go?"

I told him and he said:

"There is no bus from here that will take you to the Bronx."

He asked if I could get to the Bronx if he showed me where to get the trains.

I told him,

"I know the No. 2 and No. 5 trains run where my friend lives."

He asked me to get on his bus and he did not even make me pay; he felt so sorry for me. (People like these help to reinforce my faith in humanity). He took me to Times Square in 42nd street, the end of his bus route. Then he showed me where to go downstairs and follow the signs to get the trains to the Bronx. I did not have words enough to thank him for his kindness, and I wish him God's blessings.

Leila had called Roxanne's home and she was frantic because she did not know where I could be this long. She was very relieved when I got to her apartment and we soon got a phone call from my friend's husband. He would come to pick me up, but it would be when he **dropped the officiating priest back home. The service was over.** I would miss it after all my efforts.

Anyway, my friend still invited me to go over, as this was the first time she would be seeing me since I arrived. We had only spoken to each other over the phone. I visited her and stayed over on Sunday evening. On Monday morning, I took the bus from Queens back to the Bronx as everyone had to go to work and I did not expect them to drive me back.

I sometimes looked back on these incidents and thanked God that I could speak English. I also reflected on how much more difficult it would be for someone coming to this country for the first time and not being able to speak or read and write English. I was getting my feet wet with traveling, using Public transportation and eventually,

I would become such a pro. Many people on my various jobs later would always come to me if they needed to go somewhere strange, using MTA. I had learnt to read the maps and to figure out whether I was going "Uptown" or "Downtown."

I was very conscious of the fact that Leila's apartment was very small and even though they were still warm and loving, I felt like such a 'fifth wheel to a coach". When Leila first invited me to stay at her home we had never discussed how long this would be for or what, if any contributions I would need to make. She and her husband would not hear of any such thing.

How could they take money from me, for only staying with them for two days? Moreover, she said, I cleaned up and did her laundry on Mondays, so she felt she was getting the best of both worlds. I begged to differ; they were offering me the whole world.

However, I had to live with my conscience, and I constantly felt as if I should be tyring to find somewhere else to stay. The idea of living alone was daunting, especially since I was only home for two days, but I could not continue to take advantage of Leila's generosity. I finally found a solution when I learnt about a brother and sister who would be willing to have me share a basement apartment with them.

This was not just any brother and sister. These were family friends from back home, in whose home both my brother and I had stayed in the city to go to College. At this point his daughters and my son were also staying with this family to go to Queens College. Eventually, I convinced Leila that it would be best for all concerned that I go and share the apartment with Joey and Shani. So, I arrived at my new abode with my suitcase, and some additional belongings, in two large black garbage bags.

On Tuesday morning, I had to take a new route to NJ and I wrote down all the details. It was a longer route now, because I had to take two trains to GW Bridge where I would get the bus to NJ. The girls were now back to school and I rose early in the morning to make sure that they got on their bus in time. The drudgery of my existence continued as usual.

It was over six months since I had been in the States and I approached Mrs. W. about the possibility of sponsoring me as a Babysitter/Housekepter. She told me that her brother was an immigration attorney and that she would discuss it with him. I called my nephew and told him and he advised me to find out about an attorney who would probably have my best interests at heart, rather than Mrs. Ws. Interest.

I spoke to the women on the bus and I was told that there was a female attorney, who lived in NJ and who worked very hard for her clients. I took her number and decided to call the following week. She was indeed working in the best interests of her clients. After some routine questions, she told me that I should look for another job, if I wanted to be sponsored.

"Why?" I asked, perplexed.

She explained that if I was to be sponsored by a family as a live-in babysitter I would need to be working with younger children. My two girls were already eleven and sixteen. If I was to be working for a family as a live-in housekeeper then my boss would have to be employed full time. My circumstances did not meet any of those requirements. I was scared.

"Do you mean to tell me that I have wasted six months of my time?"

"No" she said, "your current employer could give you references to show experience in this country, but I am telling you, it would be very difficult to convince the Immigration Officials that this family needed someone to live in. Add to the fact that your papers would take about three to four years to process, then your girls would become older and your chances even more complicated."

I was in a quandary now. Would Mrs. W. want to give me a reference? I know how grueling a taskmaster she could be, and she had never been very affectionate toward me, how would she react to this situation?

She was livid. She wanted the lawyer's number. I was scared now, and when she sensed that I was a little hesitant; she looked up the telephone directory and found her. She started quietly enough, but soon she was yelling at the top of her lungs.

"I would make sure that you do not get any more clients. Why are you doing this to people like us? Do you realize how influential we are?"

I could not hear the lawyer on the other end of the line, but I could tell that she was not letting Mrs. W. get the better of her and she soon hung up. The next day I called the lawyer and told her that I was sorry for everything and she said that I should not apologize, but I should really get out of that situation, especially since she had spoken to Mrs. W.

She told me that I should not be scared and that she would always, no matter how many Mrs. Ws. threatened her; she would always put her clients' interests first.

Mrs. W. was really mad and she got on the phone and I heard her calling an agency to find someone to work for her. She told me that I had to wait at least two weeks and that I would have to train the person who would replace me. I felt very uncomfortable in her presence; she made me feel as if I had committed some sort of crime.

Chapter Five

Everything happens for a Reason

All I was doing was to try to find out about my sponsorship. Now that I was convinced that a sponsorship by the Wilheim family may jeopardize my future, I decided to try to find other employment. I asked around and soon found someone whose situation seemed ideal.

I met with her and she had a relatively small house. She was a professor working full time in Manhattan and she had a daughter who was four years old. She gave me a tour of the house and showed me the room that I would occupy. It was quite comfortable and it had a sewing machine, which she said I was free to use.

I told her that I needed to give my current employer two weeks notice and she was fine with that, since she said that her other baby sitter would not be leaving until that time, anyway. Everything seemed to be fitting into place, perfectly. Too perfect maybe?

I had trained someone for Mrs. W. She was satisfied and glad that this person was also from my country. My time was up with her and I should have been happy to leave, but in spite of her being such a hard taskmaster, it had been a major part of my life since coming to the States. I might also never get to see Mrs. Limbeck again. I would truly miss working for her.

Besides, I was really going to miss the girls. We had built a very special relationship, to the point where Aleya used to tell me her little "girlie" secrets, about the boy on whom she had a crush. She would come home and discuss her Social Studies projects with me and we had wonderful conversations about different cultures and religions, etc.

Kayla still used to come to my room, but we had this agreement to get her up as soon as her mom was home. When she first got her braces, she was crying and I hugged her and comforted her quite often. This period brought us closer together and I would pick flowers for her from the backyard if she were having a bad day. However, even though I was attached to the girls, I had to think of my true purpose of doing this type of job, which was to secure a sponsorship for my family and me.

I said my goodbyes to the girls. The girls and I cried and hugged each other and I tried to apologize for leaving, hoping they would understand. On the side, Mrs. W. asked me whom I thought would miss me more and when I answered that Aleya would, she was shocked that I was so right. She could not believe that I knew her girls that well. She thought I would say Kayla. I told her if ever she needed someone to stay over on an emergency basis on a weekend, she should give me a call, I would be happy to come and stay with the girls.

I went home with the intention of starting my new job the following Tuesday. The Professor did not work on Mondays, so my workweek would be the same – Tuesday mornings to Sunday mornings. I was looking forward to a more secure position where I could be sponsored and I hoped a less strenuous job. I was in for a big shock!

Ms. Professor called me on Sunday afternoon, to tell me that she was sorry, but that she would not need me, as her former baby sitter had decided to stay on. I held the phone in my hand, looking at it as if a monster was on the other end of the line.

"Why are you doing this to me?" I asked.

"Do you realize that I have already quit my other job? I did not continue my search because you promised me that I would start with you on Tuesday?"

She was very apologotic and told me that I should not despair. She had a friend who needed someone immediately. I could start with her on Tuesday. She would tell her friend that she interviewed me and that she recommended me highly. I had some reservations but I was not at leisure to pick and choose. I asked her if she could tell me a little about her friend.

It turned out that her friend had three daughters, ages 7 to 3 years old. She gave me directions and told me that her friend would pick me up at the Bus stop at 8:30 a.m. on Tuesday. I told her that I would be there.

It was not until I hung up the phone that I realized from patching bits and pieces of conversations on the bus, that I had just been set up. Ms. Professor was the ploy to interview me and her circumstances being so enticing, I would readily agree to work for her. Her friend, who was desperate for someone would accept me willingly when the other job fell through.

Anyhow, even though I realized this, I decided to try it. I was picked up at the bus stop by my new employer and she seemed pleasant enough. When I got to the house, I was overwhelmed. I thought Mrs. W. had a huge house. This one was double the size. It seemed that Mrs. Shimmel's father was a building contractor and every time he came up with another innovation in building technology, he built an extra wing on her house to reflect this.

Three different sections were connected with glassy walkways and canopied awnings. It was very impressive if you were not thinking,

"Oh my God, here I go again; I have to clean all of this!"

I soon met the girls who were very pretty and seemed quite well behaved. There was also an older woman from the neighborhood, who came by to help with the girls. She smiled very kindly and gave me a hug. It seemed that all would be well, after all!

Tuesday soon passed with doing regular chores. I did laundry, vacuuming and mopping the kitchen, etc. I did not have too much to do with the girls as both mom and the older woman were home. At night, I went down to my room, wondering when someone would say that it was time for dinner.

I soon got a call to come up and straighten up the kitchen after dinner, but when I looked around, I did not see anything left for me. I did not ask. I looked in the refrigerator and I took a bunch of grapes to my room. Luckily, I went through this before, and so I had brought some food from home. Unfortunately, I could not go back up to the kitchen to heat it up, and so I ate it cold.

On Wednesday evening, Mrs. Shimmel was anxious to go out. A teenager would come over to assist with the girls. I did not think it would be necessary; after all, they were three young girls. Thank God she made that contingency plan. The girls were taking their showers and getting themselves ready for bed. I was with the youngest one in the sitting room and then I heard screaming. One of them was cursing at the top of her lungs.

"You shut up! I know what your mother and father do in the bathtub before they go to bed at night."

This tirade continued and they started to chase each other around the living room. There was a center table with a glass top and one of them was banging on it. All the while, she was spewing out expletives that you would not expect from a five year old. She lunged at the older one and I tried to get in between. I tried pulling them apart, but I was no match for these rambunctious youngsters.

Thankfully, just in time, the teenager from next door appeared as if out of nowhere. I grabbed hold of one, and she held the other. I would always consider that teenager to be an angel sent just to help me that night. She yelled at them to shut up and finish their bath and get dressed for bed. They gave her some really nasty looks and continued mumbling under their breath, but they eventually got ready for bed.

Finally, the ordeal was over. Mr. and Mrs. Shimmel returned home and I could go down to my room. I was shaken. I did not anticipate that babysitting could be reduced to mayhem and craziness. I took some more fruit down to my room and ate it before going to sleep. I woke up during the night and I was thinking about my circumstances. Even though I needed a job desperately, would I be able to handle this job for three or four years that it would take to get me sponsored? I did not think I could.

On Thursday, I had a routine day until the girls got home from school. Mrs. Shimmel had gone shopping and Lydia, the older woman had come over. She and I were making some chicken breasts for dinner and by the time we cleaned up Mrs. Shimmel came home. I was thinking that I was doing her a favor by telling her ahead of time so that she could try to make other arrangements, but it backfired on me - "Big Time."

I told Mrs. Shimmel that I found it difficult to stay on with her because the little three year old reminded me too much of my daughter, and that when I left this weekend, she would need to find someone else.

She paused for a minute and then she looked at me and said,

"OK, go pack your bags; I will take you to the bus stop."

It was almost 7:00 p.m. and I had to go all the way to Queens. I looked at her confused.

I stammered, "I did not mean that I wanted to leave now."

She said,

"I am telling you this one more time, pack your stuff and I will take you to the bus stop."

I went downstairs and I put my few things together. While she went to her room to get money to pay me, Lydia, the older woman knowing that I had not eaten much during the day, put a few pieces of the chicken we had baked in a little foil wrap and snuck it into my bag. Mrs. Shimmel paid me for the three days and took me to the bus stop.

It was windy and dark already. I prayed to God to help me and protect me. As if in answer to my prayers, a woman was dropped off by her employers and she soon joined me in the bus stop. I felt less petrified. We soon started talking and she said that she was going to Manhattan, and we could travel together. Once I got to Manhattan, I knew how to get on the trains into Queens. I arrived home to a shocked Joey and Shani at 10:45 p.m. that evening.

I tried as best as I could to explain why I was home at that time of the night without being melodramatic, but all I wanted to do was to shout and scream at someone, anyone for what was happening to me at this point in time. Later, I would find out that you could not be too honest in these job situations if you wanted to succeed. Many times when people wanted to leave one job for another, they would say that they had an emergency back home and that they had to leave. In this way, if the other job did not work out, they could always come back to the first one.

I had never been one to play around with people and their children and so I never learnt that game and I had to pay the consequences, not once but many times over. I still never regret being honest in all my dealings with people. I still hold on to the principle that the truth shall set you free.

During the month, with all the confusion surrounding the sponsorship issue, I had called several agencies and was forwarded to Catholic Charities. This organization had a special Immigration section. I was forwarded to a gentleman who invited me to come and meet with him and he said that he knew of the political circumstances in my country and we could probably file a petition for a refugee status. He did not know if it would be granted, but he could try.

Who was I to complain? I was eager for any means to get through with my papers so that I could have my children join me. I was not having a grand old time with babysitting prospects. I seemed to have the worst luck in the world when it came to finding good jobs in this field.

Here I was once again, having to search for a job. I walked the avenues up and down, thinking that I would find some part time jobs while I continued interviewing for a better babysitting position. Well those were some long, unproductive days. No one would hire me without my papers and even if they were willing to, they needed a male who could climb and carry heavy loads. So, I kept looking through the papers and calling to make appointments.

I had an appointment for a babysitting job for a seven year old in New Jersey. I wrote down the address and left home on a Tuesday morning. From Times Square, I had to take two buses to the Darwin's home. At the back of the first bus, I saw this couple. I did not pay too much attention to them. However, when we joined the next bus, they were again on this bus. When I got off at my designated stop, they also got off.

As I was walking up the street to look for the building number, I saw them sitting under a tree. I said to myself,

"Do you mean to tell me that they would come all this way to just 'make out'"?

Anyhow, the house number seemed to disappear into thin air. You could see the numbers preceding and following it, but not this number. Lo and behold, the number was written on some concrete steps on the street corner. The house was sitting on top of a hill and it was huge. Eventually, the couple made their way along with me to the front door. We started talking and realized that both the girl and I were going after the same job. We had both seen the house, but we thought it was a factory of some sort; it was that huge.

There was a grueling interview process and we had to fill out forms. Mrs. Darwin had two boutiques in Manhattan and Mr. Darwin was a writer. When Mrs. Darwin was about to give us a tour of the house, she told us to remember where we were leaving our jackets.

At first, I thought, "How hard could it be to remember where you left your jacket?"

She knew why she told us that. Sometimes a door would open to a completely different wing of the house and I could see how you could not find where you had put something down. The biggest set back in this job was that the family owned two enormous dogs that had to be walked and fed by the household help.

I was scared of dogs and the fact that one of them slept with the little girl in her bedroom did not encourage me either. It was explained that the dog slept in her room to protect her. Thieves were always breaking in, as Mrs. Darwin would often bringt home cash with her.

I was glad that I never heard back from the Darwins. The other girl was lucky because the guy with her, her husband told her as soon as we left that there was no way he would let her do a job like that. Even if he had to work two jobs to make ends met. That was the difference in having someone with you as opposed to being alone. I arrived home before Shani and Joey and I made dinner for everyone. When they realized how poorly my job search was going, they told me not to worry; they would always be there for me.

As she had gotten older, my daughter's philosophy in life was that everything happened for a reason. I guess this was one of those times, because the attorney from Catholic Charities needed to me to go to his office quite often to fill out a lot of paperwork. If I had been working full time in NJ, there was no way I could have followed through with his requests. Eventually, he got a notice from INS that I should go to 26 Federal Plaza for an Interview.

I was so nervous; I could not sleep the night before or eat any breakfast before I left to meet the attorney. I got off at Brooklyn Bridge stop and I was going around in circles before I finally made my way to Federal Plaza on October 26, 1988. I soon met the attorney and we went in for my interview. The interviewing officer was very sympathetic, and she granted me a work permit, while the case was being reviewed. I was ecstatic, but confused. What did all this mean?

The lawyer explained that this was great news. I could work in any company and I would be given a social security card, but with restrictions. However, he thought this would be a very difficult case. It was understood that there was political unrest and harassment in my country, but it was very difficult to prove. Based on what the interviewing officer had said, you would need newspaper clippings and threatening letters of violence in order to be granted political asylum or refugee status.

Nevertheless, we would try to follow up with all their requests and who knew, maybe my case could be adjudicated successfully. I was happy and sad all at the same time. If I was successful in this petition, I could have my family join me, but I could never return to my country. How would I get to see my parents? I decided to cross that bridge when the time came, and gratefully accepted the boon that was being offered to me.

My job search went in a different direction now. I was looking at the classified ads for secretarial positions, clerks and any other office positions. I had quite a few leads but many of them were for real estate offices and they wanted to pay me below minimum wage, which at that time was $4.25 an hour.

Luckily, I saw this advertisement for a secretary in a Non-profit organization in Queens. I called and set up an appointment. I had to take a spelling, alphabetizing and a typing test. This was where my typing practice at the Wilheim's home would come in beneficial to me. I aced all my tests and went home on the promise that I would get a call from them.

Finally, I got the highly anticipated phone call. They would hire me, but I needed to go to the Main Office in Manhattan to fill out all the necessary paperwork. I got traveling directions and made my way into Manhattan on November 1, 1988. I was told that I had to go out through a revolving exit once I got off the train. I missed this exit by one train car and I had to pay the penalty.

It made a huge difference which exit you got out from a subway station.

According to the directions, once I got off at the exit, I would only have to walk to the end of the block and the building would be the second to last one. I kept asking people for the building address and the street name, and they would say, it was right around the corner or at the end of the block. Many of them did not even know.

It was the first day of November, and I had not bought true winter clothes yet. Needless to say, I was freezing and soon it started to rain. I was not a tea or coffee drinker, but I bought a cup of tea just to warm my hands around the cup. Eventually, I made my way into the building, wet and cold.

I filled out all the necessary paperwork and the Business Administrator was very complimentary about my handwriting. All documents signed, I made my way back to Queens. Walking from the Main Office back to the subway, I realized how simple it was if I had gotten out at the right exit. When I got to the Queens Office, my supervisor took one look at my cold, wet, bedraggled appearance and told me to go home and she would see me the next day.

On November 2, 1988, I commenced my fulfilling and rewarding job as a secretary. I was soon learning the ropes and created a notebook, writing down everything that I learnt. A few years later, my notebook would be used to create a Procedures manual for the agency. It included city and state regulations that needed to be followed as well as internal processes that were to be utilized.

At first, I did not talk too much to the other workers, but soon everyone and I became friendly and I still maintain some friendships that were started in that office. The most valuable of them, was my supervisor, who would soon become my mentor, a mother figure and someone whose widsom and advice I have learnt to depend on through the years.

My life took on a new pattern. I was still very lonely and missing my children and my entire family back home, but on the surface, I seemed to be doing pretty well. I tried to learn anything and everything associated with my job. I had organized the office and was typing away rapidly on CWA reports, Adoptive Home studies and if I may say so myself, from all feedback that I was getting, everyone was happy with my performance.

It was the Holiday season and the entire city was lit up and looked very beautiful. There were so many sales and the stores looked really festive with their elaborate decorations and pictures of Santa. I took advantage of lots of the sales, but the other stuff had little meaning for me. I did not seem capable of enjoying a lot without my children. All I wanted was for the weekend to come so that I could call and speak with them and make sure that they were doing OK.

Had I opened a Bank account with AT&T; (I think at this time, it was the only long distance phone carrier to my country) I would have been very rich. But I used to console myself with the fact that had I not been paying these exhorbitant phone bills, I might have been paying the money on doctor's bills. Hearing their voices made such a big difference to my emotional well being.

I had worked out an arrangement with their dad, that if by Saturday afternoon they did not hear from me on our home phone then he would bring them to the Leonora telephone exchange so that I could speak with them on Sunday morning. Being that it was a Holiday weekend, I told him to bring them on the Saturday evening so that I could speak with them.

These were the times of phone calls not going through and dialing and re-dialing for hours before you could get through with long distance calls. It was cold in NY and it was pouring rain in Guyana which made matters worse. They were waiting for me and I was dialing and could not get through.

There was no way I could get a message to them to go home and so Zara fell asleep while waiting. Her clothes had got wet from the rain and when she fell asleep they had to wrap her up in newspaper and when this did not work, they wrapped her in an old flag that was sitting on the cupboard in order to keep her warm. I did not know this until much later.

Anyhow, I kept calling and calling without any luck. Shani and I eventually went to bed and she started praying out loud asking God to please let me get through to my children or else she knew I would be miserable and she would not be able to be festive around me. After a while she fell asleep and I got up to go into the kitchen to call so as not to disturb her. Her brother Joey had gone out with friends to a Christmas party.

Around 2:00 a.m. I was still sitting in the kitchen intermittently tyring to dial home. I heard the key in the lock but then I heard Joey running back up the basement steps. I called out to him to ask if he was OK. He came into the apartment all breathless and saying that he thought he had seen a ghost. I can still laugh as I write this but he was literally shaking.

Apparently, from the passageway to where I was seated at the kitchen table all he could see was my head. Earlier that day I had washed my hair and it was still open and he thought he was seeing a ghost – people from my country were very afraid of ghosts. We tried to make light of the situation and he went to his room. The next morning when we woke up, his keys were still in the door to show how scared he was, neither of us thought about getting his keys out of the lock.

I then went to the room that I shared with Shani and tried as quietly as I could to continue dialing home, thinking that it being the wee hours of the morning, the circuits might be less busy. No luck. I kept getting busy tones. I could not take this torture any more and around 5:30 a.m. I finally dialed for operator assistance. You may want to ask why I waited this long. We had been told that the same circuits that were available to us were the same ones that the operators used but the rates were much higher if the operator assisted you with your phone call. Therefore, we avoided using the operators as much as possible.

Anyway, I was put through to our home phone and I was able to speak with the kids around 5:30 a.m. They were still a little sleepy but we were very happy and so after speaking to them for less than 20 minutes I hung up before finally going to sleep. At 7:30 a.m. the phone rang and I was a bit confused as I was roused out of a deep sleep.

The operator who had assisted me had gone on his break. He came back to find the meter still recording the call as if I were still on the phone. He thought it was unusual for someone to be on the phone for over two hours especially knowing how expensive these calls were.

Once I was fully up and understood who was calling and why he was calling I could not thank him enough. I told him honestly that I had not spent more than 20 minutes on the phone. (I was later told that I could have lied and said five minutes, but with him being so kind, how could I?) He said,

"OK, I will make sure that you are not charged for more than 20 minutes."

How could I not believe that there was a God and that he was looking out for me, when he was sending people like this in my life?

With all of this out of the way, Shani and her brother and I spent a quiet Holiday weekend. Nothing too festive, but we bought a cake and cooked some of our special ethnic dishes. Shani also rented Indian/Bollywood movies and we attempted to watch them. It was not easy to watch a movie with her, because she would keep fast forwarding or rewinding to the songs or to a part that she really liked while you were waiting, tyring to get the movie flowing so that you could get the entire story in one viewing.

The holidays were soon over and little by little I took on more responsibilities from the current Administrative Assistant. As a result, I was sending reports to the Main Office. They were impressed with my precise accounts and updated information on movement of the kids. These details made it easy to monitor payments to foster parents and checks were made out accurately the first time around. Everyone was also very impressed with my handwriting and the neat way in which my work was presented.

On one of my visits to the lawyer's office, I told them of my new job and they were thrilled. They suggested that I ask my employers about the possibility of sponsoring me as a Secretary. I had all the necessary qualifications to be sponsored for this job. I was excited once again, and yet scared at the same time. I was not sure if this agency would be willing to do this for me.

As soon as I got back, I discussed this with my Supervisor, Rhonda. She said that she would set up an appointment with the Executive Director and she would present my case. She reassured me that whatever she could do to make this happen, she would leave no stone unturned. Here was another perfect example of God's emissaries to help us in this world.

Ms. Rhonda, my supervisor returned from one of her visits to the Main Office and could not wait to give me the good news. The Executive Director wanted to meet with me to discuss the procedure involved in sponsoring me. I called the lawyers and requested all the information that I needed to provide to him before going to the appointment.

Finally, the day of my appointment with him arrived. I made my way to the city, with less trouble this time. His Assistant was very warm and inviting and soon I was in the waiting room to see him. He was such a gentleman. He shook my hand and welcomed me with such sincerity, that I was instantly at ease. I must say that he had the voice of a Roman orator. I could understand why he was such a successful Pastor – I thought people would enjoy listening to him endlessly.

I provided him with all the details that the lawyers had given me and because it was a Non-Profit organization, he was relieved that the agency would not incur any expenses to sponsor me. I assured him that I would take on all the financial responsibilities to see this process through. He was happy that they were able to help me as I thanked him wholeheartedly.

I was on cloud nine. I did not know how long it would take to be reunited with my family, as part of my sponsorship would enable me to have them join me. However, the fact that I could be sponsored as a Secretary and I was able to work in a field that I was qualified for was amazing. On top of that I truly enjoyed my work. I hurried back to the office to tell Ms. Rhonda the good news. I was so happy reporting it to her that I shed tears of joy.

All the necessary paperwork was submitted on my behalf and then we got a letter from the Labor Department asking us to show that this job was posted in the Newspapers. Also needed to show that there were not enough responses from American citizens who were interested; why an alien immigrant had to accept this position.

Luckily, the job had been posted! Unfortunately, no one had expected this and the newspapers were thrown out. Undaunted, I went to the Library and was shown how to operate a Microfiche machine to pull up material that was filed away. Apparently, after a certain time all the periodicals and newspapers were microfiched for storage and reference. It was a little awkward operating this machine at first, but I soon got the hang of it and soon, wallah, I found the job postings that I was looking for. Happy day!

I immediately took this requested information to the lawyer's office and they submitted everything to the Labor Dept. Still, they sent back for more paperwork. They needed documentation to show that the salary that was being agreed upon was average and not too low for this profession. They suggested doing a Labor survey.

I was very perturbed about all of this and felt very despondent. Ms. Rhonda told me not to give up; we would do whatever it took. The lawyers did not have the time to do a Labor survey and so I took it upon myself to conduct a Labor survey. Ms. Rhonda gave me her backing.

I visited and called at least 60 Companies in and around the Queens locality. I did Non-Profit as well as commercial businesses and was happy to find that very few companies were paying more than the agency had agreed to pay me. I took this back to the Lawyer. He was very impressed and wanted to know if the agency would pay tuition fees so that I could study to become a lawyer. I thought that was too far fetched and never followed up on that line of thinking.

In the paperwork that was coming back from the Labor Dept. was the name and number of an adjudicator. I called him and he was kind enough to speak with me. Through communications with him, I was advised that they were satisfied with all the documentation provided and that he had approved my case. The only thing needed now was for his supervisor to sign off on the final approval.

Then, as my luck or my curse would have it, there was a semi recession in the USA and all Labor certifications were put on hold. I spoke to the lawyers. They were very disappointed and they did not know what to say to me. I was bewildered and confused and to say the least at my wits end. I had done everything they requested and now at the "nth" hour, when everything was going great, this had to happen. I had to wait, yet again. This would be the pattern of my existence for a very long time to come.

If only I could shut myself away and give up on everything. However, I could not. Two innocent little children were depending on me to be strong. If I ran home with my tail between my legs, all the agony that we had gone through so far would be for naught. I had to be brave and I had to SURVIVE. Even if I could not live, I must exist to see this to the end.

Thus, I continued my dreary life, one day at a time. I know that I was not the only person who had been separated from their family but the hardest part of this torture was that it was self-imposed. It was as if I had inflicted a jail sentence on myself and the only freedom for me would be to be reunited with my family.

I suppose some would say that I could have gone back at any time, but then I felt as if I would be succumbing to being a loser after enduring all this hardship. How would I face my children and tell them that I had shattered our dreams when I was the one who caused them to build those dreams?

I had to confess: there were several occasions that I had felt so down and depressed that I thought of ending it all. However, my children were always the beckoning light at the end of my tunnel. I would always; from somewhere deep within my soul have the presence of mind to think of what would happen to them if I were permanently gone. To this day, I consider them my greatest blessing; they were the very essence of my being and I treasure them as God's greatest gift to me.

I could easily have given in to these fits of depression and gone over the edge. However, I was conscious that my job was important and I focused all my energy toward being an excellent employee. I could tell that I was succeeding, because very soon, I was promoted as an Administrative Assistant and I got my own little office. In this position, I was required to send a lot more reports to the Main Office in the city and the Comptroller was very impressed with my work.

He scheduled a meeting with my supervisor and discussed with her the possibility of me working in the Business Services Section of the Main Office. She was not to say anything to me, but as soon as she returned to our office, she called me. She told me that I had to pretend that I did not hear this before, but she felt obligated to give me a "heads up".

She then said the sweetest thing to me. She said that she would never expect to get someone like me again, but that because she loved me and wanted only the very best for me, she would let me go to the Main office without any reservations. I did not know how to respond. I never expected anything like this and I was scared and excited all at once. I was so comfortable working here I was not sure if I really welcomed this big change at this time. I decided to wait and see how the situation developed.

Very soon, I was invited to a meeting with the Comptroller in the Main Office. I had heard that this man was very mean. I was very nervous and up to this point, I did not know if I was going to say yes. I met with him and the meeting went very well. I asked him for some time to discuss it with my husband who of course he knew was back home in my country. He told me to take all the time that I needed.

I then did the unthinkable and to this day, when I recalled this incident, I still feel embarrassed that I could have made such a fool of myself. I knew the Comptroller was not married and ever conscious of not putting myself in a compromising situation, I asked someone in the office if he was the type of person who was known to have affairs. Innocent enough, you might think!

Nevertheless, not so bright, if you found out later that the person whom I asked was the person with whom he was allegedly having an affair!!!

Anyway, I think they understood that I asked in all innocence and it never came back to haunt me except in my mind. So, as promised I called and discussed the issue with my husband who wanted to know if I was going to work for a male or female and after a few probing questions gave me the go ahead.

Chapter Six

"Infinity" and "The Trip"

The following week was my son's birthday, and even though I spoke with both of my children during the phone call to their dad, I liked to speak to them on their birthday itself. So, I called in the city where he stayed to go to school all week. After I wished him a happy birthday and we talked for a little while, I said to him that I loved him very, very much.

He then said, "I love you very, very much mom'" and then he said,

"Oh wait, I love you to 'Infinity' Mom."

You could tell this had me "boo hoo ing", but I did not let him know that I was crying, I said to him that that was so sweet. He then explained that he had just been learning about long division and infinity in his math classes. This then became a very special word between us and because of this among other reasons; my son now drives an "Infinity" car.

Eventually, I started my new job in the Main Office in the Business Services Department. I could say in all honesty that I enjoyed working in that department and I learnt so much about the inner workings of an HR department that it has been beneficial to me throughout my career.

All my fears about the Comptroller were unfounded. I never, ever had an unpleasant encounter with him. I had mentioned on one occasion that if he ever yelled at me I would burst into tears and I was told that I was the last person he would yell at. Working around him and getting to know him, I realized that he was a lonely person and he sort of did not allow people to get close to him by being harsh. Deep down inside he was all "mush".

My personal life as I knew it also went through a drastic change. Joey, one of the cousins with whom I was sharing the basement apartment had met his girlfriend and they were planning on getting married. They thought that after marriage, she would come and live there, at least for a little while.

I did not wait to be told that the apartment would then become overcrowded and so I started making some enquiries about a new place to stay. I was still hesitant about getting an apartment on my own.

Luckily, my brother-in-law on my husband's side had migrated to the states with his family and they now had their own apartment in Brooklyn. During one of our conversations, they suggested that I should come and stay with them and after thinking about it for a little while, I accepted graciously.

I had to move yet again, and this time after a few years, it was amazing to see how much stuff I had accumulated as opposed to when I had moved from Leila's apartment to Queens. There were bags and bags of stuff that needed to be transported from Queens to Brooklyn. Joey and my sisiter-in-laws sister made a few trips back and forth in their cars before I was finally moved.

I was getting settled and accustomed to the waiting game. My evenings were not as boring as before because my two nephews-in-law occupied a lot of my time when I got home. We shared a room as well as stories and jokes about our day. There was a scar on my leg and I told them that I got that scar while I was in the war. I thought they realized that I was joking until I heard one of them ask his mother, how come she was not in the war like his aunty was.

The younger one had just started kindergarten and when he came home he told us that his class had "black" "white" and "green" children. He could not put a definitive color to the Hispanic kids, so he said they were green.

Our routine consisted of us getting dressed in the morning (Their mom left home much earlier than I did) and dropping them off to their grandmother next door where they would stay until their grandfather dropped them off to school.

In the afternoons I would pick them up and they would be all excited when I would sometimes pick up Pizza on my way home. After dinner, we would watch Wheel of Fortune and Jeopardy and the younger one would always fall asleep on my lap. It is amazing how grown up they are now, but I still have a very close relationship with them.

One evening as my sister-in-law was cutting coupons as she does to this day, she looked up and said to me ...

"Why don't you do this trip? You have been working non-stop and you really should do something to relax a little."

"What are you talking about?" I asked.

She then explained to me that Amtrak was having a country wide sale where they had divided the country into three regions and you could do a round trip of one of the regions at a really reduced fare. My ears perked up a little. Could I really do this? Would I allow myself to go on a trip? Would I not be wasting valuable dollars that I could be using to purchase stuff to send for my kids? This was all my mindset in those days.

I guess I was ready to be adventurous or I really did need a break because it did not take too much persuasion on Shahida's part before I finally made up my mind. I was going to do the smallest of the regions which would take me from New York, stopping in Chicago, New Orleans, Atlanta, Washington DC and back to New York in one week. All I knew about this stuff was the costs based on the round trip ticket price that was quoted.

As I was getting out of the subway on my way to work the next Monday morning, I saw a travel agency just by the exit. It did not miraculously appear; I could assure you. It was always there, but I never noticed it, because I had no interest in travel. Since it was not yet opened I promised myself that I would come back on my lunch break and see if they could help in any way to plan my trip.

As I thought about my trip I started to get a little excited and then I started to feel guilty. How could I be excited about going away? Was I a bad mother; was I being selfish or what was going on with me? All these mixed emotions were making me waver in my decision but I convinced myself that I should do it. And so I went to the Travel Agency and met a really nice agent – I still remember her name – it was Pamela and she was from Trinidad. I explained to her that this was the first time I was venturing into something like this and I needed her assistance.

She was exceptionally nice to me. She recommended that from New York to Chicago where I would have to be overnight on the train that I should get a "sleeper" cabin. Thank God I went to her. I had never realized that there were sleeper cabins on a train. In New Orleans she booked a relatively cheap hotel for me in the French Quarters. It was called "A Creole House" and it was on Ann Street.

The hotel was not far from Bourbon Street (a very famous street in New Orleans) and within walking distance of the board walk and the steam boat Ferry. In Atlanta she booked me in the Days Inn which was not very far from the Amtrak station. I did not plan to overnight in Washington DC and from there I could take any train back to New York as they left every hour on the hour.

I graciously thanked her as I think she had done a really great job of getting me the best deals in terms of comfort; my finances and my safety. I went back to work and then I told my co-workers who at first expressed surprise that I was doing this; and then encouragement. They all thought that I really deserved a break and that they were proud of me for doing this. A few of them even brought books for me to read on the train.

When I got home that evening I told my sister-n-law what I had done during the day. She was also very excited. She insisted that we go and get me some clothes that would be road worthy – namely a few pairs of jeans. This may seem odd to you – why would you need to buy jeans - you should really be wearing your old jeans for a road trip.

The truth was that I never wore jeans or pants. Do not ask me why but I did not own a pair of jeans. I was always in dresses and skirts. During the winter time, I would wear leg warmers and thick socks. That was just me. Many times during the winter, I would be told that I had to drink coffee and start to wear jeans. I still do neither; to this day.

Anyway, I went with Shahida and we bought two pairs of jeans and a few tops and some other traveling necessities especially new "unmentionables". I remembered the old saying never to leave home without clean ones. Since I was going God knew where I did not want to be without new ones.

The date in February 1992 was drawing near and over the weekend I went to my nephew in New Jersey as my train left very early in the morning. He was off from work that day and offered to take me to Penn Station where I would board the Amtrak train for the first leg of my trip from New York to Chicago. We got there a little early and he bought coffee for himself and hot chocolate and bagels while we waited.

It was freezing cold and I was huddled in my winter coat outside of Penn Station. Azeez could not come in with me because it was very difficult to get parking unless you paid to park in a Parking Garage. I did not want him to go through all that hassle especially since he had gotten up early on his day off to bring me to New York.

It was now time to say goodbye and he gave me a big hug ... I was taken aback ... he said,

"Good luck and have fun but above all be careful."

I now understood the big bear hug. - He was concerned for my safety. I walked into Penn Station and it was a maze in there. How would I know which train I had to take and which platform I had to get to? Thank God for the ability to read English. I soon asked questions or read signs that pointed me in the right direction and very soon I was standing in line to hop on board. I was tingling with excitement. I was really doing this!!! Wow!!

I got on the train and my "sleeper" cabin was totally awesome. If I had seen it NOW, it would have been just OK but at that time I had never travelled much nor was I exposed to these sorts of things, so it was an enigma to me. There was a regular seat and I stashed my bag and quickly sat down. But then I jumped up again and started to look around. I was mesmerized when I turned a small metal gadget and down came a little bed - next to this were a little toilet and a small sink. I was so fascinated and thrilled to be in my own "cabin". I really did not see the comfort of it until later in the evening.

Very soon there was a whistle and we were off!! I was like a kid looking out the window and taking in everything in sight. While we were getting out of the Station there was not much to look at but once we were outside the tunnel I was checking out all the buildings and tyring to read billboards and just plain enjoying the view.

As we got to the less populated areas I truly appreciated how vast and huge the United States of America was. While looking at all the "dead" trees because it was in the heart of winter, my mind went to my mother and from that point on, it was like she was sitting beside me and it was as if I was looking at it all from her eyes.

I would look at the bare trees and think about fire wood and when I saw the rolling expanses of open space I thought of all the different crops that could be planted there. And this was my mind set with every new experience I had. What would Ma think of all this? And amidst all my excitement and this vastness of space and time, I started to cry uncontrollably; missing my family so much, especially my parents and more so, my mom.

Many people complain of boredom on these long trips. Even though my friends from work had given me books to read to alleviate the boredom, I did not find the time to read a single page from any of the books. My thoughts kept me company as I took in all the landscape – much of it the same for very long periods of time, but yet I never tired of either looking out at that or into my thoughts.

I dozed off a little and woke up feeling hungry. I had brought some pastries and a sandwich from home so I did not have to worry about food. I just got some stuff from my bag and around 1:30 p.m. I ate lunch. I then relaxed and continued looking out the window sometimes lost in my day dreams about my childhood and my mom. At some point during the afternoon I took out my ticket and the other travel details and discovered that there was a "lounge car" on the train where there would be food for purchase.

A cold meal of junk food from my bag or a hot meal, what should I do? The choice was not difficult so I made my way to the lounge car and was not surprised to see that it was almost full with families and couples having dinner and chatting up a storm – some folks were even playing board games. I exchanged a few pleasantries with a couple while waiting for my food.

As soon as I got my order I skedaddled back to my cabin. From my brief observation of the lounge car it seemed as if I was the only who was travelling ALONE. It really hit me then how alone I was and I did not feel like explaining my circumstances to anyone who might be kind enough to engage me in conversation.

It got dark very early since it was February and after I had my dinner I continued looking out, but it did not make any sense. It was pitch black outside and there was not much to be seen. Once in a while a little light would appear from a house that was closer to the railway tracks but only to disappear within seconds. So, I decided to call it a night and that was when I realized the true value of my "sleeper" car.

I fidgeted with the gadget and brought the bunker down and drew the shades on the windows. At first I felt weird lying down on a moving train, but soon after I cuddled into my blanket and got accustomed to the motion of the train, I fell asleep. You might think that I would be too scared to sleep, but I guess the dark and being up since early in the morning made for perfect sleep conditions.

I woke up a few times during the night and had to take quite a few minutes to get my bearing. At first I did not know where I was until I became fully awake and focused. I had no idea of time and space during the night and when I woke up the next time I realized that it was morning as the sun shone through the blinds. I was very relieved that the night was over.

I lazed around for a little bit and then I finally got up and replaced the bed in the wall of the cabin. At first I thought I could never get it but after some persistence I was able to get everything back in its place. I freshened up a bit with the limited resources from the sink and decided to go to the lounge car for a cup of hot chocolate – I had never been one to drink coffee which I know some people would say was what I really needed at that time.

While I was standing in line for my chocolate I saw some nice warm eggs and hash browns and ordered that instead of eating cold stuff from my bag. I also did something daring – I decided to sit and eat in the lounge car by myself. I then went back to my cabin as the lounge car began to fill up with the regular hustle and bustle of families waking up and rushing around for a hot meal.

I realized that we would soon be reaching my first stop on the train as I started to see more and more houses as we swept past on the tracks. Not so many dried trees or vast expanses of land, but little towns appearing in view. Very soon the landscape turned into skyscrapers and office buildings and around 10:30 a.m. we finally arrived at the Union Square Station in Chicago.

When I got off the train I felt a little wobbly and had to steady myself against a post on the platform. I guess being on a train for about 30 hours would do that to you. I had to wait until 4:00 p.m. to board my next train so I had about five and a half hours to check out the city of Chicago. I did not want to carry my luggage around and upon investigation I found out that there were storage lockers in the Amtrak station. I had to get quarters to secure the locker and I soon had my keys and was on my way out of the station.

Here I was in a strange city for the first time and I had no clue as to what I was going to do or where I could go. The only thing I knew for sure was that I wanted to see the Sears Tower – this was the only famous landmark that I had read about in Chicago. I went outside and was excited to see quite a few buses parked in the bus depot. I explained to one of the drivers that I was waiting for my Amtrak train connection and could he advise me what I could do to pass the time.

He was very kind and explained that his route went along the water and that if I did a Round trip on his bus it would take me about an hour and a half. This was perfect for me. When it was time for him to leave a few other passengers and myself joined his bus – since it was still empty I took a window seat so that I could get a good view of the scenery.

We were soon making routine stops and I noticed that the streets were named after many of the States – like Michigan Avenue, Alabama Avenue, etc. I thought this was really cool to have the streets and Avenues named after different states of the USA. As I was looking out on the river I noticed that the sun was shining on the water and the reflection created quite a dazzling glare. I was perplexed that the water could give off this much of a glare.

I kept staring at the river and I soon realized that it was not the water that was giving off the glare – it was actually ICE. This was the first time I would see a river frozen and I got goose bumps by just looking at it. It was still winter time and I later learnt that Chicago got very cold and windy – actually it was referred to as the "Windy" city. I was still learning so many different aspects of the weather in the USA as compared to a Tropical country from where I came.

I got off the bus at the last stop to stretch my legs a little and had to keep my head down from the wind. You could tell as soon as the driver was ready to start the return trip I was the first one on the bus getting out of the cold. I made sure to sit where I could get a view of the other side of the road and this time I was looking at more residential properties. From time to time I would sneak a view of the frozen river – I was so fascinated by it.

When I finally got off the bus I thanked the driver and went back into the train station to grab a bite to eat. I could have gotten something outside, but it was much warmer in the station. After lunch I browsed around and picked up some postcards only to be reminded about the Sears tower. Now I was on a mission. I wanted to see the Sears towers, and so I ventured outside again and this time I went in a different direction from where the buses were parked.

I found myself on a bridge and when I saw a policewoman by the rail I decided to ask her if it was possible to visit the Sears tower with the remaining time I had before my train was scheduled to depart. She looked at me as if I was asking her a really silly question and I was a bit taken aback. But not for long, when I realized that the Sears tower was immediately at the end of the bridge. However, I did not know if you had ever experienced this, but you could be standing right under a building and the closer you were to it, the less you realized how high it was. This was exactly my predicament that day.

I had failed to look up and even if I did because I was so close I may not have realized how high the Sears Tower really was. And so with my new found exhilaration that I could finally get to visit this great landmark considered to be the tallest building in the world at the time of my visit – it was 110 stories tall. I made my way across the bridge and right into the lobby of the Sears Tower.

There were lots of tourists milling around and taking pictures and I tried to get in the act only to find out that the batteries in my camera were dead. How embarrassing – one would think that for someone going on a vacation they would have taken the time to make sure the camera was fully functional.

(This was something all my friends and family would learn about me and my family – we would plan parties and celebrations to the last detail, EXCEPT for having a proper camera ready- we always had to run out and purchase the instant cameras for many occasions when we failed to plan on capturing the precious moments on film) Believe me; they were captured in our hearts.

Anyway, I was able to quickly purchase the requisite batteries and the store clerk was kind enough to insert them and made sure that my camera was working properly before I ventured off again to find a tourist willing to take my picture.

I got quite a few photographs and toured a bit before realizing that I had to make my way back to the Station if I wanted to catch my train. However, I really wanted to see the building from the outside and so I gave myself enough time to walk a few blocks away and then look at the building to really appreciate its magnificence – it was a remarkable view to see it stretching into the sky – almost as if there was no end to it. I just stood there and stared at it but had to leave since the passing clouds made me kind of dizzy as if I were falling.

Reluctantly, I made my way back to the Union Station where I would now board my train for the second leg of my journey. Before entering the station I picked up a sandwich and some juice for my dinner. From Chicago I would travel to New Orleans, Louisiana and for this the travel agent had also recommended that I book a Sleeper Cabin. This was perfect.

Shortly after boarding the train and looking at the buildings as we sped by it started to get really dark and I ate my sandwich and soon turned in for the night. Even though I had done the same thing the night before, the motion of the train still made me a little uneasy until I fell into a deep sleep having had a very exhilarating day.

I was awakened very early the next morning as the sun was coming up and after a routine freshening up session I went to the Lounge car to get some breakfast. It was not quite busy yet and I did not wait around to make small talk. I just headed back to my cabin and sat by the window to take in the sights.

It was like looking at the movie "Swamp thing" - we were passing through the Bayou County and there were vast stretches of wetland and marshes. Most noticeable were the huge trees with lots of vines and stuff looking like huge birds' nests hanging into the water. I shuddered to think of all the creepy, crawly things that would be living in these surroundings.

I think at some point I dozed off and when I awoke we had passed through the Bayou County and were coming into smaller towns. I went back to the lounge car for lunch and was approached by two friends who were travelling together. We exchanged small talk and they encouraged me to go to the upper deck of the train from where I would get a better view. I had not even realized that there was an upper deck but soon found out that if you went to a few of the cars in the center of the train there was an upper deck that was enclosed by glass surroundings and I was happy to get a view from a higher vantage point.

As I had thought, it was not long before we were seeing more densely inhabited areas and the buildings were becoming larger and more urbanized. The train soon pulled into the Station in New Orleans and I was elated to disembark after such a long train ride. I collected my belongings and as I was walking to the taxi stand the same two guys who had spoken to me at breakfast asked where I was going and if I wanted to share a taxi with them.

It turned out that they were also going to the French Quarters and it was possible to share. They told me that I could ride "shot gun". This was the first time I was hearing this phrase and at first it confused me, but I would soon realize that all it meant was that I would ride in the front seat with the driver. I was soon dropped off in front of my hotel which was located on Ann Street and the guys did not even allow me to pay my cab fare. They said they would take care of it. I thanked them and we all wished each other a great time in New Orleans.

The hotel, "A Creole House" was not very imposing. I walked up to the front desk with so much fear that you would think I was about to commit a crime. You see in my country there was a misconception by country folks that the only time people went to a hotel was if they were having an illicit affair and if they were picked up off the streets by rich men to have a quick fling. Therefore no respectable young woman would go to a hotel; especially NOT ALONE!!

If the clerk could have read my mind he would have been amuzed because I was sure that he had seen many people who were not having affairs come and go everyday. But I felt only embarrassment and confusion as I signed and picked up my key. Imagine I was entering a hotel for the first time in my life and I could not take this stigma out of me that I was doing something really wrong.

Anyway, I tried to allay my fears and made my way up to my room which was decent but not sophisticated. It was just minimal and the travel agent had really worked with me in terms of being in a good location but still not paying too much. I soon made my way to the restroom and took a good long shower. It felt very relaxing and I lied down on the bed and soon fell asleep. I had no intention of going to sleep but I guess the shower and the rigors of travelling for two days had taken its toll even though I had slept a lot on the train.

I woke up with a start and when I looked at the time on the TV set, I was relieved to see that I had not slept for too long. I got dressed and decided to go out and explore the French Quarters. Could you imagine that I could wear summer clothes to go outside when I left New York in turtle neck and a heavy coat?

As I ventured out of the Hotel I soon found myself on Bourbon Street and the buildings were already being decorated in preparation for Mardi gras. There were lots of paintings and special designs on the front of the buildings and even though I had never witnessed Mardi gras, there was an air of excitement by just looking at the special decorations.

I had been told that there were boat cruises and I soon found myself on the boardwalk going towards where one of the cruise ships had docked. The "Caribbean Queen" was sitting on the docks and I was told that the earlier cruise had already left at 2:00 p.m. The next one would be the dinner cruise leaving at 6:00 p.m. I was very disappointed because I could not go since the cruise would not be back until around 9:00 p.m. I did not want to be out so late.

I looked around for other activities and saw the street cars which I joined at the corner of the street and rode for a little while. I got off at the Andrew Jackson monument and was able to find a fellow tourist to take a few pictures of me in front of the monument. I then walked around some more and I picked up some brochures where I saw that there was a steam boat that ferried people across the river.

I was excited – I really wanted to take a boat ride and since I had missed the earlier cruise I would settle for the ferry ride. I kept looking for an entrance to the boat but could not seem to find one. As I was standing next to a street vendor on a little rise in the boardwalk I asked him how to get to the steam boat – he looked at me and smiled – I was standing on the ramp that took you to the steam boat – how hilarious was that!!!!

With a little hemming and hawing to stifle my embarrassment, I thanked him and following the ramp I was able to board the ferry. This seemed to be the theme of my trip – I was always right next to where I wanted to go and I did not realize it. Remember the same thing happened to me in Chicago with the Sears Tower?

I did not think I had to purchase a ticket to get on the steam boat and I got on board among the last set of passengers. It was not that crowded as it was only around 4:00 p.m. – I guess the rush hour had not yet started and so I got a seat. As I looked out on the water a wave of nostalgia hit me like a ton of bricks. This was a very popular means of transportation in my country and there were many trips with my parents when we went from the county side into the city. I felt tears brimming in my eyes and I just had to steel myself against breaking down and giving in to my emotions.

Instead I reminded myself that I was surrounded by a host of people in broad daylight and I would look really crazy if I just started crying for no apparent reason. By then the boat had started up and I looked at the water chugging around the edges of the boat. I then let the wind blow away my tears before I turned around to view the other side of the river.

We soon reached the opposite bank and the passengers started to disembark. I did not get off because I did not know the schedule and how long it would be moored before starting back on its return journey. I stood by the rails and was pleasantly surprised to find the captain of the boat standing next to me. He then engaged me in a very educational conversation.

He told me some facts about the Mississippi River and the many battles that were fought. He even told me that his great grandfather was one of the fighters during one of the battles. He pointed out some areas of interest but they were just a blur and they did not register in my memory. He then said goodbye and wished me good luck for the remainder of my stay and went back to guide the boat on its way back to the French Quarters in New Orleans.

As I exited the steam boat I realized that I was lucky to have gone earlier because the throng of people waiting to get on was quite huge. I made my way on to the board walk and got a few more pictures taken by fellow tourists and then I headed towards my hotel since I did not want to be out after dark.

I soon got the scare of my life. As I was walking on the street towards my hotel, this guy in a red convertible drove up alongside me and tried to accost me. I ignored him as best as I could but the more I tried the more he persisted and when I tried to walk faster, he sped up his car – there was no simple way for me to get rid of him. I guess he was one of those rich guys who thought they could get anyone to do whatever they wished.

I was really panicking by this time and I kept praying that I would come to no harm. I realized that we were at a corner and as I looked across the street I saw a Delhi and just darted in there like a scared little rabbit. There were a few people in there and I thought that there would be safety in numbers. In order to allow some time to pass before I got out again, fearing that this guy may be waiting outside still, I decided to order a sandwich for my dinner. It took a little while to have my tuna sandwich made and I picked up some snacks and soda.

I furtively made my way back to the street and breathed a great sigh of relief when I did not see the red car anywhere nearby. Even so, I walked as fast as I could to my hotel and quickly made my way to my room. The nerves now set in and I started to tremble and it took quite a while before I got up from my bed and turned on the TV. For some reason the voices on the TV afforded me some sort of company and then I took a shower and had my dinner in bed. While surfing the channels I happened on Ballroom dancing and I was hooked.

I fell in love with ballroom dancing that night – it was the first time I was exposed to it and I got carried away dreaming about a fantasy world in which the women wore all these fabulous outfits and were dancing the night away. My fantasies helped me to pass the time until it was late enough for me to turn in for the night. I went to sleep but not before checking the door and the windows to my room. I did not sleep very well that night for I was really scared that something bad might happen. The encounter with the guy in the red car was the scariest part of my entire journey and thank God I was leaving very early the next morning for my next stop in Atlanta.

I got on my train to Atlanta without any mishaps and was somehow very relieved to leave New Orleans. I did have a great time during my short stay but the incident at the end of the day just made me want to be out of there. I did not have a sleeper cabin as this trip would not run into the night. As we were travelling en route to Atlanta I was amazed at the vast expanse of water over which we were passing.

It was really an awe inspiring sight. There was water on both sides of the track and the water at times was quite rough. As I looked out on the water, I would sometimes see little thatched houses way out in the ocean and the reason I knew that people lived there was that there would be clothes lines filled with clothes that were hung out to dry. I could not believe that people could live in such surroundings. I was truly relieved when we had passed through that watery portion of the train ride.

The scheduled arrival in Atlanta was around 7:30 p.m. and so I already decided not to do anything when I arrived except to go straight to my hotel which was not very far from the train station. As soon as I got out of the train and I looked around I labeled Atlanta the "Pristine" city. Do not ask me where that term came from but all the buildings looked new and shiny and the outside looked so clean and almost clinical.

I checked in to the hotel and noticed that there were lots of fast food restaurants around so I got myself dinner to take up to my room. I did not linger around. I was just going to shower and watch some TV before going to bed. I had almost all day the next day to take in the sights of Atlanta as my train to Washington DC would not leave until late in the evening!

I tried to search the TV channels for more ballroom dancing to entertain myself but was not that lucky and so I watched a few "half-hour" shows and wrote a few letters to my children. I wanted to recount many aspects of my trip while they were still fresh in my mind. I could not call them until I got home on the weekend – this was not the age of so many cell phones and I did not think that pay phones would have allowed me to make long distance phone calls.

Since I had the day to myself in Atlanta, I did not rush to get up really early and after getting breakfast from a fast food chain downstairs I got dressed and checked out of the hotel to make my way back to the train station. Here I used the lockers again to put my baggage away and then took the bus for a little ride. When I got to a train station I learnt that you could ride from bus to train without paying an extra fare and so I took the train that would take me to the Underground Market.

What an amazing atmosphere! There were long stretches of stalls with many fabulous items for sale including T-shirts, mugs, and lots of souvenirs. Not to mention the array of different food stalls of hot and cold dishes and all kinds of delicacies. My favorite of all the items on sale were the aquamarine type of costume jewelry that were in abundance. They had such a beautiful bluish green hue in so many different shapes and designs to choose from. I was overwhelmed and wanted to buy everything in sight, but with my limited resources I decided to make my way back upstairs to avoid temptation.

It was still too early for my train so I crossed the street where I was yelled at by a bus driver because there was a circle and I was crossing in the middle of the street. What could I say – I was a typical New Yorker in that instant! I did not go around as I should have to get to the traffic sign. A little shaken up by the encounter I decided to stay off the streets as much as possible and when I noticed a Museum a few blocks ahead I decided to spend the rest of my afternoon in there.

I kept looking at my time and when it was near time for my train I made my way back to the station. I picked up a hot meal to have for my dinner on the train and then collected my baggage and made my way to the platform. I was so indecisive. When I was on the train I was anxious to get off and when I was walking around I could not wait to get back on the train. I was not sure if that was because I was all alone or what contributed to that ambivalent feeling.

I was not in a sleeper cabin even though my journey was during the night. It was more expensive and since I was getting off the next morning around 9:30 a.m. the travel agent felt that I could handle the train ride by just dozing in my seat. My train soon took off and I looked out on the scenery until it got pitch dark and there was not much to see except for a few flecks of light here and there. Eventually I fell asleep like most of the other passengers in my car.

With the angle of the train I was able to see the rising sun and it reminded me of a time when my dad and I were crossing a bridge back home. The sun had come up really big and bright against a backdrop of trees and the water. This sunrise reminded me of the other one so many years ago, making me nostalgic for everyone back home. It seemed as if everywhere I turned there was something to remind me of them even though we were in such different parts of the world.

Knowing that the train would soon reach its destination I did not go to the lounge car to get breakfast but figured I would wait. We arrived as scheduled and immediately upon getting off the train I stashed my baggage again in one of the storage facilities in the station. I then ventured off to get a hot breakfast.

I remembered that a guy from my job had told me to take a certain number bus and it would pass by the White House and I really wanted to do this as I was in DC. My train was scheduled to leave at 5:00p.m.for New York and I had enough time to do a little sight seeing.

I got on the Bus and asked the driver for the closest stop where I could get a view of the White House. He promised to let me know and soon I was stepping off the Bus to get a good view of this imposing, picturesque building. I saw a guard hut and asked the guard if I could put my camera through the fence to take a really good picture. He told me that if I walked around the block I would be lucky to get on the line for the next tour of the White House.

This was beyond belief and way more that I had expected so I did as he recommended and soon found my way getting a complete tour of the White House. Wow – I felt so honored and privileged! There were so many rooms with such beautiful architecture and rich looking furniture – but most of all I was fascinated by the rugs and the dishes – as the tour guide explained all the nuances of the furniture and the dishes – which President's wife was responsible for picking the china for which room and a ton of historical facts.

This was a really unexpected, lavish treat and I got lost in the moment, forgetting all about the time!

I got out of the tour at a different spot from where I had entered and it took me a little while to get my bearang. Even though I was pressing for time I was still able to get a few pictures of the White House up close and a fellow visitor took one of me with the flag and the White House in the Background. Feeling a very great sense of accomplishment I made my way to the Bus stop for my return trip to the Amtrak Train station. From DC I would be on my final lap back to New York.

As I was getting my baggage, I remembered schedule of the trains to New York and realized that there was a train leaving every hour on the hour and that I did not have to wait until 5:00 p.m. as the travel agent had planned. I could get on the 3:00 p.m. train without any problem. This would be so much better for me as I had to take the trains to New Jersey to my nephew's home once I got back to Penn Station in New York.

It was now almost 2:45 p.m. and the next train left in 15 minutes. Since I had not expected to tour the White House there had been no time for lunch and I was starving. I had not even had something to drink since my breakfast in the morning. I looked at the track where I had to take my train and it was pulling into the station.

"What should I do?"

I ran up to the conductor and asked him if I had time to grab a bite to eat. He told me it depended on how long it would take me to get something. I looked at the McDonald's restaurant and I said to him, it did not depend on me, it depended on them. He told me to try and see what I could do, but he could not hold the train for me.

I ran to the McDonald's and looked at other fast food restaurants around and decided against it. There were lines everywhere and as I heard the whistle blowing for the final call to board the train, I just ran and got on the train, literally, seconds before it pulled out of the station. Turning around, I saw a girl had also gotten on the train just as I did. We had both gotten on to the last car of the train and we both breathed a huge sigh of relief.

She was in the same predicament as I was. She had been tyring to get something to eat at the last minute and decided to make the train instead. We put our bags in the overhead compartment and decided to go the lounge car to get something to eat. What did you know? The car was not open yet … they were now setting up the food items and there was nothing available.

We debated whether we should wait there and decided to go back to our car. As I sat down I looked over to a seat a few rows in front of me and there was this huge woman opening up a big foil wrap which she spread out on the pull out tray.

I almost fell out of my seat when I looked at the huge slabs of meat that she unfolded – she seemed to have enough barbecued ribs to feed an army and then she started taking out more and more food stuff. She had corn on the cobs and it seemed like home fries and at this point I stopped looking. I was like a hungry puppy and I could almost see myself with my tongue sticking out, panting and ogling her food! I was definitely salivating by this time.

To end the torture I went over to the girl and asked her if she was ready to go back to the lounge car. From her seat she was not able to see what I had seen. She could see the woman but not the array of food that she had spread out. Thank God she readily agreed and we made our way back to the lounge car and were able to grab something to drink while our order was being prepared. We stayed in the lounge car and finished our lunch. Since it was just a little over a two hour ride we soon made our way back to the last train car to finally disembark at Penn Station in New York.

It was already dark by the time I got out of Penn Station to walk across to the Avenue where I would get the Path Trains to New Jersey. From there I would take the train to Journal Square and from Journal Square I had to take a bus to my nehpew's home. It took another hour or so to get from New York to New Jersey and it was such a relief to be finally back, safe and sound.

I felt so happy to be home and to be welcomed so warmly by Roxanne – she had done the sweetest thing. She bought a long stemmed Peach rose and the florist had encased it in a special plastic casing (not the regular clear plastic wrap) but a specially designed plastic container for a single long stemmed rose. I kept that rose for years and years and after a couple of moves I finally had to throw it out as the casing had finally given way to wear and tear and all the petals which had dried began to fall out and make a mess.

There were so many questions both at home and at work and the more I spoke to everyone the more I realized how much of a risk I had taken in travelling all by myself. They were all now telling sordid stories of people being attacked and robbed and in the case of a woman alone; so many worse scenarios. Thank God, they had not told me all of this before I left! The one thing I was assured of was that I was considered a little heroine for doing all of this and everyone could not help expressing their admiration. Rest assured after all these negative stories, I never ventured out by myself on any long trips again.

Guyana
1990-06-25

Dear Mom,

Assalaam-o-alaikum,

I hope this letter may reach you in best of health and happiness by almighty Allah's grace. We are fine home here except for the terrible budget which land down the other day in Guyana causing everything to raise by 45% higher. For a long time I haven't heard your voice on the phone but I am listening to your voice on the cassette you send for us. How is every thing at your work place, everytime you write me you always adviceing me not to do any thing wrong, you are not write about yourself and your friends. Before you write about something interesting but your advice are a bit interesting. I apply them in several ways and I find it easy for me. You are looking like a queen in the photographs you lately took out, with the latest styles and fashion, keep it up you are looking very beautiful. I am getting impatient for few us to get through but I know your advice will be that I must have faith in Allah. Last week I started writing my end of term examination. So far I doing good which I think will please you or make you happy. Uncle Shair had an operation for his eye and since after the operation now he hasn't the strength to open them. He has to act as if he e blind. Nana and Nanoe are going fine for the time. Nanee recovered for the sickness, she's feeling a lot more stronger than she was before. Must

Dear Mom,

Assalaam-o-alaikum,

I hope you are fine when this letter reaches you. Today again the phone let us down. We left home as early as possible to get there and left there around 11:30 am and still no phone call. I think you might be very disappointed. Thanks for every thing you sent for us and thanks very much for the get fighter game

Chapter Seven

The Card and Heartbreak Central

When I came back from my trip, I sat down and wrote the same letter to my son, my father and one of my brothers. I guess the trip brought on these thoughts but I asked each one of them to read this letter to my mother – I wanted to make sure that at least one of them would read it to her. In my letter, I asked her to forgive me if anything happened to her and I did not get to come home. I also asked her if she would understand.

(I never mentioned the fact that "if she died", but they all understood what I meant when I said, "if anything happened to her").

She told them all to write back to me that I should not worry about those things. My brother also told me that the same way I tought about death, they also worried that if something were to happen to me, they would not be able to see me as well. For some reason I felt better when I heard her response yet, to this day, I had deep regrets about the events that were about to unfold.

Anyway, for the mother's day of that year, I finally did something for her that I always wanted to do. Since coming to the States, I had always wanted to send one of those really LARGE cards but I never did for fear of it bending and being destroyed. So I used to send her very pretty cards, except they were not really big.

Well, as usual I went to Hallmark, my favorite card store and bought the pretty ones that I used to send. A few days later, I went back into the Hallmark store and lo and behold, there was the ideal card. It was one of the huge ones that I always wanted to send her. It epitomized my mom to the letter. It was of a woman in a straw hat in her garden filled with flowers. My mother used to have the most beautiful flower garden in our entire village.

And so, I picked up the card and as I was paying the cashier I said to her,

"I do not have two moms, yet I am now saddled with two cards."

When she asked:

"Why?" I explained how I already purchased one card but now I had found a more ideal card.

She was all smiles – I had not gotten used to the culture of exchanging stuff. She just had me pay the difference and away went my dream card to my mom. She simply adored it. She thought, as it was my intent, that the picture on the card was a true representation of her and she was surprised that I could find a card so befitting of her. It was my last card to her!

It was the year of 1992. I had been getting letters and one or two phone calls that my mom had been having some problems with her diabetes as well as some issues with Alzheimer's. I knew she had diabetes and I had accepted that she would have problems. However, the Alzheimer's shook me up a lot.

You might ask why, since she was in her 70s. But, if you knew her as I did, then you would understand. My mom, God rest her soul, was "unlettered" – she could see her name in big neon signs and would not recognize it. However, she had a "computer" brain.

Let me try to explain what I mean. She used to sell produce from her garden and the farm to the people in our village. There was a system where you would buy "trust" (credit) but it was never documented. It was really taken on "trust". My mom would sell to people who got paid: weekly, fortnightly and monthly. When she came to "collect" her money at the end of the pay cycle, she would tell you what vegetable and how much you bought at what day and the total you owed her without it being written down anywhere.

As I grew older I started to recognize this remarkable ability in her – what a memory! SO, when I found out that she was losing her memory, it was very painful to me. She had such a sharp mind, if only she could read and write.

My mother was slowly drifting away. Her diabetes was getting worse and she became ill quite frequently. My brother wrote and let me know her condition. I went to the drug store and spoke to the pharmacist who recommended two or three different kinds of creams and anything that I thought might bring her relief. I was scared to think of the reality of it all. What would I do if she did not get better? I tried to comfort myself with the fact that many people lived with diabetes for years and years and I hoped and prayed that I would get to see her, if only, for one last time.

Alas, these were futile wishes. My nephew had been told how bad her condition was and since he could go, he visited her but did not let me know that was the reason for his visit. He just said that he was way overdue for a visit and that he needed to go to the Embassy to finalize paperwork for his parents.

Upon his return we picked him up at the airport and he told me that everyone was doing well and that his parents would be coming up soon. I was thrilled and excited that there would be some more immediate family members in the USA. I was thrown off guard thinking that this was indeed the reason for my nephew's visit. In hindsight, I should have realized that every time I brought up the subject of my mom, he kind of skirted the issue and started talking about something or someone else.

On Saturday, August 1, 1992 a very good friend was getting married and I was invited. My nephew was supposed to accompany me but since he only returned on Friday, he asked his sister-in-law to go with me instead. I did not know if some inner voice was telling me that all was not right, but I was so lethargic and gloomy that I had no energy and just wanted to sit in the dark and not do anything.

Imagine the wedding was supposed to start at 4:00 p.m. in Jamaica, Queens and we did not even leave New Jersey until 4:45p.m.

The bottom line was we did get to the ceremony which believe it or not was delayed for three hours – the bridge in the Bronx was open and the bride was stuck there. Going through the motions I think I spoke appropriately and did what was expected, but my heart was not in the wedding. I could not shake this feeling of desolation that was gripping me and I could not explain it either.

On Sunday, I stayed over by my nephew and we went to a friend's house for a BBQ. A cousin of mine was there and he came over to me and asked me what was wrong. He said he just looked at me knew that I was not my normal self. But even at this point, I just told him that I was fine, because, I really could not express what I was feeling, or exactly what was bothering me. I just knew that I did not want to be where I was or anywhere for that matter.

On Sunday evening, I had the strangest dream around 3:00 a.m. I dreamt that an old man, with a long white beard came to my parents' house and was asking for my father. I was a young girl in this dream and I told him that my father was not at home and could he tell me what he needed.

He replied that I was too young and would not be able to deal with the information he needed to give my father. (Later I found out that this was around the time my mom was dying – did not know if there was any correlation – I just thought it was very strange).

I woke up with a start with this dream in my head. It felt very real and I could almost see this elderly man. I was a little scared and then after tossing and turning around for about a half hour, I finally fell asleep; only to have to wake up and get dressed to go to work. It was Monday morning and the bills were waiting to be paid.

If only I could have known, my world as I knew it was being ripped to shreds. This was August 3, 1992, a National Holiday in my country. The Holiday was usually on August 1 – Labor Day, but because the first fell on a Saturday, the Monday was declared a National Holiday.

On Tuesday morning, I woke up in my normal dwelling in Brooklyn and decided to call home. The phone in our home was not working and so I called across the road to the Telecommunications Outpost. My son soon came over and as I was talking to him his father was there and I heard him say,

"Should I tell Ma?"

I said, "Tell Ma what son?"

And then, my son said to me,

"Ma, Naani died and the funeral was yesterday."

I stood with the phone in my hand and the first thought in my head was that I was imagining things. I asked my son to repeat what he said and I knew I had heard him correctly the second time.

He said, "Ma, are you OK?"

And then my baby boy started to cry. He said, "Ma I am really sorry. Please do not cry Ma. Ma, say something, Ma, are you there?"

I did not know how long I stood there and then his father took the phone from my son. I was not sure if I should yell at him or rant and rave at myself, for even thinking that he would do the decent thing by calling to tell me that my mom had passed away.

I do not know if I would ever be able to forgive my husband for this, but I was sure that I would never be able to forget the fact that he did not think it appropriate to call and let me know, much less try to console me. Later, when I asked my brothers the circumstances as to why I was never told, they all told me that since we had a phone in our home and since he was my husband, they assumed, rightfully so, that he would call and let me know.

He never sent me a sympathy card or even called later to find out how I was doing. I did not know how I survived during this darkest period in my life. I really, truly felt alone. This world had suddenly become barren for me. I did not want to belong anymore. I wished that I could see her face, hear her soothing words, her comforting songs as she would run her hands through my hair which she often did while I would lie in her bed at night. I yearned and I yearned and I yearned.

After I got off the phone, I called in to work to let them know that I could not come in because my mom had passed away. They were very sympathetic and understanding. I received lots of cards and a beautiful array of flowers. I did not know what to do with myself – I think my feelings shut down as a protective mechanism and I went into zombie mode. I was home alone since everyone had already gone to work. My sister-in-law offered to come home, but I assured her that I was OK.

Then I started cleaning the apartment. This was Tuesday; the apartment had already been cleaned over the weekend. But, I still had to be doing

97

something and so I took a pale with soapy water and a rag and I went down on my knees and wiped every corner of the rug in the living room.

Imagine, this rug was supposed to get shampooed and dry-cleaned with a special machine – I did it with my bare hands. I then showered for a long time and made dinner. (Yes, I made dinner – I was doing stuff as if nothing in the world had happened - just going about my business as usual.)

Later that evening, my sister-in-law's parents and other relatives came over and we held a "wake" and everyone tried to console me. When they saw my composure, they assumed I was OK and around midnight, after the last of the mourners had left, I went to my bed. I was not sure if I was too tired, or what was happening to me, but I soon fell into a blissful sleep. Sweet escape: at least until the next day.

On Wednesday, I woke up to the usual hustle and bustle of movement in the home and soon I was home alone, as everyone had gone to work and school. Thoughts then started to crowd my brain and I started to get a blinding headache. I took two Tylenol and tried to sleep some more, but it was impossible and I decided to get up and find something to eat.

What did you do, when you were all alone in an empty apartment and your mother had just passed away? And you could not even go to her funeral to say a last goodbye? How did you cope – could you cope? I felt like running out of the apartment and screaming to the world to let them know that I was in so much pain, and then I felt like burying my head under my pillow and not face anyone.

I did neither of these things. Instead I just sat and stared in space and then I turned on the TV just to have some background noise without really knowing what I was watching. There were lots of phone calls and everyone tried their best to console me.

As was customary, we kept "wake" with family and friends coming over the next couple of nights. After they stopped coming over, I stayed up and said special prayers for my mom for forty nights. I had to be eternally grateful to my sister-in-law who stayed up with me every night and offered me great comfort and solace.

And so, the living must go on and I did, by burying myself in work. I was lucky to find a weekend job about two weeks later. Strictly by chance I overheard a co-worker mentioning that there was an opening for a weekend counselor at the Child Care Agency where she worked and she offered to take in my resume if I was interested. I was called for an interview and I was offered the job.

I started out as a temporary, weekend counselor, but due to some very bizarre circumstances, within a week or two I was made permanent.

After my first meting with the House Supervisor, she asked me if I could come over on the Thursday evening to help her with some paperwork. I did not see that as a problem and so I went willingly.

This woman brought out bags and bags of receipts – I was not exaggerating when I say bags and bags –there were at least 10 Duane Reade large shopping bags full with receipts. She asked me to sort them and I made piles of receipts for groceries, clothing, shoes, cleaning supplies and miscellaneous categories as best as I could. I was sitting on the only table and chair in the staff room while she was sitting on one of the beds rifling through a lot of papers also.

It was almost midnight and she did not seem to be getting ready to go to bed anytime soon but I was dog tired. I had to go to my regular job the next morning and so after some thought, I finally said to her that I could not do any more tonight, I would have to turn in. Without any hesitation she said OK. And so I slept as best as I could in the other bed in the staff room while she still had on the lights and I could hear her papers rustling until I fell asleep from sheer exhaustion.

The next weekend, I was scheduled to work from Friday evening and I got a call from the Supervisor to meet her at the Delhi on the corner from the Group Home. I did not see anything wrong with this request and so we met. I had brought her some flowers as during my interview I had told her that I was looking for a weekend job to keep myself busy since my mom had just passed away. She said she understood as she had recently lost her mom as well.

We ordered a light snack and made a little small talk about how we spent our week and routine stuff. Eventually she gave me an envelope with some money for petty cash for the home as well as the weekly allowance for the girls. She also gave me some tokens which I had to give the girls to go to school on Monday morning. She soon said goodbye and I went to the Group Home.

I did not realize this as yet, but I was going to be alone all weekend handling a group of teenagers whom I had not really met yet. I arrived to a very quiet house with only one resident present. It was Friday evening and all the others were out and about. I went to the staff room where I found a big notebook and I started to write down a few details. Time I arrived and condition of home, etc.

For the remainder of the weekend I documented every activity for every resident and gave a detailed account of all the monies that I distributed and the balance that was on hand. No one told me to write in the diary, but I thought to myself that I needed to give a written account of my activities, especially to account for the monies that I was given.

I just went with my instincts and I guess it did not fail me as during the week when the Director came and visited the home she was very impressed with the work I had done over the weekend, especially with no one to guide me. And so, when the supervisor told her that she wanted to make me permanent she did not hesitate to say yes.

The following Monday, I had to take a day off from my regular job and I was taken to the Head Office of the Group Home to fill out all the necessary paperwork to become a permanent, 40 hours a week counselor with all medical and benefits entitlement.

The girl who was taking my picture to get my permanent ID badge made me realize what a big deal this was. She explained to me that there were almost thirty temporary counselors who had been with the agency for over a year and she did not know how come I was being made permanent. I told her the truth – I did not know either.

It was not until I went to work the following Friday that I realized fully what was going on in the Group Home. Supposedly the supervisor who had hired me was being investigated for corruption and wrong doing with mismanagement of funds and she could not even come back to the home. That was the reason why she had met with me at the deli the weekend before. This also explained ALL the receipts I had been helping her with.

I was worried at first but then I knew that I had not done anything wrong to be overly concerned and so I did my job as best as I could. I kept my diary up to date on all the activities of the girls and I kept accurate records of the cash that I was entrusted with.

I started to bond with the girls in the home and made them my first priority. There was a lot of tension among some staff members, as it seemed that they were accusing each other of being spies for the supervisor who had left and silly stuff like that. I tried not to be a part of it as I was brand new.

So, I worked my regular job from 9:00 a.m. on Monday morning to 5:00 p.m. on Friday evenings and then I went to start my weekend job from 7:00 p.m. on Friday evenings to 7:00 a.m. on Monday mornings. I worked in the Group home with girls aging from 12 – 21 years of age, who were wards of the state.

It turned out to be a very fulfilling job as I developed a wonderful rapport with the girls. I used to cook for them on Sunday evenings, even though I was not really required to do so. I think it also brought back memories of my days as a teacher and my love for children in general. Suffice it to say, I forged a very caring and respectful relationship with them.

There was a funny incident during my tenure at this facility. On my regular tour of duty, I would eat the meats that were served in the house because they were "kosher". However, during the month of Ramadan, I was fasting and I did not feel that it was right to eat this meat since I was supposed to eat only "Halal" meats.

Well, on the Sunday afternoon when I cooked, the girls offered to wait until I broke my fast so that we could all have a nice sit down dinner at the table. They were very observant and noticed that I did not eat any of the meat dishes. When questioned, I explained to them about the "Halal" meat and we left it at that.

A few weeks later, when I arrived at work on Friday evening, as I was on the telephone advising my sister-in-law that I had arrived safely, one of the girls ran to the staff room yelling for me.

"Come quickly, come quickly, I am frying some chicken wings and I have the last set to fry. Could you come and "bless it" so that you could have some to eat later?"

My sister-in-law heard the whole outburst and thought it was hilarious. I guess the girls had not understood clearly, that the meat had to be blessed BEFORE it was slaughtered for it to be "Halal". What a sweet gesture though, just to reaffirm what a caring relationship we shared.

During this time a respected family friend, tried to convince me that I should really try some other means of getting my children. Everyone who knew me realized that I was having a very difficult time and they were all thinking of ways to help me. My sister-in-law also tried to get me to at least think about it. Everyone knew that my husband was having affairs one after the other and they felt that my marriage was in shambles anyway, so why was I still being so faithful and loyal to him?

After much consideration, I thought I would give it a try and so, I was "introduced" over the phone to someone who was supposedly a very religious person, almost to the point of being a priest. He was much older than I was though, almost by 15 years. My rationale at this time was that beggars could not be choosers and so I spoke to him with sincere gratitude.

After a couple of conversations over the phone, during one of which he asked me to recite from our Holy Scriptures for him; he seemed to be a very congenial person. So when he invited me to lunch on a Saturday, I did not have any qualms about saying yes. He picked me up and the first thing he did was to give me a gift and a small book of our Holy Scriptures. I was very touched.

He took me to a very nice restaurant and our conversation was good. I was a little perturbed though when he kept hinting that since I was alone here and that I was working two jobs then I should have a good amount of savings in the bank. I sort of shied away about the topic of money.

He was the perfect gentleman during lunch and asked if I wanted anything to take with me, since I had to go back to work that evening. Well, after lunch, he offered to take me for a drive and I did not have a problem with that, because someone was covering for me on the job until 4:30 p.m.

We drove for a little while towards Upstate New York when he suddenly pulled off the side of the road and stopped in the parking lot of a building. I saw a sign that said MOTEL. He stopped the car and then he said:

"Let's go."

I looked at him and said, "Where are we going?"

He said, "We are just going to have something to drink (neither of us drank alcohol) and talk some more."

I then looked at him and said, "I am not going in there. Please take me back to work."

102

He looked at me as if I was an alien or something. He got back into the car and I said to him,

"We just had lunch and I am not hungry or thirsty, so why do we need to go in "there"?"

He pulled out from the motel and turned the car around. I tried to get into the farthest corner of the car away from him, because he had just shattered all my hopes for any relationship with him.

When he was quite a ways from the Motel and the sign could no longer be seen, he then said to me,

"Why are you behaving this way?" I looked at him in consternation.

"What do you mean why am I behaving this way? Why did you need to take me to a motel? I may be young and naive, but I am not stupid. I know what is supposed to go on there. Is this the type of person you think I am?"

Believe me, this so called religious, almost priest like person, just sat there and said to me that if I wanted to, he could turn the car around to show me that he did not take me to a motel and that I made that up.

So then I said to him,

"Where was it that you pulled into just now?"

He said that he could take me back to show me where it was and that it was not a "bad" place.

By this time, I was in tears and all I said was "Please, just take me back to work."

He tried to engage me in conversation but I refused to speak to him and shed quite a few silent tears. I think it was more because he had disappointed me in a very big way. I always thought that priests were supposed to be people who defended your virtue and who protected you, not people who would want to seduce you and blemish your character.

When he dropped me off at my job I said good-bye and could not wait to get out of his sight. Do you think he let it be? No! Later that evening, he called at my job because he had the number and he cursed me out using really nasty slang words from my country. He said things like if I thought I was the only woman out there and that he was doing me a big favor and I then hung up the phone on him telling him not to ever call me again.

That was the end of anyone tyring to get me to "hook" up ever again!!!

I just told them that things did not work out with this guy. I could not tell them the truth of what really happened, because I did not think they would ever believe me. Here was someone who was supposed to be very religious and church going and here I was, young and all alone – people may just think I was making things up because I did not like him. So, I left it alone and prayed that God would guide me through this as well.

I continued working both jobs and wrote to my dad asking him to make preparations to go and make his pilgrimage to Hajj. I had offered to finance his trip since the year before, but I think because of my mom's condition he really did not want to go. So in my letter I even mentioned to him that he had no reason not to go and that whatever assistance he needed he should go to my brothers and let them help him with the paperwork and so on.

On Wednesday, December 2nd 1992 I called home to speak to my kids. Since the call did not go through to the house phone I tried the Telecoms across the street and as I was speaking to my son, he said to me,

"Ma Grandpa is passing to go to the Post Office."

I told him to call my dad so that I could speak to him. I was so happy to hear his voice and during our brief conversation he coughed and I asked him if he was sick. He said,

"NO, I just have this dry cough."

I still made him promise that if he needed any medication, he should not hesitate to let me know. And so we hung up not realizing that I would never hear that voice, ever, ever again.

On Friday, December 4th, 1992 my father was giving the Friday sermon in the mosque where he was the Imam. It was a very hot day and my eldest brother got up and went outside, saying to one of the other worshippers,

"What is wrong with Pa today, his service keeps going and going and going."

After the service, Pa came outside and told them that he was really thirsty before heading home. Upon reaching home he drank a glass of lemonade (actually lime water). That was it!!!! He immediately fell into a coma after complaining of a severe headache.

In the meantime, I was here going about my business as usual, unaware of any of these tumultuous events. I went into my weekend job and on Saturday evening, I spoke to my cousin's husband from Seattle who was going to Guyana. I asked him to make sure that he enlightened my dad about the Hajj experience as some members of their family had already been through this process.

On Sunday afternoon, my nephew called me on my weekend job. This was very unusual, but I did not think anything of it. His first words to me were,

"When last did you speak to them in Guyana?"

I reminded him that I had called on Wednesday and that I had subsequently called and told him about my conversation. This was a practice we shared. Once one of us called "home" we would report to the other one that everything was OK.

So, I just said to him,

"Is everything OK?"

He said,

"Yes, but I think PA has a little cold or something."

I told him,

"I know, because he was coughing when I last spoke to him."

He just said we would talk later and hung up. He did not know what else to say to me because by this time, he had received a phone call from Guyana telling him that PA was in a coma. However, even though that was the reason for his call, he did NOT tell me.

I did not know what prompted this reaction from me, but after I hung up with my nephew, I just knew that something was terribly wrong. I sat down on my bed in the staff room and when the other staff member came in she took one look at me and asked me if I was feeling OK.

She said, "You really do not look well" and she recommended that I lay down.

I took her advice but could not fall asleep. My mind kept wandering and I started to think about photographs of my parents and where I had put them. Because when my mom had died I had taken one of her photographs and enlarged it and sent a copy to all my brothers and my sister.

I kept thinking that I may have to do the same thing now. And then I had to admonish myself to stop thinking such silly thoughts, that PA only had a cold and why was I being so morose. I guess a child's instincts or whatever you may want to call it.

The next morning I arrived at my regular full time job to see a message next to my phone. The number to call back was a New Jersey number. I even asked if someone had taken this message on Friday since I had spoken to my nephew the day before. I was told that the message was from that morning.

So I called my nephew and had to wait for him to call me back.

When he called back he asked "Did you have breakfast already?"

I said "No, I am calling you back as soon as I got in."

He asked "Are you OK?"

I said "Yes."

I then asked him if everything was OK and he said yes.

I then asked "Is everything OK back home?"

He said "Yes."

So I asked him, "Is PA worse."

He said "NO."

I said "Is he in the hospital?"

He said "NO."

I then blurted out, "What are you telling me then, that PA is dead?"

And he said "YES."

The first words out of my mouth were. "Dear God, how much can one person take?" before I started shaking. A co-worker heard and came by and took the phone from me and walked me to her office.

And then I said to her, "My dad is now dead."

My mom had died only four months ago. I did not think anyone had any words with which to try to console me and so they resorted to being practical. They asked if I had anyone to come and get me and I told them that I would call my sister-in-law. I never did because she had just gone back to work way out in New Jersey after two weeks vacation. So I told them that I would meet her downstairs and I left to go home.

I went down to the train with tears streaming down my face. I just could not control them. I did not know her, and I did not think I would ever see her again, but a young girl gave me tissues and said if I needed anything else to please let her know. I took the tissues and told her thanks and that I would be fine.

I cried my way home. When I got home I could not find my keys and my brother-in-law who worked nights that week was shocked to see me at the door and wanted to know what was wrong. I just told him that my dad had died and walked straight to my room and into my bed after asking him to call and tell the relatives.

When my mom had died I had thought the world was dark, but I guess I could not fathom the true extent of darkness. Devastated was not the word to describe my feelings. I was way beyond despair and I did not know how to deal with this double whammy. I did not want to see anyone or hear anything. I just wished that I could also die or disappear and come back to find it was all a horrible dream. Unfortunately, it was REALITY and one that I had to face!

Eventually, I got up and started cleaning in preparation for relatives and friends to come over and pay their respects. I also asked my brother-in-law to pick up some extra food from the supermarket. In the evening my brother who had now arrived in the States and my nephew and his family came over. Very soon the house was full to capacity with relatives and friends who came to offer their condolences. I sat through it all and accepted their words of comfort appropriately but I was not sure what anyone said to me. I was cold and numb inside.

I even had a family friend who was expecting her baby at any time come to the "wake". She asked me for candy and apologized for not staying too late as it was uncomfortable for her to sit on the floor for too long. They left that night to go straight to the hospital. The next morning I got a phone call that she had a baby boy! The way of the world – everyday someone dies and someone is born!

Again, I am not complaining, because it is now water under the bridge, but my husband never thought to call and tell me that my father had passed. He did not even call to offer any words of solace knowing that I was the apple of my parents' eyes being the last child and all. And so four meager months after my mother passed away, my father joined her in the great beyond. All of us concluded that he died from a "broken heart".

So my father was buried on the very Monday on which he passed away. This was customary in our religion – to try to bury the dead at the earliest opportunity. I was here tormenting myself with imagination. I kept thinking: now they would be bathing his body and then dressing him and all the other rituals that needed to be performed.

When I knew it was time for him to be buried, I tried to shut that image out of my head – that here I was in America, miles and miles away and there was my dad, being laid to his final resting place. It was pure torture and I would not wish this emotional roller coaster on even my worst enemy. To this day I cannot comprehend how I survived these calamities in my life.

On Tuesday after the funeral, everyone left for work and I was home with a splitting headache. And then the heavens started to mourn with me. It was as if the Gods were angry and the skies had broken loose. There was so much rain that Coney Island overflowed and the subway system had to be shut down because of water on the tracks. It rained all week and I stayed home and buried my head in my pillow. However, I had to get up and go to the doctor because I had become physically ill.

The week after my father passed away I returned to work and was very disappointed when my supervisor told me that I had to apply for Vacation during my time of mourning. She said that the Company policy did not allow for more than two funeral days off per year. As if I had asked for both of my parents to die in the same year. Especially since I worked in the business department and knew that she could have allowed me to use "Excused" absence.

بسم الله الرحمن الرحيم

To my dearest Daughter _____

أسلام عليكم

Guiana

I hope my few lines may
not fails to reach you as it leaves my self and Ma.
quite ok Insha الله I reacived your letter and I was very
happy especialy your Ma we are very glad to hear that everything
thing is ok with you it contain a $20. U.S. (الحمد لله)
I did reacived your letter regarding my Intinsion about going
to Haj let me tell you the truth Ma was very sick at that
time I was very much worried as you know . leave. come to
and she didnt like the situation she told me that she is not going to
work so I couldnt think about going to Haj but
any how I got the information from C.I.O.G. Head office. the time then
was to short. so I clove it. My Dear in your letter you said it
is your desire to to see that if your Dear Father can get the opportunity
to go and make the Haj my Dear if (الله) so will the الله will
fulfil your desire. if I die before next year I pray الله
that He give you that blessing of your desire. I pray الله blessing
every morning I read my Fajr prayers I make special Dua for
you. what you can do If everything goes well (أنشاء الله) we will
start early next year. you should know a lady wife she is worried
daughter she is working with now much more reasonable I pay $2.00. two
hundred Doollars p week with her care ma is not messing up she gets up
and try to help her self. wife coming every day Bade her
change her close comb her hair and keep her very tidy she act as
she is her own mother please say Helo to O Family O all around .
so for now may (الله) keep you safe ma say when you qu come

Yours truly Father

سلام عليكم Stay well a Happy Edul Aza for one and all

109

Chapter Eight

Welcome Guests

And so life as it became continued. I existed and I began to EAT. I did not know how or why, but I would wake up in the middle of the night and look through the refrigerator and eat anything and everything that was in sight. I would then wake up early in the morning again and eat stuff that I never used to eat before. I started putting peanut butter and jelly on anything and everything and I was still never full. I just kept eating and eating and eating as if there were no tomorrow. Later, I realized that I was just trying to fill the void in my life with food.

When my mom had died I had read from our Holy Scriptures for 40 nights. This time around, I could not bring myself to do it, even though my dad was the one who taught us to read in Arabic. I was not sure why, but I did not want to do it even though my sister-in-law offered to sit with me. I just told her that I would do it later, but the later never came around.

Eventually I resumed my normal routine by working two jobs. I would leave on Monday morning to my regular job and then go to my weekend job on Friday evening. The girls at my weekend job were a great comfort to me and offered a lot of distraction. They told me about a situation that occurred while I was off the previous weekend. One of the girls had to be sent on respite to another home because she had broken a vase on another resident's head and she had tried to attack the Counselor who was sent to fill in for me.

And so in January 1993, on my birthday I was truly an orphan for the first time and I did not deal with it very well. I was at my weekend job and I stayed in the staff room and could not face the world. However, knowing that the girls depended upon me I took a long shower and tried to get a grip on reality.

As soon as I had finished and was drying my hair, there was a knock on the door and the girls who were home for the weekend stood there tyring to hide something from me. Then they all yelled out Happy Birthday and gave me a bunch of yellow roses. And the flood gates opened!!!

I started crying and could not stop. They were concerned and wanted to know if they had done something to cause that.

Through my tears, I said,

"NO, No, please, No, it is nothing that you guys did!"

It was just such a sweet gesture and I was feeling so down that I could not help crying. It also meant a great deal that these girls would take money from their meager allowance of $8.00 per week to buy me flowers. I realized that I had to shake this morbidness out of my system and proceeded to dress up a little.

And so the girls took a beautiful photograph of me with my yellow roses in the living room of the Group Home. It was one of my cherished memories of the great ways human beings could uplift each other. I truly treasure the time I spent with those girls. God knew I needed them as much as they needed me during that period of our lives.

As anyone who had suffered a great loss knew, the living must move on even though we felt numb inside, we continued with our basic routines. I soon recognized and appreciated the fact that work was like therapy for me. I kept myself busy between both jobs and it helped to take away lonely moments when I would revert to wallowing in self pity. I tried to take on as many assignments as possible so that I would be too tired at night to think too much before I fell asleep.

However, it was not long before realization stepped in and I started worrying that if my parents could pass away and I did not get to see them, what if me or one of my children died and we could not see each other, how would I survive then? Whenever those thoughts took over I would break out in a cold sweat and it took a lot of praying and deep breathing before I could compose myself.

With these thoughts now occupying my every waking moment, I started to take steps to see if my family could get even a visitor's Visa to come and join me earlier. There were a lot of delays in my paperwork even though I had done everything possible to have my Labor Certification Approved. I was told that there was a freeze on finalization of Labor Certifications. I was not sure where I got the strength but I kept going, one frustration after another. By this time I had developed a very serious sinus problem with a deviated septum and I needed to have surgery.

I then used this situation to my advantage by sending all the medical paperwork back home and the children went to the Embassy to see if they would get a Visa to come and visit. I guess Lady Luck decided that I had had enough bad luck for one person and so, lo and behold the children were granted visitors Visas to come and visit. They had to get a lot of paperwork together and so they could not come the very next day as I would have liked.

Fortunately or unfortunately, they could not come together as my son had already signed up to write CXC exams and we thought it prudent for him to stay and finish his studies as there were no guarantees that he would get to stay with me and go to school in the States. Nevertheless, this was great news, at least in another couple of months he would also be coming. The anticipation was making me giddy.

This was time for action. After a vigorous search I soon found a studio apartment which would suffice for the time being. I was busier now more than ever. Still maintaining both jobs, I was shopping for my new apartment. Finally, I was ready to move and I decided to take a day off to move. Another friend, Prem, who used to work with Joey and had sent me a Valentine's Day card to his loving sister also offered to help.

I started preparing dinner and Prem arrived to take whatever he could with his car as he could not help until I was finished since he had to go in to work. By the time he came I was cooking roti and luckily my sister-in-law came in at the same time and she could take over.

We carried whatever we could with his car and by the time I got back,

Leila and her husband and his brother had arrived to help me move also. They started without me and had already finished packing up the van they had rented. I was surprised at the amount of "stuff" I had accumulated over the past couple of years. She took all my clothes and put them with the hangers into huge garbage bags so that it would be very easy to unpack.

In rushing around I did not get to eat anything and I did not think to ask my sister-in-law to pack something for me to eat later. As caring as she was, Leila observed this and when we were leaving with the van, I noticed them driving away from the regular route. I asked where we were going and she fibbed and said that we were taking a different route.

She said,

"You know Azad; he knows how to get around via different routes."

I did not say anything, knowing that she was right about Azad and his ability to find his way around New York.

They stopped at a Supermarket and she picked up bread, milk, cheese, chips, eggs, sodas, and a variety of food items so that I could have dinner and at least breakfast the next morning. As soon as she got back into the van, I realized what she had done and was really grateful for her thoughtfulness.

We finally got to my new studio apartment and Leila and I were told to take a few small items and to make room for the bigger stuff. The boys brought in the heavy items and they set them down as instructed. Very soon we were all unpacked and it was time for them to go. We said our goodbyes and thank yous and I was left contemplating whether I should try to organize now or just call it a night and start early the next morning.

After about five minutes, the buzzer started going off and it took me a little while to realize that it was mine. I asked who it was only to hear Leila's voice telling me to let her in, which I did. As soon as I opened the door she hugged me and said that Azad had sent her to bring me with them.

He could not bear the thought of me sleeping on only a mattress all by myself. We both started crying and it took me a little while to convince her that whether I stayed tonight by myself or the next night, eventually I would have to stay by myself. She finally left but only after I promised to call immediately (although I did not have a phone yet) if I needed them, even if they had to come back that same night.

These were the kind of friendships I would be eternally grateful for in my life. To this day I am friends with Leila and her husband and I know that should I ever be in need, I could always depend on them.

The next day I woke up and went to the Avenue to shop for some pieces of furniture and thought I was doing myself a service by shopping at a store just two blocks away. I would soon discover the perpetual nightmare most people endure of waiting for furniture to be delivered. In spite of the promise to have the items; a day bed, an entertainment center, and a small coffee table delivered the very next day.

"Oh, do not worry; we would bring it no matter how late we come back to the store."

I finally had to literally carry the glass top of my coffee table in my hands before I could get all the stuff I had ordered.

Prem and his sisters also went with me to the hardware store and I bought some tiles and a piece of rug. I had asked the landlord and he said that if I paid him $50.00 he would install the rug for me and he would put the tiles on the floor right in front of the stove and on the wall behind the stove. Even though I was in a studio apartment I was determined to make it beautiful and clean and welcoming.

I also went by myself and bought a TV, a microwave oven a blender and a few other kitchen gadgets. I took a cab home and I was scared to ask the driver to help me bring the TV in. I asked him to help me put it by the front door and had no clue how I was going to get it into my apartment. Just then a young man who lived in the building was coming out of the door and he offered to help.

He took the TV and I carried the microwave and the other stuff. He even helped me to take the TV out of the box and the next day the super came and hooked it up. After he left I tried to open the microwave box and I cut myself on my thigh – with the blood and everything going on, I just decided to call it quits. I showered and went right to sleep. When I awoke later that evening, I willed myself and soon got the microwave on the shelf and fully operable. It might seem like a little task to most people, but for me it was a sense of accomplishment. I was really on my own now.

And so I worked my regular job from Monday to Friday and then my weekend job from Friday to Monday. As soon as I came home on Mondays I would just eat something that I had picked up from work and went straight to sleep. On Tuesdays, I would make one big pot of chicken curry and rice and would have that for most of the week. On Thursday, I would also cook something for me to take with me to my weekend job. This was my EXISTENCE during this period of my life. But it would soon change in the best possible way.

All the planning was paying off and Zara would be coming soon. I was excited and the day could not get here fast enough. On a bright Saturday afternoon in September of 1993 my darling baby daughter was able to join me. A few friends had accompanied me to the airport for this emotional reunion and as we were standing there she walked right up to me (who by this time was in tears).

One of my friends then said to her,

"How did you know which one of us was your mom?"

She replied in her "Guyanese" dialect.

"Me does see she picture."

This made everyone laugh; and it certainly lightened the mood. I was overcome with happiness – imagine I was now seeing my daughter after five and a half years. I kept hugging her and touching her face and holding on to her as if at any moment I would wake up and find her gone. My friends took me home and soon we were alone.

I had cooked a few dishes which I thought she might enjoy from the night before and I started offering them to her one after the other. I guess I was tyring to make up for all those lost years. I then gave her a shower and it was as if I was tending to my new born baby. I examined every part of her body, her toes, her fingers, her little ears, mouth, and teeth until I was satisfied that they were all intact. There was a scar on her right hand and of course I had to find out how she got it.

She told me that she had been taking the goat to graze. She was holding on to the rope when a dog started chasing the goat. She was too small to understand that she should let go of the rope and so she was dragged for a little while before a passerby was able to help her. The scar was from the bruises that she suffered that day.

In the meantime she was fascinated with all the amenities that were in my apartment. She was not accustomed to an indoor toilet and bathroom as in our country these facilities were all outside in the yard. We talked some more and soon I noticed that she was getting tired and we retired to our bed.

You must understand that I was in a Studio apartment and except for a door to the bathroom, everything was all open. I had a day bed and soon we were cuddled up together. I was not sure if I could ever have enough words to explain how my heart felt at this moment... feeling her warm body folded next to mine, I soon fell asleep, but as only a mother would, not without a thought of her brother.

On Sunday around 10:00 a.m. the phone rang and Leila said that we should not make breakfast as they were coming over to take us out. Leila and her family took us to a fancy Diner and we had pancakes and eggs and Zara was told that she could have whatever her little heart desired. She deferred and left the choice to me.

Afterwards they took her shopping and bought her a few outfits, socks and shoes. She thought she was in a Fairy Land when she went into the stores. Before we went to sleep that night we called home and she spoke with her brother telling him all the exciting things that she was experiencing.

On Monday I took off from work to take her to school. When I was waiting to get her signed up, I met with some volunteers and we chatted for a little while. She was soon assigned to a classroom. It was scary leaving her so I waited until she was settled in a little before I left.

On my way out, one of the volunteers asked me how everything went and as soon as I told her the name of the teacher she advised me to try to get my daughter out of that class room as soon as I could. I did not understand her motive and I did not pay her any mind. My primary concern at that time was to get her enrolled in school.

At 2:20 p.m. I left home to go and pick up her from school. I had never revealed this to anyone but when the doors opened and all the children were coming out, I experienced a moment of real panic. I am still embarrassed to say that I could not recognize my own daughter. All the children looked so alike, dressed with their little denim jackets and jeans and so on.

I thought,

"Dear God, please forgive me, but I do not know my child."

I was fortunate that I was standing where she could see me quite easily and she recognized me. You could imagine my relief when she broke into a big smile and started running toward me.

We got home and she was happy that I had made her favorite snack – plantain chips. She had her snack and I had an earful of her day. I looked through her books and then I took her notebooks and textbooks and covered them with gift paper. This was something we used to do back home so that our note books would stay neat and our text books would stay new so that other relatives could reuse them.

While we were coming home I had noticed a gentleman with three children going in to the house across the street from us. I said hi to them and they seemed nice. I knew that the next day I could not take off from work to take her to or pick her up from school and so I asked her if she would feel comfortable if I asked these people to pick her up.

I guess neither of us had a choice and so later that afternoon I went and knocked on the house next door. I then negotiated with the Mr. Sarjoo who was from Trinidad if he would be willing to have Zara go to school and be picked up along with his children.

And so every day after school she would spend time with these children until I got home to pick her up. Of course, this was not a free service. I had to pay Mr. Sarjoo $50.00 per week plus I had to give her snacks for when she came home from school. Under the circumstances I could not complain because I knew she was safe and she was a little too young and new to this country to become a "latch-key" kid.

Remember that I still had my weekend job at this time and the agency would not release me until I had trained someone to take over my position. So for the next three weekends I had to depend on Prem to come all the way from Brooklyn on Friday afternoon to pick up Zara. She usually fell asleep during the car ride.

In the meantime I would leave from my regular job and go to my weekend job. In the past I would leave from the weekend job back to the regular, but now I left on Sunday afternoon and went straight to Brooklyn to pick her up. Prem never let me take the train home; he would always give us a ride home to Queens.

Once I had trained someone to take over my weekend job I resigned from there. I had to really think about this decision. It was a well paying job but I had to get my priorities right. I could not work round the clock and have Zara in the USA. When would I get time to spend with her and what was the purpose of her being here with me if every weekend she had to go all the way to Brooklyn? In retrospect, I do not for one minute regret my decision to quit my weekend job. I was able to build a solid relationship with my daughter.

It was not easy at first. It took a lot of patience and dedication. She had some emotional issues to begin with. When she was in our country people used to tell her things like her mom did not love her anymore that was why she left, some of it not in spite, but out of ignorance as to what statements like these could do to a child's psyche.

Also, whenever she was suffering, (maybe her trials and tribulations would be in another book) she would ask God why her mother did not come to save her. So there were a lot of misconceptions that had to be cleared up in her head. I had to reassure her constantly that I loved her.

But little by little we worked out our little issues and reached a good compromise. I allowed her to try out a few options. One week she took a shower first and then ate and then we reviewed her homework. The other week I let her do her homework first and then shower. We decided which one she liked better and she preferred to shower, have her dinner and then we would review her homework (most of which she would have finished while she was over at the sitter). We then fell into that routine and finally after watching TV for a little while, we would cuddle up in our little "day bed" and go to sleep.

I was comfortable with her school work and I made sure that she did all her assignments so I was looking forward to her first marking period to see what her grades would be. To my surprise, her report card had "S" right down the middle. I was very concerned. I knew I was not in her classroom and I did not see her actual test scores, but I knew her assignments and everything else were well done. Thus, as soon as the "Meet the parent's night" came around, I came home early from work and went to her school.

I met with her teacher and when I asked about her grades, the teacher told me that she was advised by the principal to give grades of "S" so that the child could have an opportunity to improve by the next marking period. This did not seem right to me, and I asked her,

"What happens if the child falters, then the grade would become 'U'"?

I explained that I thought the child should be marked based on their performance. She hemmed and hawed and tried to make me feel that I did not know what I was talking about and that I had no right to be questioning her. She said she was going according to instructions and I then asked if I could speak with the Principal.

An appointment was made and I took a half day off to visit Zara's school once again. I actually met with an Assistant Principal, Mr. O'Connor who was very understanding and listened to me intently. I told him that I had lost faith in that teacher and that I was requesting that Zara be put in a different classroom.

He said it was not such an easy process and that Zara had to take some tests and based on the findings then they could make that determination. I told him that I did not mind what the procedure was, but I would really appreciate every effort to move her to another classroom. He promised to do his best.

At the end of our official visit, he turned to me and said, you sound like a very intelligent person. I THEN told him that I was a teacher in my country and I had some insights into the marking system, maybe it was different here, but I guess the basics could not differ that greatly.

He wanted to know why I had not told him earlier that I was a teacher. I explained to him that I did not want him to feel as if I was threatening his authority or that I felt I knew more than him, I just wanted what was fair for my child. He then said to me,

"This is off the record, but I admire your spirit and the way you approached the situation. I want you to promise that you would never stop fighting for the welfare of your child, whether in this school or any other institution."

I thanked him sincerely and left for work. He followed through on his promise and Zara was given a series of tests which she passed and she was then put into another classroom. From that point onward, there was no turning back for my baby. She kept blossoming from strength to strength and she soon started bringing home student of the month awards for a whole semester.

I was always grateful that I had the insight and the perseverance to see her through this transition. She became an honor student and was inducted to the Honor Society. She also graduated Valedictorian of her High School, and the lists of accomplishments went on and on......

The outcome could have been so different but for one moment in time when I made that extra commitment to visit her school and had that discussion with her teachers. Like the Assistant Principal had said,

"Do not ever stop fighting for the rights of your children".

Needless to say, there were many nights throughout our reunion that I would wake up and hold her tight to make sure that I was not dreaming and that she was really there with me. We practically lived for the end of the day when I would pick her up from the "baby-sitter" as well as our weekends together.

We became inseparable once we were not at work and school. She had become very "clingy", never letting go of me, if we went out to a party or visiting friends. However, as happy as she was being with me she was missing her brother more than anyone else back home and she started complaining of headaches.

They became overbearing some evenings and she would end up crying. By now it was getting into winter and at first I thought it was her reaction to the extreme cold. However, to be on the safe side, I took her to a pediatrician who referred me to a specialist.

Her aunt then told me that her father had a sister who had died when she was aged 12 after complaining of severe headaches. My mind was by now getting the best of me worrying whether she had inherited a genetic illness and if I would lose my baby only after just being reunited with her.

So I rushed to get an appointment with the specialist. I picked her up after work and we caught the bus to the doctor. It had snowed the day before and it was cold and dark outside. We had to take two buses to get there and then we had to search for the address which I had been given.

I had never gone to this doctor's office and you could imagine how difficult it was to find a new location especially on a cold, dark night. We kept looking for the address but could not find it. This was not the time of cell phones, so I then had to walk around before I could find a public pay phone only to be told by the receptionist that we were across the street from the office. However, we could not see the name plate on the door because it was a basement office.

My baby was cold and scared as I was since I now had a responsibility to protect her. I felt like I was doing a very poor job with this venture. Anyway, the doctor took a bunch of tests after which I had the daunting task of making our way back home. I opted for safety and asked the receptionist to call a taxi for us.

It was now around 8:00 p.m. and I was not going to wait for two buses in the blistering cold, especially now that my little girl was in tears. It had become overwhelming for her and she started crying. The taxi driver was very polite, but it did not stop him from charging us $50.00 from Ozone Park in Queens to Corona, Queens.

The next day I was relaying my experience with my co-workers when my boss overheard me and he called me into his office. He showed his true expertise as a social worker with an intricate understanding of family issues when he told me not to worry too much. He felt that the tests would turn out negative. He also opined that the headaches that Zara was suffering from were no more than a result of being separated from her brother and familiar surroundings.

I waited anxiously for the test results from the doctor's office and when she called I was literally trembling when I picked up the phone. My relief was instant when she told me that the results were negative and that should the pain persist she could refer me to a brain specialist but at this time she did not think there was any undue need for concern. She recommended aspirin and to make sure that she got enough rest.

While all this was going on, plans were going ahead for Fiyaz to join us as soon as he had finished writing his exams. We were both very anxious and could not wait for that phone call to say when he would be coming. Zara was conscious of our expenses and when we were coming home one evening, she was muttering under her breath....

So I said to her,

"What are you whispering about?"

She was like,

"I know you would get your phone bill and I was praying to God that your bill would not be too high."

She had noticed that my AT & T long distance bills used to come up to nothing less that $250.00 to $300.00 per month. I started laughing, but it made me feel happy that in her little heart she was concerned about all the bills that I had to pay. When I opened the bill, it was $237.50.

It was now the Christmas season and she was very excited about all the lights and decorations especially when we went into the stores. She was not very keen on going to see Santa and so we never went. However, I got her a Christmas tree and put it up in our small apartment and put her gifts under the tree.

You could be assured that I went overboard with gifts for her, but I was practical and wrapped stuff that she would also need for school. My friends also flooded her with gifts and she was in seventh heaven. Also, everyone commented on how much she had grown within the past couple of months.

On Christmas morning she woke up and it was indeed a Kodak moment to see her eyes light up upon seeing all her gifts under the tree. She could not wait to open them and I let her do whatever her little heart desired on this day. I had my little moment when I wished I had my whole family with me, but I was truly grateful for the blessing of having her for now.

Later that day my nephew called and said he was going to come and pick us up so that we could spend the evening with them. We got dressed and soon my nephew and my brother came and got us. We had dinner and the kids watched a movie and played with their toys while the adults chatted.

Azeez then came up to me and said,

"You do realize you have a situation on your hands." I smiled at him and said,

"I think I know what you are talking about."

(His daughter, Ferona had become very attached to me over the years and she used to sleep with me whenever I stayed over by them. I was the only one who could comb her hair without her crying histerically– she had a full head of curly hair which was easily tangled up.)

I told my nephew that I had foreseen this situation and that I had already thought of a resolution. Zara and Ferona were waiting to see where I would sleep and who I would sleep next to. I could not choose between either of them on this night, so I decided that I would sleep in the middle with both of them on either side of me. It worked for sleeping purposes, but it was funny watching the two of time "sizing" each other up.

Zara was jealous of this little girl who was sitting so close to her mother and Ferona was furious at this girl who she had never really seen before. She refused to call Zara by her name, and kept saying, "that girl with my 'gran'ma". It took about a whole year, before the two of them finally accepted that they were both a part of my life and that the animosity was unnecessary. Today they are great friends, with Ferona being the maid of honor at Zara's wedding.

Zara and I were still bonding and we were becoming very close, watching similar shows and doing our little chores and her school assignments together. She loved to hear stories about her baby days before I came away and I could not hear enough of her stories after I had left. The saddest part was when she wanted to know why she could not ride her bicycle around our new neighborhood the way she used to ride and go visit her uncles back home.

I had to explain that in our country everyone knew her and within five minutes of her leaving home, at least five different people would be able to give me an update as to her whereabouts. You had to bear in mind that I was a teacher and her father was a police officer so we had some amount of stature in society. Over here, we were just a face in a massive crowd. She kind of understood, but it was still a huge change.

The New Year soon rolled around and I was praying fervently that this would be the year when my family would be reunited. My one year lease in my apartment would be up and I was not sure if I should renew or what I should do. For me and Zara, the space was fine, but when Fiyaz came, it would not be enough.

So I kept looking out for any cheap apartments around the neighborhood. I saw one right across the street from us in a second floor window... I actually took lipstick and wrote down the number to call, since I could not find a pen quick enough in my pocketbook.

When I got home that afternoon I called the number and was amazed that the people knew who I was. The woman answering the phone said,

"Are you the girl who usually picks up your daughter in the afternoons from our neighbor?"

I never realized that people used to observe our activities. I was so into my own little world of work, school and Zara. I asked to see the apartment and was told that it was a basement apartment which at first I was skeptical, because I had a bad experience with being really cold in a basement at one time.

However, I agreed to go and see it. It was a two bedroom basement apartment with a good sized kitchen and small living room. It would be ideal for me, Fiyaz and Zara with me and Zara sharing and Fiyaz having the small bedroom. I told the lady that I was interested but could not give a definite answer as to when I would be able to move in as I was not sure when my son would be coming.

She called me later that evening and said that her husband would hold the apartment for me, no matter for how long since he really wanted us to rent it.

In February of the year 1994 we got the much anticipated phone call. Fiyaz had finished writing his exams and he had gotten a flight. He would be here SOON. Not soon enough. Zara and I started preparing for his arrival as if the King was going to visit our little cottage. Every afternoon she would take the little hand held vacuum that I had and she would vacuum the rug and I started preparing all the dishes that I knew he used to like. I was not too sure if he still enjoyed them, but I was making them anyway.

Soon the day arrived and Prem and Nadira took me and Zara to the Airport to pick him up. It had been almost six years since I had seen him and I was anxiously scanning the arriving passengers to catch a glimpse of him. I saw a young man and from recent pictures I knew it was him.

My heart was rejoicing and as I looked at this handsome person walking out from the baggage claim area, I could not hold back the tears. I rushed toward him and wrapped my arms around him before taking a step back to look at him, really look at him. He had fuzz all over his face but his eyes were all smiles as I was all tears.

We looked at each other for that quick moment before we both wanted to ask all sorts of questions. But then the others required his attention and our fleeting moment of ecstasy was no more, but forever buried in our hearts. You should have seen Zara's face when she saw her brother. She was smiling from ear to ear.

We soon got into the car and on our way home; I gave him the apple and the Cadbury that we had brought for him. He was very hungry as he had been traveling since very early in the day. Once we got home to our little studio apartment, Prem and Nadira left and I was left with my two babies, together again.

I had to take really deep breaths. I wanted to savor this moment; I wanted to feel this joy and hope it would last a lifetime. Not unless you had been separated from your family members for any length of time would you be really able to empathize with this feeling of ecstasy that I was experiencing. It would not truly sink in until I had calmed down and lay down in my bed.

I encouraged Fiyaz to take a shower and I wished I could examine his body the way I had done with Zara. However, he was a "young man" of sixteen and I furtively looked at his body tyring to discover any new scars or marks that were not there when he was little. He was so grown and so sweet looking, I could not imagine that I was really looking at him, face to face.

I remembered when I used to live in Brooklyn I would stand next to one of the nephews who was the same age group like Fiyaz and tried to picture what my son would look like. I was grateful that now I could stand next to him and actually feel him, and touch him and smell him after all these years. There were so many questions – could we ever really make up for all the lost time that we had spent apart? I would never know the answer to that question, but I would always treasure the moments we did have with each other.

We talked and we ate and we talked some more and we finally were getting ready for bed. I only had one day bed in a little studio apartment, so how did we share? We decided that we did not want to sleep apart from each other, so we moved away the coffee table and put the comforters and the pillows on the floor and went to sleep, arms and legs all over each other. It was truly a blissful night for me. I thanked God for this moment of being reunited with my children. And I cried for my parents – not being able to meet them ever again.

The next day was Sunday and we woke up but did not get up too early. We turned on the TV and lay on the floor watching: cartoons of course. This has been one of the things we would always find ourselves doing from time to time – bringing out the extra mattress and having a sleep over in the living room – each one of us giving up our room and our beds to rekindle these mushy moments that we shared in our times of need.

The voice of reason triumphed and the mom had to get up and made sure her children were fed. I made hot cocoa and put out all sorts of fancy pastries and cakes only to find that they still both liked our old fashioned bread and butter and some "plantain chips." After breakfast, we straightened up, but how much could you straighten with three people just moving around in a tiny little room. Soon the phone was ringing off the hook with everyone welcoming Fiyaz.

My friend, Leila and her husband came over from the Bronx and they took us to dinner. Before going to the restaurant and as was their usual generous nature, they bought him some clothes and I also picked up a new pair of sneakers for him. We had a fun time at dinner and everyone had doggy bags to bring home. They drove us back through Flushing Park and Fiyaz saw Shea Stadium and the Arthur Ash Tennis stadium at very close range. He was all excited because he had heard about them and seen them in movies.

He was also a very good tennis player.

Chapter 9
Skinny Delivery Boy

On Monday morning, Zara and I had to go to school and work and tried as we might, we could not get dressed without waking Fiyaz. Soon we left him and he went back to sleep. He later told us that he watched a lot of TV and also slept some more. It was a real pleasure to come home and see that he had cooked dinner for us. He was a great cook – he explained that he and his friends used to do "bush" cook back home and he was usually the one doing most of the cooking.

I started looking up the requirements for getting him into College and found out that the Exams he had written in Guyana had all the prerequisites for admission. We just had to wait on his results from Guyana. His results were excellent. He had passed six subjects at CXC and one subject at GCE so he had seven "O" level subjects all together.

This was more than the equivalent to a GED in America. However, just to be on the safe side I took him to an Immigrant School where he registered to write his GED. We got the booklet and he studied for the exams and wrote them. However, when the results were due, we were told they had lost all the exam papers. We did not think stuff like this happened in America, but it did.

And so, without the official GED results, we went to a Brooklyn

Education site and met with a very nice woman at the registrars office who acknowledged that his certificates from Guyana ensured his admission to the Colleges in the USA. He registered to start classes at BMCC in September, 1994. He took some tests and based on his results he did not need to take any remedial classes.

Things finally seemed to be looking up and it seemed only a matter of time before all my immigration paperwork would be finalized and I would have the freedom that I craved. And so my children and I settled into our little routine. I tried my best to make sure that they were well provided for.

Now that Fiyaz was here our little studio apartment was no longer appropriate. He was a young man and the only door that closed inside this apartment was the bathroom door, everything else was one room. So, I called the landlord across the street and told him that I would take the basement apartment that I had seen earlier. The timing was perfect as the one year lease on the studio apartment was about to expire.

We decided to start our new rental on the first of the month. We started packing our belongings into garbage bags and the landlord agreed to give us the keys before the official start date. And so all week we kept carrying over one or two garbage bags worth of stuff that we did not need to use immediately.

On Friday evening, the landlady called and told us that since we would be moving in, she wanted to have the exterminators come and do a thorough spraying. She felt that since the basement was empty it would get a good cleaning. She told us that on Saturday morning the guys would come at 6:00 a.m. and that by the evening it would be OK for us to be there permanently.

So on Friday evening, me, the babysitter's children, Fiyaz and Zara carried over quite a few more garbage bags worth of stuff to lighten the load on Saturday. (We made sure that the bags were sealed properly so that the insecticide or pesticide that the exterminators would use could not get in).

I put all my little savings and jewelry in my pocket book and carried it around with me for safety. Late that night we went back to our studio apartment and being very tired the children soon fell asleep. I tried to do as much as I could and was hand washing some clothes in the bathroom when I stopped dead in my movements!

What had I done with the pocketbook with all my valuables? I went numb because it had all my jewelry and over $1,500.00. This was money to pay the first and last month's rent on the basement apartment. As I tried to recollect my actions earlier in the evening, I remembered that I had put the pocketbook in a little closet in the basement – I was tyring to be so careful and now I had left it there unattended. It would have been fine, but for the fact that the exterminators would be coming to the apartment at 6:00 a.m.

It was now 1:30 a.m. and I was in a quandary. I knew I would not be able to sleep until I had procured my valuables and I did not have the heart to wake the children – they were sound asleep and I knew how tired they were. And so I did something which I was not sure I would ever do again, but without thinking rationally, I took a jacket and the keys to the basement and I went over to the apartment and grabbed my pocket book ALL BY MYSELF, at 1:40 a.m. in the morning!!!

I thought that if someone saw me going without anything in my hand and now I was returning with a package they would realize that it had to be something of value and so I had the presence of mind to hide it under my jacket. When I got back to the apartment, I began to tremble with fear at the thought of what could have happened. I tried to dismiss this and consoled myself that it was over. I continued washing the clothes and around 3:00 a.m. I finally hit the sack, too tired to think about anything except sleep.

I woke up on Saturday morning to find Zara sitting on the floor and complaining of a really bad tummy ache. I thought maybe she was hungry and I tried to make some breakfast and a hot cup of tea for her, but after drinking a few sips, she said she wanted to throw up. For most of the morning instead of concentrating on moving, we now had to worry about Zara. I sent Fiyaz to the grocery store to buy a hot bottle of ginger ale and I rubbed her stomach with baby oil (our home made remedy). We put her to sit in a corner of the apartment while we carried over more stuff.

We then tried to clean up the basement apartment, because we had to get rid of the entire residue from the exterminators and especially with Zara not feeling well, we had to do a very thorough job. The baby sitter's boys came over and helped. We wiped down the walls and putt new shelf paper in the cupboards that we used for grocery and utensils. I also used the blinds and drapes that I had in the old apartment – I had to cut and fit in some instances, but without a sewing machine, it was a very laborious job using needle and thread to hem back the edges.

With our limited resources, Fiyaz and I tried to save as much as we could and we decided to use the rug from the studio apartment to replace the one in the basement, which was quite dingy looking. Neither he nor I had done anything like this before, but all things considered we measured and cut and placed the rug on the floor. If I may say so myself; we did a very decent job putting down the rug in the basement.

I kept running back and forth while the boys were carrying over the many garbage bags and books and microwave, etc. to check on Zara; and as the day went by she started feeling much better. Very soon we had brought over all our belongings except for the furniture – the day bed, the wardrobe, the entertainment center and the TV, etc. On Saturday evening, we made our bed with comforters and slept on the floor in the studio apartment for one last time. Zara had two vomiting episodes during the night, but by Sunday morning, she was fine.

On Sunday, Prem brought over two of his nephews and his friend and they soon brought over the furniture that was left in the studio apartment. As they were coming down the basement steps with the entertainment center the sliding glass door broke and one of them got cut on his hand. There was a lot of blood but soon everyone was back to normal and eventually they set up all the furniture before leaving.

We now had two bedrooms but only one day bed and as was our habit and one which we enjoyed we made our bed again on the floor and slept through the night without much incident. We stayed like this for a week as Zara and I still had to go to work and school. Fiyaz continued to do whatever little things needed to get done as well as make dinner for us, which was a great relief.

The next weekend we decided to look for some additional furniture. The previous landlady was very kind and when I moved from the studio, realizing that I was a single mother, she offered to give me a sofa set that she had in storage. A previous tenant had left it when they were moving since they had purchased new ones. I accepted it with gratitude. It fit perfectly in our little living room and it was one less thing that I had to worry about. She also told us about a salvation army place where they sold used furniture at a very reasonable price.

I took her advice and we took the train and found the place. We bought some dark wood furniture for Fiyaz's room – a closet, an end table and a book stand. It all came up to $120.00. The items were in very good condition and I thought it was quite a bargain. We also bought some polish and as soon as we got home we polished the pieces and they looked almost new.

We then went to Jamaica Avenue and purchased a new bed with mattress and end tables, as well as a bunk bed for Fiyaz's room. I think Fiyaz suggested that we buy the bunk bed and it was a really good suggestion, because as circumstances would unfold, he would have to share his room with Zara. Along with beds came the need for sheets, pillows and all the necessary fineries which I also purchased on Jamaica Avenue.

And so we started our new life in our basement apartment quite content and I was happy that I was able to provide for my children albeit only their basic needs. We soon fell into our routine of going to work and school. I always made the apartment comfortable and I had set aside a quiet corner for them to do their homework.

And remember the headaches that Zara had been having? Well guess what; since her brother had joined us she did not experience them again. Amazing how the mind could make the body sick.

It was now the summer time and Fiyaz had signed up to start College in the fall. A family friend encouraged me to have him look for a part time job so that he could assist me with our household needs as well as save a little for his tuition. They promised to see if they could help to find something. Soon I got a phone call that someone was willing to take him as a "delivery boy" in and around Manhattan.

I was thinking that this was a job that he would be delivering important mail and maybe small packages and we accepted willingly. He started promptly the following Monday and once we figured out how he would get to work we realized that we could travel together. So he got off at 42nd street while I had to get another train to get to my job.

We arranged that in the afternoons we would wait for each other at 42nd

street and we would ride the train home together. Cell phones were not as popular at this time and so the first day after we met up we pinpointed a spot where we would meet from then on. The first day he looked fine, but on the second afternoon his eyes looked red and when I asked him what was wrong he just shrugged it off and said it was maybe the sun.

A few days later, when he came home he asked me if I had a bandage that he could use.

"What do you need with a bandage?" I asked.

"Oh Ma, my knees are hurting me a little."

So I started to look at him more closely. One afternoon as he was coming down the subway steps I noticed that he was limping but as soon as he saw me he tried to straighten up. I did not say anything at that time as the train was coming in the station and we had to rush to get on. The train was too crowded for conversation.

After dinner that night I went to his room and I sat down on his sister's bunk bed and I said to him,

"Babe, could you please tell me what exactly you have to do when you go to work?"

He was like,

"Ma, just stuff here and there," but I could not see his face as he was talking. So I got up and now I was looking at him directly and I said,

"Fiyaz, there is something that you are hiding from me. Can you please tell me what it is?"

That was when my son started to tell me that he was a "delivery boy" in the garment district and he was not delivering mail or small packages as I had been led to believe. He was actually pushing boxes and boxes of supplies including buttons, zippers and fabric from one warehouse or factory to another. He had to stack these boxes four or five at a time and push them from one location to the other. He was just sixteen years old at the time and skinny as a rake. I broke down in tears and said,

"Why did you not tell me this before?"

He said,

"Ma I know you have a hard time taking care of all of us and you have to pay the rent and everything, I did not want to disappoint you."

I assured him that he was not disappointing me.

"I admire you for tyring, but your little body cannot take on this type of work. I would not let you kill yourself like this."

The next morning when I got to work, I called and told the manager thanks for the time that he spent there but that he would not be coming back because he was having severe knee pains. This was the truth anyway.

He stayed home for the remainder of the week and I put in quite a few phone calls because he insisted that he would like to work as he was home doing nothing. Luckily one of my co-workers knew someone who would give him a job at an electronics store in downtown Manhattan.

This was quite a good fit for him as he had done a radio and electronics course as well as he had done a "Work-study" program in the Office of the President in the Photography area before he came up to the States.

During the summer he worked there full time and when he had to start school in the fall he worked part time. The manager was very impressed with his work ethics and so he was only too happy to accommodate his school schedule. It also worked to everyone's advantage that his college was only a few blocks away from the job site.

Believe it or not, his school was within walking distance from my job as well and it was like when he was a young kid back home. At lunch time if he was between classes, he would come over to my job and we would have lunch together. He had found a mango drink that he liked and he would buy and bring for me sometimes, which made my friends think of him as a little angel.

If they had projects for their school or work assignments they would ask him to draw pictures for them and enhance their presentations. He was very good at that as that was one of the subjects that he had passed at his GCE O'Levels.

Their father soon joined us as well. Being a Sergeant in the Police Force and having some vacation time, he applied for a Visa and was granted a visitors Visa. The family was fully reunited. There should be more enthusiasm in my writing at this time, but that was another story, maybe another book. Suffice it to say that we were all together once again.

It took him a couple of weeks before he was able to get a job. Once again, my friend Leila and her husband were instrumental in helping us. Azad got him a job where he worked at an oil fueling company as a mechanic's helper. He was very diligent and went to work everyday, but all the other responsibilities of caring for the children were still left on me; and also for taking care of him. It was as if I now had three children to take care of, the difference was that now I had two incomes coming into the household.

My sponsorship at my job was still pending and I was just awaiting a response from the Labor Department. If you could remember, the last I had heard from them was that due to a recession there was a hold on all Labor Certifications. I had been in contact with a very nice representative from the Department of Labor. He had signed off on my paperwork and he had just needed his supervisor's signature, when as my luck would have it, there was a freeze on approvals.

What could I do but wait, and wait and wait? We tried to live a normal life, going to work and taking care of the children with their education and fortunately they were both doing extremely well in school. One might think what more could you ask for? If you were free there would not be much. However, at the end of each day, as I lay down to sleep, I would always worry about my immigration status. When would I get my papers so that this big burden on my shoulders could be lifted?

How ironic it was that during this time, the INS asked that all companies review their personnel files to make sure that the I-9's for all their employees was up to date. Guess who was assigned the task? I was. Even though I was not a resident or a citizen part of my job responsibilities was to do personnel filing.

As I was about to begin this task, my supervisor called me and I got scared. But she only needed to confirm with the attorneys that it was OK for me to still be employed based on this new request by the INS. She was assured that based on the sponsorship by the company, that I was covered.

Phew!! You could imagine my relief and with that reassurance, I went about my task with a lot of gusto and completed it in record time. I have to admit that I really felt bad for those people who could not provide updated documentation to satisfy the INS guidelines. But, I did my job diligently with no bias or favoritism. This was all when I was in the Business Department of the Non-Profit organization where I worked.

Around this time, my very first supervisor that I had worked with in the Queens Office, was promoted and came to work in the Main Office where I was now located. I was very happy and soon rumors were that the files in the foster care section were in a mass of confusion and disarray. Everyone thought that if anyone could make it better, it was me. And so, I was approached by the head of that department and asked whether I would be willing to move downstairs and become the Administrative Assistant to the Director of Foster Care.

I thought that I was working for the same agency and wherever my services were needed I was willing to work. In hindsight, I think this decision was to cause me a lot of grief in the very near future. Remember I was in the Business Department and the Comptroller of the Company was my big boss at the time. Now I was going to a Director of Foster care who had no control about financial issues. In my innocence, I did not think of all these ramifications and I switched departments.

With the help of the secretary and working late a couple of afternoons per week, I was soon able to bring the files up to date and create a more efficient system where it was very easy to locate files and information on any given case.

My efforts were much appreciated by my new boss as well as all the other social workers who saw the immediate improvement. The agency was back on track and it prospered, unfortunately, to my detriment.

The economy was not doing well and CWA had made a lot of cutbacks requiring the agency to cut back on staff. My boss had the daunting task of visiting all the branch offices, do the exit interviews and provide a letter of recommendation to the employees who were being let go. We were all speculating as to who would go and who would stay and the general consensus among all my co-workers was that I had nothing to worry about. I was one of the best workers around. What did anyone know?

Anyhow, on a fateful Wednesday in June, 1995, my boss had gone on one of his trips to the branch office when around lunch time I received a phone call from my son. He sounded very nervous and told me that he had received a certified letter from my job. I did not know how or why, (because none of us knew what form the termination would take) but I immediately felt a sense of doom as I started trembling and asked my son to open the letter.

It was heartbreaking to have my son read the termination letter to me and at the end of it, he said to me,

"So, Ma, what are we going to do now?"

I could not answer because I did not know myself. I told him not to worry, we would figure something out. I felt like someone had punched me in the stomach and it hurt a lot to have my children find out about this even before I did. I had no time to prepare them for this.

As soon my first supervisor, Rhonda found out, she said,

"Come on lets go to the Executive Director of the Agency."

He was very sorry and he knew that I was a really great worker but that there was nothing he could do. It was then that I realized the huge mistake I had made in accepting the job downstairs. I was sure and this is still my belief to this day, that had I still been upstairs, there was no way I would have been let go.

We went back downstairs and my boss soon got back. He immediately called me into his office and most apologetically he said to me,

"I am so sorry; this was not how I wanted you to find out. I had every intention of telling you as soon as I got back today, I did not think that the letter would arrive before".

I tried to be as calm as I could and I told him that I understood and that I knew it was not his fault.

There was no way I could console myself and I could not hide my feelings from my children. When they were back home and I had disappointing news I would never let them know. When I spoke with them on the phone I would always make up some story or the other telling them that everything was OK.

I was naked now. I had no way of masking the pain I was going through and I wish I could have gone somewhere else that afternoon. Instead I had to walk into our apartment with two pairs of eyes looking to me for hope, when I had none to give. I honestly did not know what my next course of action was going to be and it was frightening. However, I tried to reassure them that I would consult the lawyers and they would be able to figure something out.

That night I cried myself to sleep and wished for some sort of miracle to free me and my family from this constant nightmare of disappointments.

It was such a sense of rejection and feeling of failure. There did not seem to be any resolutions; at least not any time soon.

I did not know where I got the will power, but will power was definitely what it took for me to go to work the next day. I had two days until my last day. The news had soon spread and if coworker morale could have changed the situation, I certainly would have had my job back. Everyone was shocked and confused.

They could not understand why I was let go and some of them thought about signing a petition on my behalf, but I discouraged them for fear of them jeopardizing their future with the company. It could not reinstate me, but their support meant a lot at this point in my life.

The events following later that day would help to take the focus away from my pain, if that was in any way possible. My boss, who had been given the dirty task of doing all the termination exits and giving people letters of recommendations was called upstairs. No one knew what was going on, but when he came back down he went to his office and closed the door.

Rhonda was then informed through the grapevine that he had just been given the axe. She was utterly disgusted at the way this situation was handled.

She came to me and said that I should give my boss twenty more minutes to himself and if he did not open the door, I should go in and make sure that he was OK. (I was the only one who could go in being his Admin. Asst)

I did as she recommended and when he did not come out, I knocked before I went into his office. I would never forget the forlorn looked on his face when he picked his head up from his desk, where he was resting it on his hands. He looked at me and said,

"Can you believe that these people are supposed to be a Public Service Company and they treat people this way?"

I had no words with which to comfort him. I honestly was at a loss for words and I said, .

"Have you told Mary yet?"

Mary was his wife and she was a stay at home mom with his two little girls. He had not – he had needed to process the information and calm himself down before he spoke to her. He tried to convince me that he was OK and I left him to make his phone call.

I felt really bad for him. The way he was told after he had been used to tell everyone else was really a low blow and it made my situation seem a little more bearable. I knew his circumstances could never compare to mine; he was a US citizen and he would soon get another job even though for now it was hard with him being the only breadwinner in his family. For me, I was being sponsored on this job – so much had been riding on this sponsorship! The future of four innocent souls had depended so heavily on this job, and now it was gone!

That Friday was a really memorable one. All the workers from both floors got together and had a farewell party for the folks who were leaving. I tend to pride myself that I was one of the chief guests. I still have some of the jewelry that I had received on that day. One of the girls gave me a check for a hundred dollars – I did not know this until I got home and opened the card. Everyone was in tears and of course, I could not get a grip on my emotions. It was a bittersweet moment – I knew everyone liked me but I never knew the extent of their affections. It bolstered my spirits, if only for a little while.

And so I was now without a job. And I did not have any paperwork to get the kind of job I had been doing. (The earlier work authorization I had been given had long since expired and the case for Political asylum had never materialized). I stayed home for a few weeks since the kids were off from school and it worked out that I did not have to find somewhere for Zara to stay during the day. Their dad was working and we were making ends meet as best as we could with some of the money I had received from the agency when I left.

I was home for the first week when school reopened and I walked Zara to the bus every morning. When she came home from school I always had a nice hot snack (you guessed it, freshly fried plantain chips) and something to drink. She was very happy until I told her that I had to find a job because funds were running really low.

She said

"Ma, you do not go to work; I will work and take care of you."

Little did she realize that she could not be going to school and working at the same time!

My only alternative was to find a babysitting job. I was referred by a friend and was hired by a family who had two daughters. The older one was three and the baby was only a year old. At the interview, the mother told me not to worry, that at no time would I be left with both children since she did not work. If only this were true. Very soon I was left with all the household chores and the two children. If we were in the house, it was fine.

It was when I had to take them out and I used a double stroller to push them around. If you had never done this, you may think, what was she complaining about? Yes, if it was pushing them on a straight smooth road, the wheels on the stroller propelled it forward. However, try pushing them around some of the bumpy corners in Manhattan and getting them up to the curb when you cross a street. It became back breaking work.

I could not complain about having to go home and preparing dinner. My son would make sure that he cooked as soon as he got home from College and it was such a joy to go home and get a hot meal.

One afternoon, after a hard day out with the two girls in the stroller I got home and went to my room. When they did not see me coming out as usual, Zara came into my room only to find me in tears – I was in so much pain, I could hardly get up – my lower back and my hips felt as if they were ready to break away from my body.

She went and told Fiyaz and he brought some dinner into my room and they told me to lie down. They begged me to leave that job and wait until I got something less strenuous. I understood their concern, but they did not understand about all the bills and everything else that needed to be taken care of. And so after a fitful night of twisting and turning in pain, I got up the next day and went to work.

I think the powers that be were looking down on me and decided that it was a little too much. That same day I received a call from the director who was with a sister company of the agency from which I was terminated. Someone had told her of my situation and she wanted to find out some more details. When I told her she said she was going to find out if there was any way in which I could work for them and if they could pick up my paperwork and continue the sponsorship.

I was very skeptical and did not want to put too much hope into anything, not with everything that had been happening recently. However, it was something to at least hold on to.

She called me back within the week and told me that yes, they could apply for me but they did not have a weekday position available, would I be willing to work a forty hour night/weekend shift – that was one of the criterias for the sponsorship. I had to have full time employment with them. I was willing to do whatever it took to make it work and so I said, absolutely. I could not thank this woman enough.

In order for the sponsorship to go through, the job had to be advertised in a prominent newspaper for a week and all the responses had to be documented and forwarded to the labor department. It would cost $1100.00 to run this ad. Without any questions, this director said she was going to put this on her credit card and I could pay her back in installments. Another angel whose intervention I would always treasure.

And so the second sponsorship started going through. One great thing that came out of that was we were all granted Work Permits. Great in that I was also then able to get a daily job in my field and not have to continue to do the babysitting job. My friends started to recommend places where I should apply.

I was fortunate to interview with an HR representative from a very renowned Private Company in Manhattan and she really liked me. However, she had no immediate full time opening. She encouraged me to take a part-time job just to "get my foot in the door" and she promised that as soon as an opening came about, she would definitely keep me in mind. I would still need to wait regarding even the Part-time job as she needed to interview more applicants.

While I was waiting on her response a school mate from back home offered me a job at the company where he was a comptroller. He knew my situation in the states, but he also knew about all my qualifications and he promised to teach me the ropes so that I could move up quite quickly within the company.

As I have come to realize over the years, when you were looking for a job or anything else, nothing came around. When it did come, everything came all at once and then you were faced with the dilemma of choosing.

SO, I fell in that same trap!! I was in my first week on the job with my school mate when I got a call from the HR rep. in Manhattan. She was offering me a part time seasonal position with the hope of getting something permanent, IF, something became available. What was I supposed to do? This was so unreliable and here I was on a full time job which was great.

Except for the fact that I had to leave home at 6:00 a.m. to get there before 7:30 a.m. when they were open for business. This was what created the problem. I now had an 11 year old daughter who I would have to leave to go to school on her own. I had been traveling quite a bit in the States now and I sometimes saw the way young girls dressed to go to school. Being from an old school of thinking, I thought students should be dressed appropriately and I did not want her to go to school without decent clothes. Also she had become a "young" lady and was having a few issues with severe stomach aches, etc.

Besides which, as part of my training/growth experience at his job I would be required to come in on at least two Saturdays every month. I did not tell my friend who had gotten me the job this part, but knowing my husband, I would have been accused of all sorts of "other" things than job related duties. And so, I took a huge risk and made the choice to accept the part-time/seasonal job knowing very well that I was leaving a permanent position. But all things considered, I felt I would have incurred more problems if I had stayed.

I needed to start training on the Monday, and all weekend I was still debating whether I was making the right decision. I called my friend and told him about my concerns for Zara and so on and even though he may have suspected that there were other reasons behind my decision, he was very supportive and wished me all the best.

To this day, we are still very great friends who have the utmost respect for each other. I considered him to be a truly great human being for not holding a grudge against me even though he had put his neck out and went to bat with his bosses to get me that job.

Chapter 10

Major Set Back and "Serenity"

And so I started with my training for the job in the city and after three days I was issued a certificate and assigned to a specific department. This area only needed me during the Christmas Holidays and the assignment would end in mid January. I tried not to worry about that and delved into my duties with my usual fervor. At the end of the day, we were required to prepare some reports which had to be sent up to the HR offices. (These reports were filled in by hand).

During the last week of December the supervisor in the Department where I was currently assigned called me aside and said to me,

"I was asked not to discuss this but I feel compelled to give you a heads up. Please pretend that you never heard it before. The folks upstairs, (meaning HR) have been asking my opinion about you. They have been looking at the handwriting on our reports and are very impressed. They may have a position that they may offer to you."

This was music to my ears and I promised not to mention this to anyone. And as anticipated, I was soon called upstairs by the HR rep. who had interviewed me. She told me that there was an opening in the Benefits Department as an Assistant Benefits Analyst.

I was a perfect fit for this position with all my qualifications and experience in my previous positions. I was ecstatic. Maybe, my luck was beginning to turn around. I told her I would be more than willing to accept the position and so on January 4, 1996 I moved upstairs to the Benefits Department.

My situation was beginning to look better and better. I was being sponsored and I now had a very fulfilling job which I loved. But do not forget that in order for me to be sponsored I had to work some evenings and most of the weekend to meet the 40 hours minimum requirement. I was not complaining, it was very taxing, but it was a means to an end.

I had to procure the services of a new attorney who was charging some exorbitant fees claiming that it was a very difficult case. I had no alternative but to pay him as I saw some results. We did get the work authorization but they had to be renewed every year. I saved quite a lot on legal fees as I was able to pick up the forms from the weekend job and filed the paperwork myself. If the attorney had to file them, it would cost us $300.00 each for the four of us.

And here came the waiting game again! I was waiting and waiting and waiting! In the meantime I was really doing well at my job. I was even conducting Benefits Orientations for new hires and sometimes going to Branch locations especially in New Jersey for Open Enrollment sessions with employees.

It may seem odd, but I got picked up from my basement apartment in Company cars to go to these offsite metings. My manager saw one day that I lived in a basement and she said to me that I should try to find a better apartment befitting my status. I did not take this as an insult or in a negative way; I thought she was just trying to state the obvious – that if I was doing such a decent job then I should live somewhere befitting my means.

Little did she realize that I may have come a really long way, but I still had to overcome that greatest of all struggles, getting my Green Card/ Permanent Residency Status and FREEDOM! Freedom: to try and find a bigger, better apartment; or even try to buy a small house. Freedom: - from being scared of would be sent back if the paperwork did not get approved.

Freedom to travel and to do so many other things; it was remarkable how we sometimes took certain things for granted.

I was in a state of limbo and I felt that it was just a matter of time before we would finally get called for our interview. On one of our routine trips to get our Work Authorization renewed, we were standing on line waiting and our files were placed on the pile to be called. I heard my name, my husband's name and Zara's name but I did not hear Fiyaz's name.

I thought – it may have slipped under someone else's and his name would be called soon. After a few names were called and I did not hear his name, I went up to the Rep. and asked why I had not heard his name. She told me that his file had been sent to another window. I was bewildered.

"Can you tell my why it was sent to another window?"

She said she did not know.

I was frantic! We had now received our Work Authorizations except for my son and even knowing that there seemed to be a major problem his dad left and went to work. I was left to deal with the problem, like always. I was tyring to figure out what could be the reason for this new development and right away a story I had heard popped into my head.

There was a couple and their two sons who had come to get their paperwork and the dad's file was handed off to another window. No one thought anything of it and she went outside to get something for the young boys to eat. She never got a chance to see her husband again, except in handcuffs as they were shipping him off to be deported.

As with any negative thought, I could not get this picture out of my mind. But Fiyaz had done nothing wrong and we were all getting work authorizations as required. What could be the problem? Dear God, not another set back!!

I went over to the Guard standing next to the other window and I asked him if he knew why files were transferred to this window. He looked at me as if I were speaking some foreign language and said,

"Why are you asking me?"

I did not know why, I just had this bad feeling in my gut. I was so scared and I told my son to sit right near to the door. I told him that if I only made a sign to go, he should leave the building right away... I was desperate now, and I guess I was not thinking of the consequences, but I was not going to stand there and see them take my son away.

With this "arrangement" between us, I went to the window and waited quite patiently until a representative came and I asked him,

"Sir, please could you tell me what is wrong with my son's file and why they sent it to this window?"

The officer asked me, "Where is your son?"

You did not do this kind of thing in an Immigration office, but I guess I was beyond being logical and so instead of answering the officer, I countered his question with a question of my own, saying,

"Is there a problem, officer?"

He asked me again for my son and I asked him again if there was a problem. We did this at least three or four times and when he saw that I was not backing down he said, there was no "problem" but that my son had "aged out". Therefore, he could no longer get his work authorization or even his green card under this current sponsorship.

He told me that I should have received a letter to this effect, but I informed him that I had not. He then told me that all he needed with my son was for him to sign a form stating that he was advised of this and that he understood.

I said,

"Are you sure that is all you need from him?"

He reassured me that that was all. I then signaled for my son to come and even as he was coming toward me, I was wondering if this officer had lied to me. But, as promised, he just had my son sign a form and we were allowed to leave.

I took my two children and we bought some lunch at a nearby buffet and we sat in the Park. As we were about to eat, I looked at Zara and realized that her eyes were settling with tears. As soon as I started talking to her she started crying and sobbing hysterically, telling me,

"Ma, I do not need my papers yet, why could they not give Bro. mine? Why are they making us suffer so much, Ma?"

It took me a while to get her to listen and I told her that the fact that her brother was going home with us, was a blessing. I told her how scared I was that they could have deported him and we would have had to be going home without him.

"Would you have preferred that, babe?"

I told her that all we had to do was to wait some more. The officer had explained to me that once I got my green card, then I would have to sponsor him all over, but that he would be "grandfathered" with our original sponsorship date.

I had a very tough time consoling Zara. She was too young to understand how fortunate we were to still have her brother with us and all she could think of was how unfair everything was. She was getting papers she did not really need, while her brother who desperately needed them was being denied. We left the park after eating just because we were hungry, we did not enjoy our food – our mood was too bleak.

There was one good thing about the whole process this morning and that was I knew for sure our paperwork was making progress. Somebody had gone into my files in order for them to terminate my son based on his age. How ironic that they would go in AFTER he had aged out and not BEFORE. The sad part was that I had sent several letters to the INS pleading with them to adjudicate our case as my son would soon turn 21.

No one bothered to reply or act upon my pleas. It was as if we did not exist, until it was time to terminate his case. What did they care?

The lawyer called one day and left a message home that I should go into his office. He had received some correspondence and he needed to explain all the details. It seemed that I would have to pay a lot of back taxes. How was this, you may ask? Hope this explained it.

I was supposed to be paid a specific wage in order to be sponsored. Being a Not-for profit organization, the agency could not afford to pay me that exact amount by the hour, and so they had put a $$$ value on the cost of room and board when I worked evenings and weekends. This was satisfactory for the sponsorship purposes. I did not actually receive this in cash, but NOW I had to show that I paid taxes on all of that compensation.

What was a poor soul to do? I either paid the taxes or not get my green card. I went to an accountant who did three years tax amendment and the total figure I would now owe the IRS was $6,854.00. I was speechless! Apparently, this increase in "wages" would put me in a different tax bracket.

I was at my wits end. I tossed and I turned all night and prayed for a miracle or something that would make me not have to pay this large sum of money.

Unfortunately, reality had to kick in and I realized that I had gone through so much to get my papers, if I did not fulfill this final obligation I would be throwing away everything. And so with a very heavy heart, I put together all my little savings and even had to borrow $2,000.00 from Prem and Nadira. I finally went to the bank to get a certified check for the full amount. Fiyaz and I went to the city – we had to look for a Main Office of the IRS located on Broadway and Duane Street not very far from 26 Federal Plaza, the Immigration Headquarters.

It was so funny that a week later after I had not seen the returned check I told Fiyaz that maybe they would not cash the check. He looked at me and laughed – he knew I was in "la la" land.

He said, "Trust me, Ma they will cash it."

We knew that they had to because the new rule now was that the IRS had to send directly to the INS that the green card applicant had paid all their taxes before they would grant an approval. However, you could pay all your taxes and meet all the requirements and yet you could be turned down. This was why I was still petrified.

What if I had paid all that money on top of everything else and still was denied. These thoughts would come to my mind and I would break out into beads of perspiration. Besides, this waiting game was driving me crazy. The uncertainty; and the waiting; just WAITING. There was no way for you to get a status update. Nowadays there was a website that you could check on the status of your case. In those times, it was just whenever you heard from them, you were lucky. I just prayed that it was not negative news.

During one of my really down days, I was coming home on the number 7 train. It had just snowed and when I looked out of the train on the elevated line the branches on the trees were laden with snow. Look at how heavy those branches were with the snow but yet they did not break and look at how after winter all those dead trees would come to life again. It looked so beautiful and serene and pristine clean and I thought to myself; just look at the miracle of nature. Just then the train stopped and as the door opened a bird flew by and I thought of that poor bird in the cold; but then I realized that it was protected.

And with those thoughts: a calm and an inner peace overcame me as I reflected on the beauty and the power of God and I consoled myself that if God could provide for the birds in the trees, why would He not provide for me and take care of me? And I vowed to leave my trust in God and that He would make everything work out. I just had to have a lot of patience.

To this day, if I was going through some troubling times, all I had to do was to conjure the image of that pristine snow in my mind and I was comforted that all things would work themselves out; it only took time and perseverance.

Our lives resumed its normal pace and I resigned myself to waiting for our Green Card but this time I knew for sure that my son would not be a part of this process. Luckily he was in school and no one was pressuring him for any paperwork. However, he was working part time and now that his work permit was not renewed, I asked him to call the HR folks to find out what his options were.

They advised that they would have to speak with the attorneys at their Headquarters and would get back to him. You could imagine our relief when they told him that since he had been working there for over three years and that I would soon be sponsoring him anyways, they did not see a problem with him continuing as normal. To this day, I was not sure if this was correct, but you did not look a gift horse in the mouth and so he continued working there.

Some of our relatives and friends were astonished that I had him speak to his employers regarding his new circumstances. They claimed that they would have let him continue to work until they found out. They did not understand how much more at peace we were when we did not have to live in fear every single day.

Both Fiyaz and I slept much better knowing that we did not have that burden of worrying every night if tomorrow would be the day that his employers would find out his true status and had to fire him.

One afternoon around 3:30 p.m. Zara came home from school and she called me all excited,

"Ma, Ma, the lawyer left a message on the machine. He said he had good news. Ma can you please call him right away and find out what the good news is?"

As soon as I hung up with her I called the lawyer's office and he told me that we had a date to go to Federal Plaza.

I said, "Does this mean we are getting our Green Card?"

He said he thought so, but we should wait and see.

Well, you could be sure that this day was not coming soon enough. But, I was not sure if you could picture how bitter sweet this was. Here we were – a family of four who had all struggled together and yet, now only three of us would get our papers. Do you know how helpless I felt as a mother knowing that my child would be hurting and I could do nothing to comfort him?

I must say that Fiyaz was very brave and not once did he ever make us feel bad about our good fortune; he always showed us that he was happy for us – even though I was sure he was sorry for himself.

Anyway, the anxiously awaited day was there and we went for the scheduled appointment. It was a very routine procedure and we all stood in line to get a stamp in our passports. This stamp indicated that we were now a Resident of the USA but the official "Green Card" would be in the mail. I then asked the officer about Fiyaz and she told me that as soon as I got the card I could go ahead and re-apply for him. She assured me that it would not be a very long process and that I should not worry too much.

We checked the mail everyday for the precious document and within a few weeks – there they were: Three "Green Cards"; even though they were more of a pinkish color. We had to go to the Social Security Office to upgrade our Social Security Cards which had said "Not Valid without Work Authorization". Our green card status would take away that special stipulation on the Social Security Card.

Immediately after these formalities, I consulted the attorney and completed the paperwork to re-apply for Fiyaz. To my surprise, within three weeks I received a notice stating that the application was received and that the process should be completed with "120 – 180 days" exact quote from the INS form. I was on cloud nine. At least he would soon get all his documents as well.

And now, I was planning for something that I had wanted to do for such a long time. I WAS GOING HOME AFTER TWELVE YEARS.

UNFORTUNATELY, it was not as I had dreamt and I was not sure how I would handle it. My parents were no more. There went my dream of pampering them and taking them to the city and doing all sorts of wonderful things with them. I had to satisfy myself with the fact that all I could do was visit their graves and ty to find some closure. Also, I had some of my brothers and all my nieces and nephews besides friends whom I would love to see again.

I planned my trip to coincide with Zara's Easter Vacation and also for her 16th birthday. She had always said that she would like to have a 16th birthday party in our backyard. She had always hoped that we would get through and probably have our own house in the USA before her 16th birthday.

Lots of shopping after work and on the weekends before our trip. Imagine I had not gone back in 12 years and I had so many relatives and friends who would all be expecting a gift, besides clothes for me and Zara.

For my brothers and my sisters-in-law and my husband's brother and his wife; and his sister and her husband; I bought a nice watch and put them in their cute little boxes. I put all the special gifts in my carry on baggage. All our clothes and other gifts I placed in the baggage that we would check and we put a very colorful ribbon on them so that they could easily be identified when we got to Guyana.

Fiyaz and one of his friends took us to the airport and we soon said our goodbyes. As usual their dad did not go to the airport with us. Imagine my dilemma when I was about to board the plane and the air hostess told me that I had to check my carry on luggage as it was too large and that there was a full flight.

I began to panic. There was no proper labeling on this piece of luggage and no identifying ribbon and it had all my most precious gifts inside. I did not want to part with it but I had no choice as I would not be allowed to board with it.

When we got on the plane Zara realized that I was sweating profusely and she said to me,

"Ma, please calm down. Talk to me she said. What are you worried about?"

I told her that not only were the items in that baggage very expensive, it was more important because it was personal gifts for my immediate relatives.

She said,

"Ma, you do believe in God! Do you think He would let your stuff get lost when you struggled so hard to buy them and also how important they are to you?"

Eventually she was able to convince me to stop worrying as it would not solve the problem since I had no control over the situation.

We were now focused on the plane taking off. Neither of us had flown since we had come to the States and this was our second time on a plane, so we were both nervous. We held each others hands and once the plane had reached its required altitude we began to relax. We talked for a bit and we both soon dozed off since we had stayed up late the night before and woke up early to get everything packed and ready for our journey.

After five and a half hours as estimated, we finally landed at the Cheddi Jagan International Airport in Guyana. We had quite a wait to clear Immigration as we were on the Resident Line as opposed to the Citizen line which was much shorter and went through much faster. I was really not concentrating much on this process; my only thoughts at this time were for my baggage that had to be checked at the last minute.

By the time we were through Immigration without any difficulty, I made a bee-line for the baggage area and lo and behold, the bag was just sitting there, next to the others that had the colorful ribbons. I still considered this to be a miracle with all the dreaded stories we used to hear of lost and damaged baggage at airports.

What a RELIEF!!! I felt like I had renewed life. The porters assisted us with our suitcases while I held on very tightly to my precious small hand luggage with my ever so precious gifts. As we walked out of the immigration section at the airport I first saw my eldest brother and he was smiling from ear to ear when he saw me.

He turned to someone else and he pointed us out to them. I then realized that three of my brothers were there with one of my nieces. I was overwhelmed with emotion and I guess too choked up to cry and so I got hugged and hugged and all of us were tyring to talk at the same time. It was truly an indescribable moment.

They were all surprised at how grown up and beautiful Zara was and she was very happy at the amount of attention and praise that she was getting. However, because she was so little when I left and she had been away now for seven years, she was much more comfortable chatting with my niece and so the two of them started bonding while my brothers and I tried to play "catch-up".

I was now seeing my brothers after twelve years and I was now returning to the land in which I was born and raised. We walked to the mini bus which belonged to my youngest brother, and once we were seated with all four suitcases stacked securely, we were on our way. While tyring to carry on a conversation with my brothers, I tried to take in the sceneries on the road side as we passed by. There were so many changes and yet so many things were still the same.

I was home and it was HOT. But I was so happy and with the windows on the bus all the way down, I was fine. Except for one thing: I was very scared of the way my brother was driving. He was not doing more than sixty miles per hour, but I felt as if any moment now he was going to crash into an oncoming vehicle. Because, you see the roads only had two lanes – one going and one coming.

Now, do not think I was being too Americanized here. But you had to admit once someone had been exposed to the kind of multi-lane highways and by-ways overseas the small roads back home seemed scary. Because there seemed to be no room for error – one vehicle getting too far into the oncoming traffic could create a major accident. I did not however, let my brothers know of my fear because this was normal routine for them and so I trusted my brother who had been driving on these roads for umpteen years and I desisted from looking at the oncoming traffic.

Ever so often my brothers wanted to stop and buy all kinds of things for us to eat and drink – fresh fruits and young coconut water and sugar cane juice. I told them that we were fine; all we wanted was to reach home. There were some really huge buildings and businesses that were new to the area and my eldest brother who was sitting closest to me gave me details about them.

Finally, we reached home to my village and to my fifth brother's house where we would be staying for now. My other brother who did not make it to the airport was waiting for us to arrive along with a few other family members. It would have been a much bigger welcoming party but everyone did not know if our flight would be delayed and it was already 7:00 p.m.

A feast had been prepared for us .... All kinds of local delicacies and dishes that they thought we might enjoy: Curried duck and dholl and rice; roti and chicken curry and fried fish, etc. I was too excited to eat a lot, but I was hungry and it was really a special dinner with my four brothers and my four sisters-in-law and a few of my nieces along with Zara.

During this time I gave them each the gift that I had brought for them – for each of my four brothers and their wives along with the watch I had bought I gave them some $$. I then related the story of how I had thought I would lose all of it when we were to board the plane in NY. They all reassured me that it would not have mattered – they would have understood.

We talked way into the night even though I was tired, but soon they realized that I needed to get some rest and we retired for the night after taking a shower. The water was a "waker upper". This was something new – almost every middle class family was able to afford an overhead water tank and the water from this system was really cold.

The next morning, I woke up late and my sister-in-law had already invited a few of my other nieces as well as my brother-in-law and his wife on my husband's side to come and assist with the distribution of the gifts and items that we had brought for everyone. Of course they were given their gifts that were brought specifically for them. My brother-in-law and his wife received the same gift that I gave to my brothers and their wives. My husband's sister, who lived quite a few villages away, would get hers a few days later.

Soon after breakfast we were all sitting on the floor with little shopping bags, tapes and markers and having a fun time tyring to make packages for everyone. Those who were present of course had first dips at the fancy stuff and we tried to do a fair distribution of things like Cadbury chocolate, apples, cookies, corned beef, sardines, clothes – it was "who do you think this would fit?" and so a parcel was started for that individual.

On Friday was the special Jumah prayers and my brothers and I planned that after Jumah prayer they would accompany me to my parents' gravesite.

So after all the goodies were parceled off to be distributed I took a long shower. This time, my niece offered to heat up some water for me to lessen the shock of the cold water from the overhead tanks. I was so pampered!!

Anyway, when my brothers came by after the Friday prayers two of them opted out of going with me, because they could not bear to see my reaction or deal with the emotional turmoil. It ended up with my eldest brother, my youngest brother, my nephew's son, me and Zara who went to the gravesite.

We had to make our way very carefully through the grass and deep "cow holes" in the burial ground because the rains had been falling steadily and the entire ground was soggy and muddy. Arman, my nephew's son held my hands while I held on to Zara as we made our way to the actual site of my parents' graves.

It was very convenient that my brothers were able to get their burial patches head to head of each other and so they had put wrought iron fence around both their graves making it look like one really long grave.

My eldest brother deferred to my youngest brother who was asked to say special prayers for my parents. All this while I was like a zombie, being led and tyring not to think. As soon as my brother started to pray my emotions took over. I could honestly say that to this day I had never felt a pain as severe as I felt on that fateful day. It was as if a heavy band of steel was pressing against my chest and it kept tightening, and tightening and I felt as if I could no longer breathe.

In the meantime, tears were streaming down my face and I could not sustain this anguish any longer. I let it out but still tyring not to bawl and scream as I really wanted to, because I had to be considerate of my brother saying the prayers.

I did not realize it but I started to shake and my shoulders were heaving in my effort not to rant and rave and scream and shout, and so Zara held on to me really tight – I could feel her tyring to comfort me without words and I could barely stand by this time. Arman held me on the other side and he took my scarf and with such a tender touch he tried to wipe away my tears. I would always remember him for that moment in my life.

I think I blacked out from the sheer raw emotional pain, but because Zara and Arman were holding on to me so tightly I did not drop to the ground. Eventually I came back to the reality of my brother as he finished the prayers and I asked them for a moment alone. Zara stayed with me – she did not trust to leave me alone, less I fall down.

In my heart I was begging my parents to forgive me for not being there with them when they passed away and not being able to attend their funeral. I begged them to release me from all the guilt and torture that I was inflicting on myself and to help me to heal. I begged their understanding and above all, I thanked them for everything they did for me since I was a baby to the day that I was standing there.

Had it not been for their strong moral upbringing I did not know how I could have withstood all the hardships I had gone through all by myself. I also thanked them from the bottom of my heart for giving me a sound education because that was what had helped me in a foreign land.

Eventually my youngest brother came and got me, saying that it was time for us to go. We then went to the graves of other relatives who were buried nearby and he said a prayer for them as well, among them one of my brothers who had passed away under very tragic circumstances.

I was emotionally spent and just sat silent on our way back to my brother's house. Zara held my hand and it was the best thing she could have done for me at the time; she did not need to say anything – I knew she was tyring to comfort me.

When we got out of the minivan, my relatives took one look at me and recognized that I was not in a mood to talk much and so I went upstairs. My sister-in-law came up shortly after and encouraged me to take a bath as was customary after returning from the cemetery. I took a long bath and cried a lot more. The cold water invigorated my body, but there was no invigorating my soul. I had to dig deep into the dregs of my being to come out of the depressive state that I was in.

As I was toweling myself dry, I prayed and asked God to give me the strength to act normal and not to make the people around me feel uncomfortable. He indeed answered my prayers. I came downstairs and told Zara to go and take a bath as well. I then slowly got back into the conversations going on around us and soon after we all had dinner before retiring for the evening.

I was extremely tired, emotionally and physically and soon fell asleep only to dream about my parents. In my dreams I was a little girl and for whatever reason they were always getting into one means of transportation or another and I was being left behind. I was always crying for them to take me, but they both said that where they were going was not for little girls and that I should go back home with my sister and not give her too much trouble.

Saturday was a big day and it was Zara's 16th Birthday! I woke up early, spending some quiet "lovey dovey" time with Zara, wishing her a Very Happy Birthday. After I gave her a special pearl bracelet that I had bought in the States for her I went downstairs and soon got into the swing of things.

There was a lot going on with relatives arriving from different parts of the country to overnight so that they could assist in the preparations for the upcoming religious function I had planned for my two children. It was called an Aqeeqah function and when you were blessed with a child, you usually gave thanks to God with this ceremony. I should have done this since the kids were babies, but I could not have afforded it at that time.

There were huge preparations to be made. There were over 500 guests consisting of family members, relatives and friends from other parts of the country as well as everyone from our village. My brother had made all the arrangements ahead of time and a bull was slaughtered for some of the guests; and for those who did not eat beef; a hundred chickens were prepared.

While the male relatives were taking care of the meat, the female relatives were busy preparing delicacies/sweets which were served during these religious functions. Some of them were also involved in cooking dholl puri and roti which was very time consuming to prepare and so it had to be done the night before.

For Zara's birthday celebration, we invited all the kids in the family and in the neighborhood and held a little party in our backyard. She had always dreamed of having her 16th birthday in her backyard, but she had hoped it would have in her backyard in the USA. I joked with her and said,

"Your dream is being fulfilled – your birthday celebration is in our backyard."

Yes we did have our own house still, and you may be asking why I did not stay there instead of at my brother's house. The reason was because my brother-in-law was living there and I had never met his new wife. I also felt that all the other relatives might feel more comfortable visiting me at my brother's house and everyone could spend as much time as they wanted.

The children had a spectacular time and they made me laugh so hard that I was crying. It was exactly what the doctor ordered. It was very heartwarming to spend such a wonderful afternoon and to see the kids playing and dancing around. The innocence and freedom was a joy to watch. Zara thoroughly enjoyed herself.

After the kids went home, we visited some of our neighbors and took over food for them. By now it was really dark and we had to walk back to my brother's house. It was hilarious to see how many times we walked into puddles of muddy water since it was the rainy season and the road was full of pot holes. Every time someone made a big splash we would start laughing only to have someone splash some more. We were a royal mess by the time we got home, but we did not mind – it was all so much fun!

We tried to get to bed early but it was impossible with so many activities going on and with so many relatives sharing stories and jokes. Eventually, we turned in around 1:00 a.m. knowing that we had a full day ahead with the big "Aqeeqah" function coming up on Sunday starting at 9:00 a.m. I prayed that everything would go well before I finally fell asleep. Much needed sleep I might add after a long tiring day – but very "happy" tired.

I woke up on Sunday morning to a lot of hustle and bustle – a houseful of folks tyring to cook, shower and get dressed in order to make it on time to the religious function. I may not have mentioned this before, but this was not being held at anyone's home, but at the village mosque, where my father had been the priest before he passed away. One of my brothers was now the officiating priest and my other brothers all had a role in the administration.

I jumped right away into the mêlée of everyone tyring to iron, shower; dress; and have breakfast in a very limited space and time. Eventually, we made it to the mosque about fifteen minutes late. In relation to "Guyana" time, this was excellent. We had a joke in the States about how notorious we were for being late, that when we got an invitation we usually asked,

"Is this in Guyana time, or US time?"

My brother started the function at 9:30 a.m. and we had to be finished by 12:00 noon. The weather was just beautiful – the sun was shining but it was not too hot and there was a refreshing breeze. It was a picture perfect setting and later, many friends and relatives commented that they felt the presence of my parents in the atmosphere.

The whole program went without a hitch and then it was my turn to give the vote of thanks. I tried to be as brief as possible but by the time I was finished there was not a dry eye in the audience. Everyone was crying as they felt my pain about missing my parents and not having them present for my big "homecoming."

We then served a very scrumptious lunch with everyone partaking of lots of delicacies and everyone was fascinated when they were each given a bottle of soda with a straw. Some of the dishes were dholl and rice with either curried beef or curried chicken along with chowmein and dholl puri. There were also sweet meats such as mitthai, phulow, cake, jello and ice cream.

While lunch was being served, I went around and met with a lot of the guests and gave little gifts to the elderly. This was customary in our society and we always tried to do this with the hope of getting a lot more blessings by providing for the poor and needy.

By 3:00 p.m. everyone had left and the place had been cleaned up with all the dishes washed and put away. We did not have sanitary plates – these were enamel plates that belonged to the mosque and they were washed and dried and packed away. All the huge pots which were used to cook a whole cow and about one hundred chickens were also washed and stored away.

To this day, Zara still marvels at how efficiently and quickly everything got done. She had never seen any big function like this – all she had been accustomed to were little gatherings at someone's apartment in the States. And it always seemed too congested to feed about 40 – 50 people.

On this day, Easter Sunday, (she was actually born on an Easter Sunday) she saw about 500 people having lunch, dishes washed and put away and the entire mosque compound swept and put back to normal as if nothing had taken place. After cleaning up, some of the immediate relatives sat under the ladies section of the mosque and chatted for another hour or so. We waited until everyone had left, before finally heading back to my brother's house.

Chapter Eleven

The Grass is always Greener

It was difficult to explain but when you grew up in a small society and everyone knew each other, you felt such joy being back among them. Our family was well respected in our community and having been a teacher before I left even though I was much younger, I was also well respected. Sometimes I felt that we were revered and if it were possible people would worship the ground we walked on. I felt all that affection on this day and to leave an environment like this was very difficult.

But, the grass was always greener on the other side. I had to sacrifice all this open space and comaraderie and go back to the States for a better financial and educational future for myself and my children.

Monday was Easter Monday. This was a day of festivities in my country. It was supposed to be the resurrection of Christ – religious significance. For us, it was a day to fly our kites and have picnics on the beach and lots of little fun and game activities. As a child growing up, I could remember how we used to pray that it did not rain on this day, as we did not want our kites to get "salt bread" - wet from the rain. If the kite got wet, it would not be able to "fly".

There were all kinds of kites – huge ones that took weeks to frame and paste with intricate diamond shaped designs and small ones which older brothers put together with a few pointer brooms. The ones with the pointer brooms were very easy and in this way they could get the little ones out of the way. There were some in the shape of birds and men and lots of ingenious ideas and some of them would be entered into competitions that were held along the seashore. Most of the kites had to be flown along the sea walls to avoid them getting tangled up with the electric wires.

Sometimes there would be organized games at different venues and they would also have fun stuff like donkey and goat races. The one thing that was the most fascinating to watch was the "greasy pole" where a log that was covered with grease would be placed across a trench and someone had to cross it over without falling off into the trench.

At the end of the pole would be the prize of usually a large bottle of rum. It was tons of fun to watch when people fell into the trench with a big splash. Once the water got on the pole it became more slippery and harder to get across. One of my uncles was very good at this sport and most of the time he would be the winner.

My sister's sons who lived a couple of villages away had invited us for lunch and we all packed into a mini bus and went over. My nephews had taken out the seats the weekend before in order to transport some large items and no one ever had the time to put it back.

We put little benches and empty cans on which we sat and no one complained. We got there around 1:00 p.m. They had prepared lots of goodies – too much to eat. The dishes were really delicious and they made special homemade lemonade which was very thirst quenching on a hot day.

After a very mouthwatering lunch I lay in a hammock and it was heaven to have the fresh sea breeze blowing in my face and keeping me cool. I think I dozed off a little and did not want to get up to go to visit more relatives who lived in the city. However, duty called and prevailed. Soon we were on our way to Georgotown to visit the relatives where my brother and I had stayed when we went to College and where also his daughters and my son had stayed to go to High School in the city.

On our way, we saw a relative on her veranda and stopped to say hello. As luck would have it, one of my other nephews saw us and stopped to find out where we were headed. He was also going to the city and he had a new mini bus. So we transferred to the new Mini bus and had a more pleasant ride into the city while my other nephews stayed in the previous bus. They had to accompany us since the new mini bus was not coming back until the next day.

We arrived at our destination in the city and everyone was surprised that we had taken the time to go visit even though they had seen us the day before at the Function that we had. I explained that Fiyaz had specifically asked us to visit and report to him how everyone was doing, especially Aunty Alice who used to cook and take care of him. The first words out of her mouth were,

"When will I see my Fiyaz?"

Unfortunately, they would never get to see each other as she would pass away a year later.

On our way back, my nephews took the sea wall route so that we could see Easter festivities. Wow, it was beyond compare and on a much grander scale then before I had left for the States. There were huge music sets and loud music blaring with the latest song hits and everyone was just having a jolly good time. There was dancing and kite flying and drinking of beer (a lot of this was done openly). The sky was dotted with lots of kites and with the sea in the background; it was really a pleasure to take it all in.

Before crossing the Bridge to go back home, we stopped to buy ice cream and freshly baked bread and cheese (for breakfast the next morning). It was very late by now and my nephew was speeding along as best as he could (remember we were in the old bus with no seats and we kept bumping around on our makeshift seats. Jokes and laughter filled the bus and then one of my nephews decided to sing and bang on one of the empty cans as his drumming accompaniment.

As soon as he started to sing, (I still had this picture in my head anytime I heard this song) we heard a bang and the bus started to swerve. My nephew who was driving did a great job controlling the bus and soon we came to a stop. What would you know? We had a flat – instead of fussing and getting upset, we all started laughing and told my nephew that he should never sing again, because he was the one who caused this to happen.

On a serious note, however, his wife had to run to the corner of the road and she started to throw up. I got very concerned and then their secret was out. She was pregnant and had not told anyone yet, but now she had to say something. Once the punctured tire was replaced, we continued on home, but with a lot more caution as we were very concerned about her well being and did not want the bus to bounce up and down too much.

Finally we arrived home worn and tired! We were also very hungry wtih all the drama on the road and so even though it was after 10:00 p.m. we all began scrounging for food. My sister-in-law had lots of leftovers and so we all sat and ate but it was a rushed affair. Soon after my nephews and their families went home we showered and went to bed. Oh, the beds were calling our names.

On Tuesday, I stayed home and slept as I had started to develop a fever. I think all the excitement and never ending activities as well as the emotional upheaval was finally taking its toll. Zara and her cousins went to the city. She had a great time as they took her to the museum, the zoo and after lunch they went to see an Indian movie on the big screen at the Liberty Cinema in Georgotown.

She was exhausted but quite excited when she got home. She had so many stories to tell me. She had seen the "Kissing Bridge" in the botanical gardens and the water lilies and the manatee and lots of other flora and fauna indigenous to our country.

When the sun had cooled down for the afternoon I took a shower and as this was the last day before I returned to the States I decided to visit my parents' gravesite one more time. It was heartbreaking, but not as tumultuous as the first time when I had gone. I shed lots of silent tears and tried to reason with them in my own way and asked their forgiveness for not being there with them to the end. In my heart I knew they understood but I still had this huge regret and I think there was nothing I could say or do to make it go away.

On our way back I stopped and chatted with people from the village and finally returned home to a houseful of immediate relatives. These included my brothers and their families which consisted of lots of nieces and nephews and their families. They were busy packing anything and everything that they thought we would pass through Immigration with into our suitcases. They had fried lots of fish and shrimps and no matter how much we told them that we got all those things in the States, they insisted that these would be fresh and better. I could not win this battle, so I gave up.

We talked and talked way into the night, but everyone had to go to work the next day and I had to return home. Saying goodbye was really difficult and I tried my best not to cry – actually they would not let me as they joked about stuff as soon as they saw me getting sentimental.

The last day of my visit was finally here and I had to do something that I had not done yet. You would probably notice that I had mentioned going to the burial ground, my brothers' homes and lots of different places, but so far, I had not gone to my parents' home. I got up with a very heavy heart – I knew I had to go back to America which was my home now, but who of these people that I was leaving would I get to see again? Albeit my circumstances were different now, God willing if something were to happen, I could always come, but it was still very difficult to leave.

I got dressed in preparation for leaving and then my brother who lived across the street from where my parents lived said,

"I know you have been avoiding this, but I guess you have to do it."

He accompanied me to my parents' home where I really broke down as soon as I walked in the front door. My brother could not take my grief and he tried to console me by hugging me really tight, but then we both started crying.

It was as if all my pent up emotions got unleashed. As I looked around at the familiar surroundings and the chairs in which they used to sit, I could not help but remember my growing years within these walls. I could picture my mom or my dad sitting there waiting for me and the last conversation I had with my parents flashed back in my mind. Did I think it would have come to this? Absolutely, Not!

Anyway I finally went into their bedroom and it was almost like I could smell them – it felt so real and yet so surreal. I opened their wardrobe, and yes there was the patch that was put over the bottom when I had punctured it as a child playing hide and seek. I touched it and wished my mom and dad would just appear for one last time so that I could get that much needed hug from them.

Unfortunately, that was never to be as long as I lived on the face of this earth. All I had now were memories of them. I took a talisman from my dad's dresser and a scarf which my mom used to wear very often. I did not need these to remember them by, but I took them as a keepsake anyways.

I finally was able to compose myself; I guess the persona that I wanted to face the world with, but my heart felt like a big lump of stone. I was able to say my goodbyes and because I took longer than I had anticipated at my parents' home, we were pushing for time to get to the airport and thus did not get to eat a proper lunch. My favorite niece had made some egg balls and other delicacies when we visited her but time did not permit and so she wrapped them and we had our little "to go" bag.

We had to leave in order to avoid getting caught with the bridge closing (the bridge across the river usually closed to allow ships to go by) and if you got caught you could be stuck for over an hour sometimes. We made it through without any incident and were at the airport on time for our 3:00 p.m. flight. We were checked in quite efficiently and all my relatives who had accompanied us to the airport (two minibuses) left to return home after a final farewell. They could not accompany us any further.

When we got to the Immigration counter, the Officer kept giving us some very weird looks. He took our Green Cards – We both had the same first and last names but our middle names were different. I was very scared because it was the first time we were travelling since receiving our Green Cards. He turned over our cards and looked at them and then he went over to another officer who did the same thing.

I tried to ask him if something was wrong but he did not give me an opportunity. He then went to a third Officer who came back and asked me for another form of identification besides my passport. Luckily, I had my US driver's license and when I produced that he took a final look at me and Zara and our Green Cards before allowing us to go through. Whew, what a relief!!

There was no prior announcement or any indication of a delay in our flights but our scheduled 3:00 p.m. did not leave until around 9:00 p.m. You could imagine how hungry Zara and I were since we had not had any decent lunch. We went to the Cafeteria in the Airport to check what they had but we could only purchase two sodas as everything else had some sort of meat in it and we could not partake of meat that was not "halal".

And now for the egg balls and other stuff my niece had packed. We were so grateful that she had the presence of mind to do that, or else we would have had to suffice on a pack of chips or something else from the canteen. We ate and soon Zara put her head on my shoulders and fell asleep. I dozed off also, because there was nothing else to do and we were both very tired.

The waiting was very frustrating. They kept changing the time of departure every hour but finally we saw that they were getting ready to board the plane. With the reception we had with the Immigration Officers on this end, I was beginning to get worried about what would happen when I had to clear immigration in the USA. I did not let Zara know about any of my anxieties in this regard as I did not want to burden her with unnecessary stuff.

We boarded the plane and we took off without any further delays. It was too dark to see much outside and we held each other's hands for the take off. I was way more nervous than Zara. Once we hit the appropriate altitude and that initial feeling of having your "gut come up in your throat" had passed we tried to cuddle up as best as we could. We slept on and off and sometimes while we were both awake we would talk about something someone had said or done during our trip.

The flight of five and a half hours felt like a lifetime. When I was awake I kept thinking about so many aspects of my life that I had spent in my home country. My thoughts took me back to years and years of happy childhood days and to a loving mother who could not read or write but who instilled a great quest for knowledge in all of her children. And of my dad, who could read and write and who had the neatest handwriting of anyone in his age group that I knew.

I said many a prayer for them and thanked them for the moral values on which they had raised me. These were the values that kept me grounded and helped me through all my trials and tribulations. I could easily have succumbed to lots of temptations. Believe me; they came from the most unexpected sources. People who should have been there to help and protect you were willing to take advantage of your circumstances.

We eventually arrived at JFK International Airport at around 2:20 a.m. on Thursday morning and it was with some amount of trepidation that I made my way to the Immigration line. I knew I had not done anything wrong, but still with the reception we had at Cheddi Jagan Airport and this being our first time using our Green Card, I did not know what to expect.

I filled out my Declaration form with nothing but the truth. I said that I had some fruits and sea food which my relatives insisted on packing and which I hoped I would be allowed to pass through with. Everyone said that I should have just lied on the form and that they would let you through.

Not with my luck! Everyone else might get away with things like that and then it was not in my nature to be on the wrong side of the law. Once we got up to the line to clear Immigration, the Officer took our cards, and looked at them and checked in the Computer and stamped our passports as re-entering the country. No hassles, no unusual questions, no looking at us over and over!!! This was a load off my mind.

Unfortunately, I did not fare quite well in the Customs department. They looked at my Declaration form and told me to join another line while I saw tons of people who I was sure had more stuff than I did were allowed to go free. The officer was a tiny little girl and she checked my bags and took out the golden apples which had been peeled and sprinkled with salt and pepper.

She also took out some "same" (vegetable like string beans) which had been precooked but she said they did not look as if they were cooked and she threw them out. At least she only threw out a few of the things – there were lots more that she could have thrown away.

We were the last ones to get out of the Airport and it was such a relief to finally be through with all of the red tape and to see Fiyaz and one of his friends waiting for us. We lived a good 45 minutes away from the airport but at that time of the morning there was not much traffic and soon we were home, exhausted and hungry.

I could not immediately take a shower and go to sleep as I really would have liked to. I had to unpack the suitcases – at least take out all the edibles that we brought. Fiyaz helped me while Zara went and took a shower. We had to make room in the refrigerator and stack the stuff that we had brought including fried fish and shrimps as well as some of the curried beef that had been saved from the bull that was killed for the Aqeekah function. While doing this we kept talking about our trip in hushed tones as his father was still sleeping and we could not be too noisy to wake him up.

Once we were through with that I ate some leftover food from dinner, took a shower and hit the sack. I was not scheduled to be back at work until the next day. There were too many stories of people being stuck and flights being delayed for me not to have taken an extra day off from my job. When I woke up later in the day I did some routine cleaning and completed unpacking our suitcases. I made dinner and then prepared for work the following day. Zara could sleep some more as she had to be back at school until Monday.

And so after the much anticipated and emotional roller coaster trip to my country, I was back to my normal routine within a short period of time. I had thought that visiting my parents' gravesite would put closure to the torment and pain that I felt. It helped, but it would never completely go away. I did not think anything would take away this emptiness I felt whenever I thought about my parents, which was quite often. I tried to move on with my life and all I could do was pray that they rested peacefully.

As mentioned earlier, I had received a response from the Immigration Department regarding the new application I filed for Fiyaz. I was elated when they said that it should not take more than six months before he would finally get his green card. With that hope I went about my daily routine and our situation was looking better.

Both of the children were in school and getting mostly A's on their tests and assignments. Both parents were working and we were tyring to save a few dollars to eventually move out from the basement apartment and find better living quarters for all of us. The children were now sixteen and twenty two and they still shared a bunk bed and a bedroom. I had to say that not once did they complain about these constraints – I was blessed in this regard. They knew our circumstances and they were very content to make do with whatever.

I had also moved on from one job to another. At my previous job, there was no room for growth within the department and I felt that as I got older it would be more difficult to find a decent job. I decided to find a similar job in another company and so when the opportunity presented itself, I seized it with open arms. Of course there were some anxious moments as to whether I was doing the right thing. However, when I looked at the new job situation, I did not think I could go wrong. It was a big sports Arena and I felt if I was looking for stability in a job, there could be no better place.

So here I was getting settled and within a few months of working here, the really horrific tragedy of September 11 took place. I was at work on that fateful day. There was sudden pandemonium as people were yelling to look at the TV and with that I got up and ran to the break room, just in time to see the second tower crumble.

I stood there mesmerized. Was this a TV gimmick, or was this real? It was very traumatic to look at the TV and hear the sirens blaring and see people running amok on the streets of downtown New York. All of us who were standing in the break room were scared and some people were openly crying and wondering what would happen next.

Many people started calling home to their loved ones to let them know that they were OK. My friend from the Bronx saw the news and immediately called to see if we were affected at my job. Fiyaz also called to make sure that I was safe. He then told me that there was no way he could get into the city any time soon – traffic and everything had started with the domino effect.

Very soon some folks at work started to mobilize a safety and rescue situation and they started to hand out bottles of water and whoever had snacks shared with others. I was offered a ride to the Queensboro Bridge – someone had drove in to work and could get me to the other side of the bridge and from there hopefully the trains were still running and I could get home.

I had to decline this offer; since Zara was in school in Manhattan as well, there was no way that I was going to Queens and leave her in Manhattan. The buses had stopped running and so I started walking to her school. I walked from 7th Avenue and 32nd street to 50th street and 11th Avenue where her school was. I was allowed to sign and take her with me. If I signed for them, the teachers would allow me to take two of her friends with us. I readily did this as her friends' parents lived all the way in Brooklyn.

Now that my baby was secure and we were together, I was still scared and nervous, but at least we were together. We walked on 50th Street toward the 59th Street Bridge and since it was about lunch time, we stopped at a Pizza parlor and we had Pizza. I could barely eat, but I guess the kids had not seen what happened, they had only heard; it did not impact them as much and they ate quite normally.

The TV was on and we heard then that some buses had resumed their schedule and the girls could get a bus from Second Avenue into Brooklyn. We walked then to Second Avenue and waited with them until they got on the bus. When I say we walked from 11th Avenue to Second Avenue, it may not make such an impact on you unless you knew the layout of Manhattan. The Avenues were really long and this was practically walking almost the entire breadth of Manhattan. For me who had already walked from my job to Zara's school it was a lot of walking, especially for someone who was not a great walker.

We were now on Second Avenue and there was the Bridge to take us across from Manhattan to Queens, but no public transportation. There was no alternative but to start walking. Zara was much younger and she was able to deal with this far better than I was. I was almost to the point of crawling my way across – I could barely lift my feet – finally we saw the end of the bridge.

What a remarkable sight to see volunteers standing with truckloads of water to hand out to weary people as they made their way across the bridge. Some were by now bare feet as they had on heels at their job and had to take them off because they could not go the distance in heels over the metal bridge. Many folks were ill prepared and it took its toll. Some people just plopped down at the end of the bridge and sat there in order to catch their breaths and waited for family members to come and get them or for public transportation to start operating again.

It was not long before the No. 7 train resumed operation. It was painful to get up the steps and up to the platform to board the train, but now was no time for complaining and in order to get on the train you had to climb those stairs. Climb it we did. It was such a relief to be on the last leg of our journey and to finally be close to home.

When my son came home that night, I hugged my children really tightly and thanked God that we were all safe. I also said a prayer for all the people who lost their lives on this unforgottable day. I sincerely hope that we would never have to go through an experience like this ever again in our lives and in the history of our country.

Life would never be the same again for many people, especially those awaiting their green cards and much more so if they had a Muslim name. Whether we accept it or not, the events of 9/11 would have a very great impact on the way the world perceived Muslims, even though not all Muslims were terrorists. But, just having a Muslim name put you under more scrutiny and rigid background checks than someone without a Muslim name.

Unfortunately, once again, Fiyaz had to suffer because of circumstances beyond our control. I could not say for certain that the delay in his paperwork was a direct result of him being a Muslim, but I know for sure that his paper work was delayed way longer than anticipated. Based on correspondence we received, it had been expected to be completed within 2 to 6 months. Believe me, it took over six LONG, AGONIZING YEARS!!

Chapter Twelve
Rewards and Dramatic Changes

We were playing the waiting game and there was nothing anyone could do to help. I wrote to the Senators and visited the Congressmen's offices both in Queens and in Brooklyn. There was nothing that anyone would recommend that I did not follow through on. All to no avail. Everyone just said we had to wait.

By this time, the Immigration Services was changed to USCIS and they had appointed an Ombudsman to facilitate and expedite Immigration issues. I wrote to the Ombudsman as well. I diligently watched any and every show on Immigration – no matter what I was doing on Sunday mornings at 10:30 a.m. I would run to the TV to watch a fifteen minute "Immigration" program that was on an Indian Channel.

I thought I could be an Immigration attorney by this time with all the knowledge I had accumulated on this subject. Needless to say, none of this could help as no new laws were coming out which would benefit Fiyaz. It broke my heart when he would sometimes come home and say to me,

"Ma, I feel as if I am carrying a 50 ton weight on my shoulders."

I tried to be very supportive and encouraging, always giving him hope, that soon, everything would be OK. I tried to get him to see the positive side of things – at least we were together, he was in school and no one was harassing us. I pleaded with both of them to take full advantage of their educational opportunities and to be as productive as possible.

Fiyaz had by now transferred from BMCC to the College of Aeronautics. As part of his course work and for final graduation grades, they had a major project to complete. He did such a wonderful job that it is still on display to this day at his school. He started small and as he progressed it became more and more elaborate until the final product was outstanding.

His professor was very impressed and offered to have him join the staff at the College of Aeronautics. You know that he could not accept such an offer. He did not have that document called a Green Card. And so, he had to politely decline much to the disappointment of his Professor. If only he knew!!

Fiyaz graduated from College of Aeronautics with his Bachelor's degree as Magna cum Laude – he missed being Magna Sum Laude by 1/10 of a point. My heart swelled with pride as his name was called and he went up to receive his certificate. He also received a special pin. After his graduation we went to lunch and a few weeks later, I threw a little party for him to celebrate his success.

We tried very hard to surprise him but it was not to be. He suspected and to keep us on our toes, he refused to change into decent clothes saying that wherever we were taking him, he was going just as he was. Eventually, we had to tell him that lots of his friends would be there and that it was a party for his graduation. He started laughing at us and said he knew he would get us to spill the beans. To this day, no one could surprise either of my two children – they always knew.

I even said to Zara once, "could you not pretend?"

She was like, "Maybe, next time."

You could imagine my elation when Zara called one day from school and said to me,

"Ma, guess what? I have great news!!"

(I could not fathom what she was about to tell me. I knew she was getting excellent grades, but I had never thought it would come to this). So, I begged her to end the suspense and tell me.

Then she said, "Ma, one of my teachers just told me that I am the Valedictorian of my graduating class." I was so choked up that I could not answer her immediately.

Eventually, I blurted out –

"What did you say?"

And then she repeated it. I said congratulations and she hung up as she had only been allowed a quick phone call. I just sat there and cried openly – all tears of sheer joy and I guess pride. At least some of my struggles were now paying off. I went to the washroom and pulled myself together and then I wanted to tell the world but only told a few of my co-workers who were around. I then called Fiyaz and told him before calling her father and telling him as well.

I did not have an opportunity to buy anything with which to reward her that afternoon because I had to run from the train to the bus to get home and I was so anxious to get home and give her a big hug. But, her brother did not disappoint. When he came home from work, he had a huge bouquet of flowers for her. I was very thankful for his generosity and his thoughtfulness. Sad to say, her father did not even try to get her anything.

Over the years, I have always admired the bond and the loving relationship the two of them shared. He had always been a very doting big brother, always helping her with her school work and buying her little things here and there. I used to laugh when she wanted him to do something that was really last minute or very difficult and she would say,

"You are my favorite brother" and he would always respond and say,

"I am your only brother".

In the meantime, my life besides our Immigration issues was falling apart. My relationship with my husband had become unbearable. I wished that my marriage could have been so different but I knew I did not leave any stone unturned to make it work. There were lots of abuse and ridicule that I had endured and which I did not deserve. So, for my peace of mind and my sanity, I finally conjured up enough courage to do something which I should have done a really long time ago.

We went our separate ways and the children became my sole purpose for living. Working and providing for them became my therapy. Believe me, it was not easy to go back to Square one all over again, but I had to do it. I now had to contend again with one income and paying a higher rent, since we were now in a three bedroom apartment – my children deserved to have better living conditions.

Our immigration woes were put on the back burner. We were in a happy mode preparing for Zara's graduation. She was going to be the star and unlike her brother who was OK with a regular suit and tie, girls had to be so much more "dolled up". I guess I was more excited about getting her dressed up than she was. We got all her stuff together for the big day!

And it was finally here! My baby had grown up and she was graduating from High School in such a prestigious manner. We were soon on our way to the venue, but we had to stop and pick up her father. We barely made it in time and she was whisked away to be with her fellow graduating students. They were all in their caps and gowns and could barely be differentiated.

I waited with bated breath until the moment when she had to give her speech. Not having heard her speech before, I was taken aback by the sentiments she expressed. She paid full tribute to her mother and the sacrifices I had made. She said when she came to this country she made up her mind not to let her mother's efforts go in vain. Today was a testament to that fact.

She mentioned her years without me in our country and how when she came here first and saw that I was working two jobs, she realized how difficult life had been for me, but that I never complained and that I made sure she was well taken care of. She also thanked her brother for his endless support.

I could not help but cry and my tears just came freely. I was very touched by her actions and I could not have been more proud. At the end of the program lots of people wanted to meet me and I felt overwhelmed. It felt as if they were tyring to meet a celebrity or something. I had to rush to the bathroom because I was having some women's issues on that day and also I really needed to wash away the tears from my face.

She was caught up in a flurry of activities with her teachers and her friends; tyring to take pictures and writing in each others auto-graph books. Some of her teachers gave her little gifts and in the middle of all of this she had to leave. We had to drop her father back to work and he could not be late. She was very disappointed, but we had become accustomed to this by now. He could have taken a day off, but he chose not to.

Once we dropped him off, we stopped and had lunch at her favorite restaurant. I could not help staring at her – she looked so beautiful – she was simply glowing. She caught me once and as I tried to look away she wanted to know why I was staring at her.

I said, "You look so radiant, so beautiful, I cannot believe that you are my child and that I could feel so proud."

She just brushed it off and said, "You are my mother; you have to say that I am beautiful."

(If you get to know us, both my daughter and I do not know how to deal with compliments very well.)

Once we had finished lunch we dropped her home as she was exhausted. Her brother and I went back to the store to pick up groceries, paper goods and goodies for the "surprise" party we were having for her the following Saturday. We had both taken the day off from work and decided to do the shopping as we had the time, because we would be quite busy cooking and preparing for her party. Exhausted we came back home and relaxed a little in between congratulatory phone calls.

On Saturday morning we had arranged with her friends to take her out so that we could do all the necessary preparations, and we felt we were still keeping the surprise.

However, before leaving she said,

"Ma what are you going to do with all the seasoned chicken that you have in the fridge?"

By then I knew that the game was up ... she knew. She went ahead with her friends and we started scurrying around tyring to get everything ready by 5:00 p.m.

She had a great time at the party which we were allowed by our landlords to keep in their huge backyard. The guests included lots of relatives and friends from her school as well. She had a fabulousl time and there were lots of speeches and well wishes which had me in tears a lot of the time. They were happy tears, though!!

After all this running around, it took a little while to get back to the normal routine of life. This time around I had some help with the household chores as Zara was home and she would start dinner before I got home from work. It was such a joy rushing home to spend time with her and Fiyaz, who sometimes came home much later, because he had a fluctuating schedule.

Soon it was time for Zara to go back to school and now she was all grown up and going to College. Not just any College. She had been accepted at Fordham Universaty with a partial scholarship. Being the Valedictorian of her graduating class would also allow her to get a stipend towards her tuition, so I had to come up with the other half of her tuition which amounted to about $12,000.00 per year since she was a non-resident student. The cost was daunting being a single parent all over again, but for her future I was willing to make the sacrifice.

We travelled together every morning until I got to Manhattan and then she continued on to the Bronx. Her total commute time from Queens to the Bronx was about two hours, but she did it without complaining too much. She realized that she was privileged to be going to such a high profile school and that I could not afford a car for her at this time. Many of her friends were driving to school if they were not resident students.

I was slowly but surely tyring to get a grip on my finances and we were barely making it, but Zara was in school and we were paying our rent and putting food on the table. And then the unthinkable happened!!!! There were lots of cutbacks at my job and lo and behold, being the last to join the staff, I no longer had a job. Zara was in the middle of exams and I went home and did not say anything to either of the children.

When she did not see me getting up the next morning to get dressed for work as usual, I just told her that I was taking a few days off. She even said that how come I did not tell her before. I hemmed and hawed and she did not even realize that I had not given her a proper answer. She went to school for the remainder of the week while I tried to make lots of doctors' appointments for both of us as my medical and dental benefits would expire by the end of the month.

It seemed as if I were locked in a square box with no air and I kept, trying to claw my way out only to be dragged back down. I had no job and now I had more expenses because the apartment that we were renting was a three bedroom apartment and I had a young lady in college with very high tuition fees. Fiyaz was working – this was a saving grace, but he was a young man with College loans, and he did his best to help wherever possible.

As resourceful as she was, Zara realized that I would have a very difficult time paying her tuition and she went to the Finance Office at Fordham and told them of her situation. She had been on the Dean's list since she started and she told them that she was willing to work longer hours at school. I knew there were other forces at work on our behalf, because she was told to bring proof that I had lost my job and to have me write a letter to this effect.

I wrote this letter and provided a copy of my termination letter with little expectation of a positive outcome. A few days later she came home; very excited and all out of breath.

"Ma, you would not believe this! I was called to the office today and they told me that they would waive my tuition fees for this semester if I could maintain my grades!! Can you believe it, Ma?"

I hugged her and could not express enough gratitude at how smart she was. I would never have thought to do something like what she did. What a relief – it was one of my major concerns that she may have had to leave school because I could not afford her tuition.

And so I started the dreary task of looking for work and filing for unemployment and the whole nine yards. I visited the Unemployment Office and went through the routine procedure. I filled out paperwork to get all the necessary assistance – use of the computers and counselors to assist with job search, etc. I had to complete a journal of all the places I applied for work in order to continue receiving my unemployment checks. I did whatever was required with due diligence.

I hit the road, the computer and friends and relatives in my job search. I had a friend who took it upon herself to send out one hundred resumes and I signed up on every available website where I could post my resume and apply on line. I also contacted several Head Hunters who had been calling me when I was working, but now they did not have available openings.

I started to receive my Unemployment benefits and for anyone who had been down this path, it was nothing compared to your regular earnings, and in the State of New York it could not exceed $405.00 or 50% of your earnings. I was grateful and tried to stretch those dollars as I did not think

I had ever done before. I made sure that I paid my rent before I did anything else.

I got into a routine of waking up everyday and going on the computer and then later in the day I would cook and have a hot meal waiting for the kids when they got home. However, some days it was very cheap fare. I had found these packets of noodle soups that were sometimes on sale five for a dollar. The chili flavored one was a hit with us and once I found them on sale, I would buy and stock them up.

Another favorite that I found quite cheap to prepare a decent meal for us was to cook curried eggs with potatoes and rice. I must say that I would mix and match and tried to change up the same things in different ways and we survived. I could not ask for more acceptance from my kids during this time. They never complained about our dire circumstances.

I tried not to go anywhere too much except on job interviews or to the Labor Department, because I found that going outside meant spending money which I did not have. I also did not go as often to the religious social gatherings that I was a part of because I did not want to be pitied.

However, one Sunday when one of the older women who used to attend these sessions did not see me, and she found out that I was not working she called me as soon as she got home. We chatted for a while and she hung up. The next weekend she called and said that since she was in the neighborhood, could she stop by to say hello.

I said, "Sure, no problem."

Soon a car drove up into the landlord's driveway and I heard her knocking on the door. After the usual hugs and kisses, she said,

"Please come with me to the car, I have a few things for you."

You could imagine my surprise when she opened the trunk of the car – it was full of all sorts of grocery supplies and snacks for me and the children. I was speechless. I kept saying,

"Oh my God, why did you do this?"

And she calmly replied, "Because I wanted to."

After we brought in all the stuff, she came in with two gift bags. She had some clothes for me and a little perfume set for Zara. The clothes she brought for me were not old clothes – they were brand new with the labels on them. How did you thank someone for such acts of kindness who was not even a relative?

This was not the only acts of kindness that I was showered with during this dark and dismal period in my life. My sister-in-law would always send a check now and then with a little note to buy stuff for Zara that she needed for school. I had a few cousins and a very dear family friend who would also send some small contributions.

I really felt hopeless and I had a hard time accepting these "gifts", but I had to set aside my pride. I was young and strong but my circumstances forced me to accept with gratitude. I always felt that the young should give to the old and needy. I was extremely grateful but constantly embarrassed to be in this situation.

The total extent of my circumstances was pummeled into me when one of my cousins called and said she wanted to ask me something very important. It was coming on to Ramadan (the Holy month of Fasting for us) and during this month, we were required to give "Zakat" (charity – a stipulated percentage of whatever savings you had accumulated during the year). Her question was that since I was not working she had spoken to her brothers and they all wanted to know if they could send me "Zakat" instead of giving to strangers.

This was hard for me to deal with. When we were growing up, the recipients of Zakat were the old and feeble, the destitute or widows and orphans. Here I was being asked if I would accept "Zakat". I told her that I did not think I could bring myself to accept "Zakat" as I felt I would be denying someone who was more in need.

However, after she hung up, I called my brother in Guyana and told him about the conversation. At first he did not answer and when I said,

"Are you there?" I realized that he was crying. He then begged me,

"Please babe if you can avoid it, please do not accept "Zakat." Please tell me what you need and I will send it to you."

Wonderful thought, but not very practical as everyone in my country was struggling to make ends meet. He said that Ma and Pa would turn over in their graves if they knew that their baby girl was struggling so much that she had to accept charity.

The fact that I called my brother to get his opinion showed how tempting this offer was. However, I could not bring myself to do it. I rehashed lots of thoughts running through my mind before I finally called my cousin and gracefully declined her offer, but at the same time thanking her for thinking about me and recognizing my need.

After six months my unemployment benefits were about to expire, but because of the nature of the job market at the time especially in my specific field, it was extended for another three months. I guess I had complied with all the rules and regulations of the Labor Department by documenting my job search and going ever so often to report my progress – thus it was automatically extended to the maximum allotment of 39 weeks.

With the final unemployment payments soon coming up, I became desperate and I started to go and do cleaning jobs with a family friend from time to time. She used to get part time cleaning and she would take two houses and we would go out to Long Island and clean and she would pay me on the same day.

On one occasion the house was so dirty that we had to use lots of extra cleaning supplies to spray the bath tub and the toilet bowl as well as the stove top, etc. It was cold outside and so we had not opened the windows. I started sneezing and soon I was hyperventilating and then she had to open the windows.

I had had sinus surgery and since then I could not tolerate the smell of strong cleaning supplies. Very soon I had to lie down a little and then she tried to give me some milk to see if I would feel better. She needed me to clean; she did not need to have a sick person on her hands. She tried to help me feel better and I tried to suppress my feelings as best as I could and continued to assist her with cleaning the apartment.

It took us longer than usual with all the disruption and she did not say anything negative when she paid me but after that every time I asked her she would make some sort of excuse. So I lost that little source of income which had been very helpful.

You know what they say, when it rains, it pours. This could never be truer in our present circumstances. One Saturday morning Fiyaz left for work as usual.

Immediately after, I got a call from him asking if I had gone outside the day before.

I said, "No, why?"

He said that there was a "For Sale" sign at the front of the house where we were renting one of the apartments.

It was so early in the morning and I was just waking up, so I asked him to repeat what he said. Soon it registered what he was saying and I aked him if the landlord could sell the house and not tell us that we had to move. He asked me to call upstairs and find out, but I told him I thought it was too early. He was so anxious that he called himself and blocked his phone number. He spoke to our landlady who confirmed that the house was for sale. He immediately called me back to tell me this.

What was a poor soul to do? Where was I going to get Realtor fees, first and last month's rent to get a new apartment? As you could imagine, panic set in. I had to get up. I could not stay in bed any longer. I had to move, I had to do something, or I might lose my mind. And so, without waking Zara, I changed my clothes and took the bus to Richmond Hill where I was hoping that I could see a "for rent" sign and hopefully get a cheap apartment.

It was too early and many of the real estate places were not opened yet. I walked around a few blocks that were next to the train station and tried to see if there any signs in people's windows. Do not ask me why I did this. In hindsight I realized that the phone and computer would have been more practical ways of looking for an apartment, but you had to understand that I was jolted awake by this news and I was not thinking rationally.

I was now getting some severe pains in my chest and in the back of my neck. I kept walking but the pain was getting worse. I had to get something to drink or sit down, if not I felt as if I would collapse in the street. I looked around frantically and there was a stoop to someone's house that was covered by the shade of a nearby tree.

Here I was sitting down on someone's step with no clue in the world as to what my next course of action was. I felt like a homeless person or one of those people who had lost their minds and wandered the streets aimlessly. Besides which, it felt as if I was having a heart attack. Please, do not let me die in the street. Was this what it would all come down to? All my years of sacrifice and hard work, was I going to die here like a pauper?

I tried as best as I could to calm down and I started to breathe slowly and deeply, one breath at a time. I was sweating profusely even though it was still early in the morning. After a few minutes which felt like a lifetime I was capable of using my cell phone to call Zara. She answered my second call and woke up all confused. Why was I calling from the cell phone and where was I? How come I did not wake her to tell her that I was going outside?

I told her that I could not explain everything right now, but that I was not feeling well. She said,

"Ma, do you want me to call, 911?" I assured her that I did not think that was necessary as the chest pains had subsided by now. She told me to stay where I was and that she would call me right back. She then called Prem and Nadira and they in turned called me back on the cell.

"Listen to us carefully'" they said.

"Look around you and try to tell us exactly where you are."

I had been walking around without paying attention to where I was.

Anyway, I was conscious enough to see the number on the house and in less than no time they came to get me. They came straight to where I was instead of going to pick Zara up and then coming to get me. They figured that this way would save more time. Nadira had the presence of mind to bring a bottle of water and soon they had me in the car on my way home. They were sensitive enough and did not push me to talk too much, but encouraged me to try to relax.

In the meantime Zara had called Fiyaz and he may have told her about the "For sale" sign in the front yard. Even though she understood how I could react that way she admonished me and told me that I should never do something like that again without letting them know where I was going. I could not say anything because I had done something that could have jeopardized my safety.

Prem and Nadira stayed with us until I had something hot to eat and I had taken a shower. They made me promise that I would stay in bed and relax before they finally left. When I recalled this incident I count my blessings that I was still safe today. I was this close to either being dead or becoming insane from stress and worry. I was really shaken up and tried to take things one day at a time from then on. Worrying would not make it better; it would only make it worse.

When Fiyaz came home that night he was very concerned and worried about our future. He told me to call again upstairs and find out what they were saying about the "for sale" sign. When I spoke to the Landlady she told me that her husband was making these signs as part of a job assignment and that they just put it up there to see how it would look. Fiyaz was speechless because only this morning she had even quoted a price to him about selling the house.

He then said to me,

"Ma, I do not trust this situation. Now that you are home, please call around and see if you could find another apartment. It might even be better if you went with real estate agents and started looking at houses."

We both knew that we could not afford to buy a house at this time, but I think he was tyring to get me involved in something so that my mind would not have too much time to worry.

I went on quite a few of these property searches and I was even offered an opportunity to become a real estate agent. Showing the property and doing the paperwork, I felt I could handle. But I had heard so many stories of how real estate agents were not the most honest people and that you had to lie about certain aspects of a home in order to get it sold, that I did not feel comfortable doing it.

I could not bring myself to cheat poor people out of their hard earned money. Besides which I did not drive and I felt that was a prerequisite for moving around and showing properties to prospective buyers.

In the meantime during the next couple of months I was religiously following any leads with regards to finding a job. A few false alarms and I would get all excited and then it would amount to nothing all over again. I went through so many disappointments that after a while I tried not to build up my hopes. But I was human and I was desperate so everytime something seemed remotely possible, there I went, thinking, this would be it.

I never thought that I would be out of work for such a long period of time. Zara was still committed to being a part of my nephew's wedding which had been planned quite a while back and which was soon coming up. Because his wife to be did not have a lot of young female relatives she had asked Zara to be her maid of honor and since I had been working at the time we did not hesitate to say yes.

But being a bridesmaid cost a lot of money and now it was too late to back out. The wedding was just around the corner. I was still praying that

I would get a job before the big day but the chances were looking slimmer and slimmer. On a Friday afternoon Nadira called and asked if I would be home the Saturday afternoon.

I said, "Yes, do you need me to do something for you guys?"

"No, no, we would just stop by to say hello as we had some errands to run around your neighborhood."

However, after I spoke with her, I got another call from the relative asking if I would go and do some cleaning job with her. I was hesitant because of my previous experience, but I said yes. The cleaning was not very extensive and so it went without mishap. As we were coming home I mentioned that I had to rush because my friends said they would come over.

Her reaction was, "You always have to rush and do stuff for your friends." I did not react too much – I just let her have her say.

I got home in time and I made a few sandwiches just to have something to offer them. I had showered and was so tired that I was about to fall asleep when they arrived. We chit chatted for a little and then they had to leave as they had some appointment; or so they claimed. After they had left, Zara came to me and asked me if I had put an envelope on her dresser.

"What envelope?" I asked. She said there was an envelope on her dresser and I asked her to bring it. When we opened it, there was $150.00 inside. I was a little confused.

She said, "Ma, I think Aunty Nadira left it there, because when you were in the kitchen I saw her coming out of my room."

Well, I could not wait for them to get home to call. As soon as I called she said,

"Please understand why we did that. We knew that you would not take it if we gave it to you in your hands, so we left it on Zara's dresser. Prem wanted Zara to go to the wedding and look beautiful and this was to help her."

Could I still not believe in angels and the beauty of friendships? How could you thank people who did these kinds of things for you?

Another friend then told me about an elderly woman who was in a Rehabilitation Center and that her daughter was looking for someone to sit with her a few afternoons per week. I jumped at the opportunity. I was required to sit with her, or push her around in her wheelchair and if she attempted to walk to be by her side for about three hours in the afternoon, twice a week. I was very patient and never late. I made sure that I got the bus and was there earlier than expected. I admired Ms. Cheryl very much. She was 82 years old but could still read without her glasses and was very independent.

She used to tell me stories about her youth and that how one of her sisters had been taken away in the Jewish Holocaust. However, as witty as she was she suffered from dementia and from time to time she would ask who I was and where her daughter was and why she was not there. These episodes made me remember my mom a lot. I guess I tried to put her in my mom's place and I was extra attentive to her.

In the meantime, I was still going on interviews which were not very abundant and I went on one where they wanted me to start right away, but they were going to pay me minimum wage. I was ready to take it even though I had to take three buses to get there. However, when I got home, the children told me to have a little more patience – something a little more lucrative would come up soon.

The next evening Zara came and sat next to me. She said, "Ma, I really don't know how you are managing financially, but please do not take a job where you would be extremely underpaid and overworked."

She then said,

"Ma, if we have to eat bread and water three times per day, we would make it, so please do not worry too much."

I do not think if I had scripted this, I could have asked for better words of comfort and it was the most reassuring thing anyone could have said to me at that time.

Yet she was still a child. How much could I burden her with financial issues? How could I tell her that I had not received any unemployment checks for the past three months and whatever little savings I had, were almost depleted? Try as I might to stretch the monies that I had cashed out from my 401K when I had lost my job, it too was now almost gone.

What was I to do? It was not that I was lazy and did not want to work; it was just that the field in which I had built my experience had very limited job openings. I was even willing to do any other kind of job but those were not even available. I was still doing a few afternoons per week with Ms. Cheryl and going on interviews.

I was on one such interview when Ms. Cheryl's daughter called me on my cell phone. She needed my help in shopping. She had just had a brand new grandson in Israel and she did not have enough time to do all the shopping she needed. She was leaving for Israel the next day.

I arranged to meet her at the Baby Department Store and as soon as she saw me she was very surprised.

"Oh my God!" she said, "You look so different."

I was dressed in very formal business attire as I had gone on an Interview in Manhattan. This was the first time that I would tell her that my true line of work was not what I did for her family, but that I had been in the HR field for quite some time. We did not have too much time to dwell on my life story as she was really strapped for time and we soon got started on shopping.

I swear Mrs. Dora bought one set of everything that was in the store or so it seemed. She could not get enough of all the fanciest clothes for her grandson. By the time we got to the register, her bill had been more than $950.00. For someone who had been out of work and with no source of income for quite a while, it seemed very extravagant to spend so much on a brand new baby. But I guess when you had it and you were so excited about being a grandmother for the first time, it may seem like nothing.

Before leaving for Israel, Mrs. Dora introduced me to her brother who would now be responsible for his mother's care until she came back. He was very business like and I was a little intimidated especially since Mrs. Dora had always been very soft and kind to me. Anyway, I did not have to deal with him too much since he had his own people who would sit with his mom while Mrs. Dora was away.

Chapter 13

Euphoria

After two long weeks, Mrs. Dora came back from Israel and immediately called me with a proposal. Her mother was to be discharged from the Rehab. Center and did not want to stay with either of her children. She wanted to go back to her own Apartment in Manhattan. Would I take on the job of being her live-in caretaker? I would go in on Monday mornings and come back on Friday evenings.

I had always been of the belief that there was no shame in doing any kind of job once you were making an honest living. My dilemma now, was that I had Zara, a young lady who I would have to leave at home all week while I was away working. I knew she had her brother, but it was still not the same. Also his schedule was very flexible and some days he did not get home until 10:00 p.m.

However, beggars could not be choosers and it was not as if I had a ton of jobs lining up from which to choose. I negotiated with Mrs. Dora about my weekly wage and we agreed that I would take the job. This was a Tuesday evening and I would not start a full week until the following Monday.

However, for Wednesday, she needed me to go to her brother's house and be with Ms. Cheryl. When her brother came home in the afternoon he would take us to her apartment in Manhattan. I would help her to clean up and got her stuff together and on Friday her brother had a taxi service which would pick us up and bring us back to Queens.

I packed a little overnight bag and on Wednesday morning before Zara left for school she kissed me a lingering good-bye. We did not say much but she knew that I was not expected to come back home that evening. During the afternoon the rain started to pour and there was a severe thunderstorm so by the time Ms. Cheryl's son came home, he did not want to drive to Manhattan.

He had a very difficult time dissuading his mother from going to her apartment, because her bags had been packed and she had been waiting patiently all day to get going. She was like a little child ... he tried everything to pacify her and eventually he told her that her grandson was coming back from his vacation and she should wait to meet him. I guess by now she realized she was not going anywhere and she went back to her room.

A little while later the rain subsided. Mr. Neil offered to take me home as it was on his way to wherever he was going. On our way home he asked me if I could come back on the Thursday to sit with her since the original plan had been for us to be in Manhattan. I told him I did not have a problem and I would be there. He then paid me for both days with a check even though I had not worked on the Thursday as yet.

I dropped my over night bag by the door way and ran straight to the bathroom – a habit I had since I was a little kid. No matter where I was coming from, I had to run to the bathroom as soon as I got home. (My mom used to laugh about this habit of mine, asking me if there were no bathrooms where I had been all day).

Immediately after that the phone rang and I got distracted so as soon as Zara came home from school she saw the bag by the door. She started yelling out to me.

"Ma, are you home?"

Her face lit up with a big smile and she gave me a big bear hug. She had been expecting to walk into an empty apartment and here I was, home!

We did our routine stuff and when we were ready to go to sleep she came into my room and as she lay in my bed next to me, she started talking to me as if she were ninety years old.

"Ma, I know times are hard and you may not have any money right now, but please Ma, do not go backwards. You have struggled so much and could we please wait a little while longer? Ma, please do not go back to being a live-in help. Ma you are so educated and now you have your Green Card, Ma, please don't do this to yourself."

I tried my best to reassure her that this was only for a little while and that hopefully I would get something in my field very soon. And then my baby girl started crying and we both cried ourselves to sleep – she did not even get up to go to her own room.

My heart was breaking for her. She did not cry easily and when she cried, I always felt helpless. Was there some relief in sight or how much longer did we have to suffer? I prayed to God with every ounce of my being that night and begged him to please take away this nightmare and that I could wake up to something positive. Please, God, kindly shed some light into these dark days for us.

And so because of a rain storm that caused me not to be in Manhattan my world would change in a very dramatic manner. On Thursday, while I was sitting in the living room with Ms. Cheryl, my cell phone rang and it was one of the Recruiters that I had interviewed with.

When I interviewed with Ms. Sophia, it had been for a full time Benefits position and she had really been impressed with my resume. However, she had cautioned me that since she was a headhunter, the final decision did not rest with her as to whether I would get the job. Before leaving her office, she asked me would I consider a Temporary assignment should it become available. I told her that at that time, I would be willing to take anything.

Ms. Sophia asked if I was available to go to a Temporary Assignment in a very imposing building in Manhattan. I think she believed that since the HR department had placed the request, that it was an HR position. It did not matter to me and so I said, of course I would go to the assignment.

Could you imagine, if I had gone the day before with Ms. Cheryl to Manhattan, there was no way I could have accepted this assignment – **I could not have left Ms. Cheryl alone in her apartment.**

I was so excited that I was shaking, but there was no one I could tell at this moment. The kids were in school and at work and I had to keep my good news to myself. I felt like I was about to burst with exuberance but I had to calm myself down, reminding myself that this was only a temporary assignment.

However, I just had this great feeling of elation. I could not explain this burst of optimism. On Thursday when I left, I told Ms. Cheryl's son that I would not be coming in on Friday. It was not such a big deal as her grandson was now home and they had expected her back on Friday, anyways.

On Friday morning I woke up very early as I wanted to give myself enough time to find my way to the job site. The night before, I had called the Transit number to find out the best way to get to my destination. I dressed carefully and took extra time with my appearance. I felt very rusty and nervous as I had been out of the professional workforce for 13 1/2 months by now.

Without any mishap I got to the building but went down an escalator where I got to a Whole Foods store. Upon inquiry, I was told that the employee entrance to the building was around the corner. I soon found my way to the reception area and once I had given them the details they told me to wait for the HR person to come and get me. Very soon a very pretty and friendly young lady came to get me and she took me to the 21st floor.

Shortly after another young lady came and got me and she was even prettier and friendlier. She introduced me to a few of the employees who were now beginning to arrive and I was enthralled. Eventually she took me down to the cafeteria and offered to get me breakfast but I declined since I had eaten before I left home.

As the work day started I was taken to a Library to do some organizing of lots of booklets; periodicals and files. I set to work with gusto as I felt I needed to prove myself. By the end of the day the same pretty young lady came back and was very impressed with how much I had accomplished.

Before I left for the day, I asked her if I had to come back on Monday and she said, "Of course."

I was very happy but I had a big obligation to fulfill. I had committed to going to work for Ms. Cheryl and now this came up. AS ALWAYS – choices now had to be made. I knew this was "temporary" but it was in my line of work and I was in my comfort zone.

So on Friday evening as soon as I got home, I called a few friends and enquired if they knew of anyone looking for a live-in situation. Lo and behold, Prem knew of someone!

I called Ms, Cheryl's daughter and I explained to her the situation. She was very understanding and very happy for me. I gave her all the details of the interested party and told her that the rest was up to them. She asked me a few questions and once she found out that the other person was from my country, she said that they would interview her.

I felt relieved. I did not want to turn my back on Ms. Cheryl and her family and I felt I had done my due diligence by recommending someone to take my place. She got the job!!

Having done that, I came back to my temporary assignment on the following Monday. To this day, I still consider this to be my "miracle" job as within a couple of weeks, I was made permanent.

There were a lot of decisions that I had to make. As this was a temporary assignment, I was still interviewing for a full time position. And what do you know? As soon as I was offered a job at another reputable company in the Benefits Department, I was offered this job in a full time capacity.

Can you believe that now I had to choose between two jobs when just a month or so ago, I was at my wits end to find one? And as usual I turned to my kids and we tried to weigh all the options. I felt comfortable here and my boss was just the most adorable person to work with.

You guessed right. I chose to stay and this is where I still am today, very happy and content.

As usual, once everything went back to normal the mind went back to worrying about Fiyaz's papers and the frustration of waiting. By now, it was almost five years since we had received our Green Cards and we could now apply for our citizenship. Their father applied first – he actually sent his form for me to complete and mail in and he got called without any delays and soon he was sworn in as a citizen. Great news for him!

I thought, wow, as soon as I got my citizenship I could upgrade Fiyaz's papers and thus expedite his Green Card process.

You probably already know what I was about to say. Not so fast!! With our luck, nothing was as easy as one; two; three. I applied for myself and Zara and we both got appointments to take our fingerprints on the same day.

No problem. We then got our appointment letter to go for our Interview at 711 Stewart Avenue, in Garden City, Long Island.

By now, we had saved some money from Zara working part-time at school and we had bought her a little "hooptie" – her first car which we bought for her 21st birthday. She was so excited even though it was such an outdated, old car, but all she cared about at that time, was that it could take her from point A to point B. She still took the train to school because parking and gas costs were too much for our budget.

So, on the date of our appointment, since Fiyaz could not get off from work, Zara decided to drive us to Garden city. I was very apprehensive since it would be her first long trip and it was pouring rain on that day. I should not have worried. She followed the instructions given by her brother and we were there in record time. I was highly impressed!

We went through the normal procedures until it was time for our interview. The same officer interviewed both of us, but separately. When it was my turn, she had a Trainee with her and the first thing she did, was ask the Trainee if she recognized some code that was in the front of my file. I could not understand clearly what they were saying as they were speaking very softly, but right away, my heart started thumping.

I did the writing test and answered the requisite civic questions and was told that I had passed with a hundred percent. However, she could not give me an appointment date for my swearing in process as the "computer was down".

For some reason, this alarmed me. However, when Zara came out, she said the exact same thing. We were both given two forms and they both had the exact same check marks. So it seemed OK. Yet, I had a premonition. Call it woman's intuition or our experience with the Immigration process, but I felt that all was not as simple as it seemed.

I asked Zara to wait a little so that I could see if the folks who were interviewed after us had been given the same response. The next person to come out of the interviewing room was an elderly, bearded man. He had been given the same response. Why did I still not feel right?

I tried to wait a little longer so that I could ask the next person.

Zara then said to me, "Ma stop this, you are scaring me."

She could sense my anxiety, even though I could not really explain what my fear was. Anyway, she insisted that we left and so in the pouring rain we made our way back home and I must say she did an excellent job driving us there and back. She was beaming – you could tell she felt all grown up and proud.

I tried to shake off this feeling of uneasiness and to some degree I succeeded. The next day I went to work as usual. Since I was out the day before, there was so much work to do, that I did not have a chance to brood too much. We went for the Interview on a Tuesday and by Friday, Zara had received her appointment letter to appear for her swearing in ceremony on the following Tuesday. I tried to brush it off by thinking that within the next day or two, my letter of appointment would arrive in the mail.

By the date of her appointment, my letter had still not arrived. I refused to believe that there was no letter forthcoming and I accompanied her to Cadman Plaza. I would have gone with her anyway, but this time I was going to make sure that there was no mistake and that my letter just got lost in the mail. I went to the representatives and asked them to please look through the Certificates but there was none for me, only for Zara.

I was extremely disappointed and now I was beginning to panic. At first I was thinking it was the mail, but now it had been confirmed that no letter was sent to me. What could be the problem? Why did I not receive my letter and subsequently my Citizenship Certificate? It seemed as if my fears were justified and the unfairness of it all made no sense. Here I was, anxiously awaiting my citizenship so that I could update Fiyaz's Green Card application and yet mine was not here.

I tried to put my feelings aside and be there for Zara. It was a grand moment for her and as I stood there at the back of the room listening to them being sworn it, I cried and cried – I felt as if I was being sworn in, because for the life of me, I thought that I should really have been on that list. I thought I had paid my dues and that I should not have to suffer any more, but I guess like always, I had no control over these issues.

As soon as we got outside, she started making fun of me at how much I was crying which lightened my mood. I resolved to try and be happy for her. We discussed the ceremony and how impressed we were with the judge. She told a story of how her grandmother had come to Ellis Island and could not read or write, yet she raised her children and they all had excellent jobs.

Before getting on the train we looked around the neighborhood and found a little restaurant were we had lunch. I then brought Zara with me to my job as I had only requested a half day off.

And so began the waiting game AGAIN!!! After a few weeks of waiting without any letter in the mail, I wrote to the Interviewing Officer directly (her name was on the paper that she had given to both myself and Zara). I went to the Post Office and made sure that I sent the letter certified, return receipt. I did receive the card back with the signature of the recipient. NO response. After another month of waiting I sent another letter; still NO response.

The Holidays came and went. It was now the New Year and yet I had not heard from the Immigration Department as to the status of my citizenship application. Needless to say, neither had Fiyaz heard anything about his Green Card Application. We decided to go in person and one winter morning Fiyaz and I left home early so that we could be there as soon as they opened at 7:30 a.m.

We had a hard time to get by the Security Officers because we did not have an official appointment letter. Eventually a Supervisor allowed me to go after I showed him the checklist form I had received from the Interviewing Officer. I explained to him that I had written several letters without getting any response. If they would not reply in writing and I could not go in person, I pleaded, how could I get a status update?

We waited our turn and finally got up to the front desk where they took the paper I had. The representative cross referenced it with their computer records. The guy looked at me and he looked back at the computer.

He said, "I am sorry ma'am, but there is nothing that I can tell you. It just says that the decision is still pending. All you have to do, is wait."

What else was new!!!! Dear God, if I heard the word "wait" one more time, I might throw something at someone.

Anyway, I was almost immune to the waiting and if this was what it took, then this was what I had to do. On the way to drop me off to the nearest train station so that I could go to work, my son was really quiet. I had no words to comfort myself or him and I tried to make small talk about anything and everything except what was on both our minds – what did we do so wrong that we had to struggle so much for everything?

As I was leaving the car to go down to the subway, I said,

"Why don't you ask your dad to sponsor you since he is now a citizen?"

He looked at me and said, "Ma, I would rather wait."

So, we waited for three more months and then with great reluctance, but with not much alternative, Fiyaz asked his dad to sponsor him.

He said, "Sure, you are my son, why not?"

Yet, we had to pay all the filing fees. We did all the necessary paperwork and submitted the application. Within less than a month we received a "Receipt Notice".

This was a little reassuring as I considered this to be a back-up plan because I could see no reason why my citizenship application was taking so long to be approved. And like always, life went on. Zara had graduated with her Bachelor's Degree from Fordham Universaty and as I stood and watched her accept her degree, I felt a tremendous sense of gratification. At least, this was worth it. My baby had not let me down and very soon she enrolled in the Master's Program for Teaching.

In September of the following year, almost a year after I had applied for my citizenship, I received a letter of approval. It was like an anti-climax for me. I guess I had waited so long that the joy in receiving it was taken away. I was still grateful for a major reason – I could NOW update Fiyaz's green card application.

Call me paranoid or whatever you would, but I decided that I was not going to play around with this last leg of his journey. We had faced too many setbacks for me to set myself up for another one. So I decided to procure the services of an attorney to file his paperwork, even though I knew I could do it myself.

When we took all his documents and all the certificates that he had accumulated along the way, the lawyer's secretary was amazed and very sympathetic at the same time. She kept saying that it was so sad for someone to be so qualified and be stuck in a dead end job just because of his "green card" status.

The attorney was very efficient and submitted all the necessary paperwork in a very timely manner. His fees were a little exorbitant, to the tune of $4,500.00 but I figured that we had spent so much money on

Immigration fees we may as well work and save and pay this last set of fees. Hopefully, it would really be the last set.

Within a couple of days we received the official "Notice of Receipt". When I opened the mail box and saw the official envelope, I got so excited only to realize that it was just an acknowledgement. Nevertheless, I now knew that his papers were filed as promised by the attorney.

Two months later, we received another letter, giving us hope, but it was only a Fingerprinting appointment. Whatever came our way, we were willing to accept. At least they were working on his papers and progress was being made. When the appointed date came, I went with him very early to the processing center and it was such an easy and streamlined process that we were finished before 9:30 a.m. We were advised that the results would be forwarded electronically to the USCIS office and that we should be hearing from them soon.

Excitement and fear all at the same time. The much awaited "interview" letter was here. I immediately called the attorney's office and it was confirmed that they had received the notice as well. The attorney said that he would meet us at the USCIS office on the appointed date and time.

I was sweating and then I got cold. I knew there was no logical reason for them to deny his application, yet with all the hardships we had gone through, I was no longer confident about anything. And with us, it seemed that anything and everything that could go wrong would go wrong. I spent quite a few sleepless nights before the "D" day, and as always, I resorted to prayer to help me through this nervewracking time.

The morning of the Interview came around and we were at the office anxiously looking around for the attorney. We took a seat and within less than ten minutes we saw him coming through the door. It was such a relief to see him, it was as if he could waive a magic wand and everything would turn out great. If only that were so!

We went through the usual moving from one section to another section as our numbers were called and we were finally at the last waiting station to get called by the Interviewing Officer. I was so nervous that I started twitching and shaking my feet so bad that my son had to say,

"Ma, stop; you are making me more nervous."

I was always the calm one, and here I was giving way to my emotions.

You might have thought that I would be immune to this by now, but I guess I was not – if anything I was worse.

By now conversation was impossible. If we had to say anything to each other, we just whispered and then shut up. The room was very, very tense as the fate of all these people was in the balance and was being held in the hands of a few Interviewing Officers. I wondered what it was like to have so much power and control over people's lives.

And then his name was called. I said a silent prayer as I got up mechanically to follow but then sat back down. The officer who called his name was a young girl and when she saw me attempt to get up, she said to me that if I wanted to, I could come in.

"Really?" I gushed!

This was a good sign to me. She seemed very compassionate. I started to relax a little and went in to her office along with the attorney and my son.

However, it was as if I was not there. The attorney motioned to me that I should stay quiet – which I did. She asked my son a lot of questions and I must say that I was proud of the way he answered them. She then asked him if he had any affiliations with any religious organizations and he said no, but that his mom did. I used to be a part of a Ladies organization and I always filled that out in my Immigration forms.

Her reaction made me wince. Immediately, I knew that there would be some problems. I was finally able to get a semblance as to what the problem was with my citizenship application delay: "My affiliation with a religious organization!" She continued by asking one or two more questions and then she said that she would let us know. The attorney then spoke for the first time.

He said,

"Have you made a decision?"

She replied that she had to get some clarification and then we should be hearing from them.

Since the attorney did not say anything further, we all said thank you and left the office. Once we were outside, the attorney became very angry and vociferous. What in God's name did she need to clarify and why could she not tell him right there. Anyway, he assured us that if she wanted a "fight" she was going to get one from him and that we should not worry.

Here came the waiting game, AGAIN!! My system had been through this so many times that it should be second nature, yet once it happened; the pain and the anxiety started all over. After a month or two without any word from the USCIS office, I called the attorney's office and he promised to send off a letter requesting a status update.

One afternoon as I opened the mail box I saw a USCIS envelope. I was very excited and thought that it was his approval letter but it was just an appointment for him to get fingerprinted, AGAIN! Six months had passed since his fingerprints were taken the last time. I prayed feverishly that this would be the last time and that this would lead to some positive results.

This time I did not go with him for the fingerprinting appointment because we knew by now that the procedure was very straightforward. All that was required was to present your letter of appointment with proper identification and the whole process was a breeze.

It was now getting close to his birthday and I kept joking with him that he would get a really BIG birthday gift that year. His response, was always,

"Yeah, right, Ma."

Nevertheless, I kept saying this. I did not know why because this was something I never joked about and I did not want to get his hopes up too high, but I had this feeling – "mother's instinct' – "woman's intuition" – whatever you wanted to call it, it was in me.

And so, one afternoon, I was at work when Fiyaz called and sounded very excited.

"Ma, guess what?"

Right away I knew, but I did not really expect THIS.

"You got your letter of approval, right?"

"No," he said, and my bubble was burst, but just for a second.

He said, "MA, I GOT MY GREEN CARD."

"Are you sure?"

"Yes, Ma, I have it in my hands."

And the tears started flowing. I could not believe it. No letter, but right away the Green Card? I wish I were next to my son to give him a huge hug, but he knew how elated I was for him.

I rushed home that afternoon and it seemed as if the train could not go fast enough. As soon as I walked in the door my son rushed toward me and he hugged me and picked me up (as far as he could)

"WOW!! Ma, it's finally here. Can you imagine Ma, that after waiting all these years I now have my Green Card?"

Once we calmed down he then said to me.

"Ma, do you believe that when I opened the mail box, this envelope with my Green Card was not even sealed?"

The flap on the envelope was open and there was no evidence that someone had tried to open it. It was just never sealed because the glue on the envelope was fresh and untouched. This was how it was mailed out from the USCIS office.

I was not complaining. For us this was a life changing event. For the folks at the USCIS office, it was all in a day's work. For us this meant freedom. Freedom to travel, freedom to choose a job better suited to your qualifications and your expertise. Freedom to do so many things that many people who were born Americans took for granted. This one little card that weighed no more than an ounce had taken a ton of weight off our shoulders.

And as I predicted, joked and said over and over within the past couple of months, Fiyaz got the biggest and best birthday present he could have wished for. His green card actually came TWO days before his birthday. This was not an exaggeration, but it was the honest to goodness, truth!

Joyfully, we went to dinner to celebrate. This time, Fiyaz, his sister and I were not only celebrating his birthday, but it was as if we were celebrating his REBIRTH. As soon as his sister tried to make a little toast I started crying and she said,

"Ma, please don't. You have shed enough tears over the years and you should be celebrating tonight."

I tried to dry my tears and I told her that, I was truly happy. These were not tears of sadness, but they were tears of joy – overwhelming joy! It took me quite a while to get here – Lord knew it did, but I now felt as if I was finally HOME. I had finally reached the light at the end of my tunnel. I had finally come to rest on the side where the Grass was Greener.

Epilogue

Thank you for staying with me to the end of my journey. I am not sure how you feel after reading my story, but I would like to ask a very big favor of you and anyone who find themselves in a better financial situation than many of us who come to the United States to try to build a brighter future.

PLEASE, DO NOT just think of us as a number with no name and no face and above all, NO FEELINGS!

We are human beings just like anyone of you. Our circumstances may be different, but we smile and laugh when we are happy and we cry when we feel pain. If you cut us, our blood would be just as red as yours.

We may be poor, but we are rich when it comes to integrity and loyalty. We have very strong work ethics and if you treat us right: with respect and give us a sense of pride and dignity, we would bend over backwards to go above and beyond for you.

You should know that we are a people, who could be trusted, if not, you would not leave your most precious possessions, your children, with us for most of their waking hours. We cuddle them, we nurture them and we treat them as the little angels that they are.

We are very grateful for the opportunity that you give us. An opportunity to work for you and in so doing eventually get our permanent papers to live and work in the United States of America – a land of dreams and promises fulfilled where the grass is greener MOST of the time!